Oedipus
on the
Road

Oedipus
ON
the
Road

A
Novel
by

Henry
Bauchau

Translated
from the French by
Anne-Marie Glasheen

Arcade
Publishing
New York

FIRST U.S. EDITION

Originally published under the title *Oedipe sur la route*.
First published in Great Britain by Quartet Books, Ltd.

ISBN 1-55970-382-2
Library of Congress Catalog Card Number 97-72130
Library of Congress Cataloging-in-Publication information is available.

Published in the United States by Arcade Publishing, Inc., New York
Distributed by Little, Brown and Company

10 9 8 7 6 5 4 3 2 1

BP

PRINTED IN THE UNITED STATES OF AMERICA

Contents

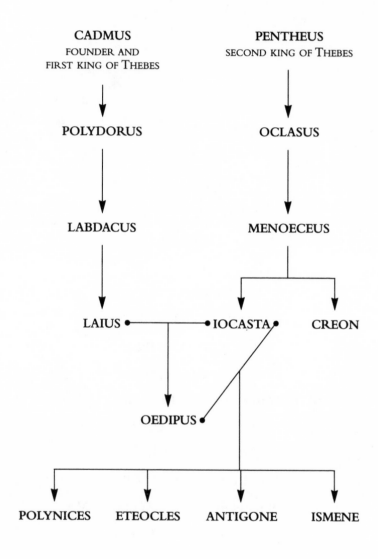

To Laure

Oedipus on the Road

I

THE EYES OF OEDIPUS

The wounds of Oedipus's eyes which have bled for so long are beginning to heal. Black tears no longer course down his cheeks, inspiring the horrific feeling in others that these are their own bloodied tears. The appalling chaos that has reigned over the palace since the death of Iocasta is subsiding. Creon has reinstated the customs and ceremonies of old but everyone in Thebes is aware of the persistence of a secret and ominous rift.

It has taken Oedipus a long time, almost a year, to understand. If at times his sons are restless and quarrelsome, if at times a muted murmur of distress rises from the city; then Creon who holds the reins of power, remains patient, very patient. For he knows that one day Oedipus will not be able to wait any longer. But what is he waiting for?

That night, the huge white seagull hovering over Corinth, the sight of which has helped Oedipus endure the interminable days and nights, does not appear in his dream. In its place, he sees an eagle alternately masking and unmasking the stars as it glides overhead. With one majestic movement, it swoops towards the

1

earth beating its wings, terrorizing its prey as it draws nearer. Oedipus is that prey. He leaps aside and escapes the eagle's talons. He wakes, his senses alert, ready to fight.

At dawn, despite her brothers having forbidden her to do so, and the guard's obstructiveness, Antigone enters his room: 'Father, you are calling me, you have no right.'

He has not spoken since that terrible day, so she is surprised, taken aback, when he replies: 'I do have the right, but I have called no one.' She looks questioningly at the guard, who ascertains with a slight movement that Oedipus has not called. She leaves the room.

A few hours later she returns: 'Father, you are calling me, you are calling me continually – with your heart.' She is not crying. He feels she knows how to control herself.

'Tomorrow, at dawn, I shall leave. You and Ismene will lead me to the Northern Gate.'

'Where will you go?'

In a terrifying voice, he roars: 'Nowhere! Anywhere! Away from Thebes!' He calms down and with a flick of his hand, dismisses her. He prefers to say no more, for the guard has left, no doubt to alert Creon or the two brothers, who at this hour, are to be found in the Great Hall, eyeing one another malevolently.

The next day, it is obvious that the soldiers have been thorough in forewarning the inhabitants, for the city is deserted, all doors and shutters closed.

Ismene gives Oedipus a gourd and attaches it to his belt, and Antigone hands him a staff. He weighs it in his hand and finds pleasure in the familiar contact. It is the wood of his favourite spear. He thinks: 'This is a farewell gift from my sons.' He forgets that Antigone, like the boys, can handle the pike and the spear and that no weapon is unknown to her. The streets are silent except for the sound of their footsteps and the tap of Oedipus's staff as he fumbles across the flagstones. They arrive at the Northern Gate. Polynices emerges from the shadows. Single-handed, he unbars the enormous bronze reinforced gates. On the ramparts above them, Eteocles is armed, keeping watch over the city and the road that winds northwards through gardens and fields to become, very quickly, a track full of ruts and holes.

Ismene, who generally behaves well, has not stopped snivelling since they left the palace. Antigone, dry-eyed, is torn, troubled by something small and yet absurdly terrifying. With one hand she guides her father, with the other she carries the bag she prepared the evening before, along with the water bottle Ismene has given him. A beggar's bag to go nowhere. The idea, the image of Oedipus the King begging, is unbearable. She could not bring herself to give him the bag when they were in the palace, and now that he is leaving them, for good perhaps, now that he is about to pass through the formidable gateway, she still cannot do it. However, time presses, since Oedipus obviously wants to curtail his farewells. He kisses them, briefly says something which she cannot understand, and turns away. He is through the gate, his step and staff reverberating differently on the paving stones of the road, from on the flagstones of the city. She watches his broad back, his tall figure moving off into the distance. She wrings her hands. Wretched, she clutches the absurd bag which was to enable her father to be a beggar like any other. Still she does not cry; she sobs without tears. Then she, proud Antigone, howls with all her might. Ismene is appalled, she stammers: 'Come! Let's go back,' while their father, blind and alone, begins his journey to nowhere. Antigone pushes away Polynices who is holding her back. She shouts: 'Wait for me!' springs forward and runs down the road. Breathless, she catches up with Oedipus, drained by the run and her emotions. She can neither speak nor give him the bag. He stops: 'Go back Antigone, no one can come with me!' and sets off again. She is chilled by his tone, for his words are not so much a father's command as the sentence of a city and the fearsome gods that watch over her. She turns and runs back to where Polynices is waiting for her in front of the gates. What a relief, he has not closed them! Crying, she throws herself into his open arms. Like Oedipus, he is tall, virile, handsome. But unlike him, he does not reject her. She loves him. Polynices, in his boyish, princely and ambitious way, loves her too. He strokes her hair, her shoulders – flatters her, soothing her with his caresses as he does his horses. He tells her they must respect Oedipus's decision and not interfere. He does not question whether it really is his decision. He takes her by the arm, tries to drag her back into the city. She resists. She wants to stay on this side of the gates – to cry and cry and cry. He is patient but the time allocated for Oedipus's departure has passed, he asks her to go and join Ismene so that he can close the gates. She wants to know why. He explains that all the gates of Thebes must be closed and remain closed that day and over the next three days for the ceremony of purification. It has been decreed. Suddenly she understands. It is the decree, passed the previous evening, forbidding Oedipus access to the city and the possibility of ever returning. It is their decree, the one she cannot accept and will never accept. Losing patience, Polynices pushes her towards the threshold of the city and tries to force her to across it.

This is no way to deal with the wayward girl who, catching her brother unawares, frees herself with a sudden movement. Staring at him, she moves backwards slowly, ready to fight. His despondency over his error of judgement soon turns to anger for he has run out of time and the decree is mandatory.

Above them, Eteocles is supervizing the closure of the gates, ready to report the slightest delay. Let her experience the life of the wanderer, a life of subterfuge. She'll be back. However, a surge of affection makes him take a beautiful object from his belt: 'Have this. You'll need it!' Fearing a trap, she leaps back, like a young animal, and catches the object in flight. She looks at it: it is Polynices's finest dagger, the one she has always coveted. She thanks him with the mocking little curtsey that is so much a part of their ritual games but he does not respond with one of his grotesque grimaces. He is busy shutting the gates, barring them noisily behind him. Mournfully, Antigone looks at the ornamental bronze reinforcements that she had been so proud to see each time she returned to the city. She hears her brother dragging away Ismene, who by now is wailing loudly. She turns around. All she is carrying is Polynices's dagger and Oedipus's begging bag. She thinks: 'I'll be the one who'll beg for him.' Seeing her move away, Eteocles, from high up on the ramparts, calls after her several times. She does not turn around but hurries one; their father is already out of sight.

Antigone does not run, she knows she only needs to walk to catch up with Oedipus. She follows him but there is a yearning inside her, pulling her not towards him but back to Thebes. Ahead, her father's tall figure advances with difficulty, with that insane obstinacy he has always had. Anger explodes within her. Why did he call her with his heart if it was only to reject her? Why did he stay so long in Thebes, humiliated and dejected, if he was to leave so abruptly? The consequences of this are all too obvious: with her two brothers' aspirations to the kingdom stronger than ever there is now open hostility between them; like an animal, Oedipus has been banished from the palace, from the city, and she, unable to endure this tragedy, is following him, with neither walking shoes nor overcoat, abandoning Ismene to the struggles and intrigues of the palace. Only too aware that she knows nothing of life beyond the useless things taught to a king's daughter, Antigone is frightened and bitter. Anything that was of value in Thebes, everything that gave them an aura of import-ance is now lost, engulfed in what Eteocles refers to as their father's mad, ludicrous adventure.

As she catches up with that great stooping figure advancing ahead of her, stumbling over stones and falling into potholes, Antigone's fury increases as she thinks of those who drove him out, especially the man who manipulated them all: Creon! Creon who loves Ismene so much because of her likeness to Iocasta; while she, Antigone, has inherited from her father her height, too tall for a girl, and her face, now blotchy and graceless. Her mother used to say: 'You look like your father, be patient, you will be beautiful, very beautiful even.'

She is not far from Oedipus, who advances with difficulty; hesitating, ceaselessly tapping on the ground with his staff. She is hungry and thirsty, like him she is burnt by the sun, but by walking faster she can now and then stop and rest in the shade.

Oedipus is nearing a well; a peasant woman, holding a child by the hand, arrives at the same time. Orders must have been sent out from Thebes for she is the first person he has come across. Living in an isolated spot, this woman cannot have been warned. She sees he is blind and gives him water. She fills his gourd and he asks her to pour some water over his head. She laughs: 'Like the soldiers do?'

He sighs: 'As I used to once.'

She looks at him with a mixture of pity and respect. He thanks her. Despite the band over his eyes, he still has a wonderful smile. He sets off once more.

Antigone goes up to the well and announces her name; the woman responds by giving hers: Ilyssa. She fills the bowl left on the lip of the well and the two of them drink. Is Antigone with the blind man? Yes, she is.

'You shouldn't let him go off alone like that, he'll fall and hurt himself.'

'It's what he wants.'

'It's what he wants, what he wants! He could so easily sprain his ankle. You must take charge, my girl!'

Antigone is horrified: 'Take charge?'

'Yes, take charge, he might be glad to have someone leading him. Has he been off on his own like this for long?'

'He was thrown out of Thebes this morning.'

'So he's the old tyrant who killed his father! I shouldn't have spoken to him. I'll have to purify myself and my son too. What should I do?'

Antigone, who is familiar with the rites of Thebes, helps her perform them faithfully. Reassured, Ilyssa gets ready to leave. At last, Antigone has the courage to ask her for something to eat. Ilyssa brings her some bread from her house. She smiles, but does not approach her. She throws the bread on the ground. Antigone bends down and picks it up.

Oedipus is dizzy. It began when he first left the shady city streets to plunge unprotected into the wind and the harshness of the road. Is it the effect of the brilliance of the sun on his scarred eyes, or the result of being in the open air after all those months of inactivity, seated on the ground at the foot of a pillar in a small anteroom of the palace? He feels as if he is crossing a red fog streaked with dark lightning, or as if he is entering a suddenly bright zone with immediate painful consequences. With every step he takes he veers to the left or the right, hoping, expecting to follow the movement, exaggerating it until he loses his balance. He hurries, not because he is anxious to arrive somewhere, for he does not know, no longer wants to know where he might go. He hurries because he is Oedipus who has always hurried, who has always been hurried by others, by events and by the oracle. Except when the event, or was it the oracle, was Iocasta, when together they put themselves beyond what we know as time.

As Ilyssa poured the water over his head he thought how a similarly icy destiny had befallen him and what he referred to in those days as his happiness. Since then facts have become confused, unconnected events have sprung from nowhere. Like the dream of the eagle, which dragged him out of that humiliating corner of the palace where he could at least refuse to face up to the future. He can no longer allow himself to do this and must find a simple, empty place, where he can crumble and disappear. By following and hounding him like a last intrusive presence from Thebes, Antigone is threatening, challenging this aim so compatible with his vertigo.

He finds it increasingly difficult to continue on his way. His body aches from having lost the habit of walking. When he no longer feels the sun's heat on his brow he leaves the road and stretches out on the ground. An automatic reflex from his military life makes him take off his sandals and put down his staff and gourd.

Light steps approach, a hand slips a little grass and some leaves under his head and places a piece of bread in his hand. Antigone says: 'That's all I have. I've already eaten the other half.' He does not refuse it but eats the bread which, though hard, tastes good. He hands her the gourd; with the next day in mind she takes a few sips only. He drinks, careful in turn to leave half the water. He too is thinking ahead. What misery! He says: 'Antigone, tomorrow you must return to Thebes. It's what I want.' She says nothing and moves away. He tells himself he has no way of protecting her. As always, he falls asleep suddenly.

There is very little moonlight and Antigone is frightened of the dark. She daren't lie down at the side of the road like Oedipus. There is a vineyard a little further on. Between two rows of vines she will be hidden. She lies down in a furrow and wonders what she will do in the morning. She realizes she has no idea. He wants me to go back to Thebes, and I, with all my soul, long to also. But where does this longing come from? For I can hear another voice speaking to me at the same time, saying: Go with him, no matter where. That 'no matter where' fills me with dread and yet attracts me. She is exhausted, no longer able to think clearly. She looks up at the thin crescent moon – without doubt a goddess. A little dazed she thinks of all the goddesses, all the gods to whom she has offered libations, made sacrifices, for whom she has sung, danced and who are now with her, drowsy as she is with sleep, far from home, from Thebes, where they all existed.

She wakes early, numbed by the morning chill, aching from her night on the hard ground. The sun on the horizon is barely visible through the mist. Her father has not yet set off. He wakes and stretches in the grass. Trees grow between the rows of vines. Whereas the grapes are only just beginning to ripen, the fruit on the trees is ready to eat. She picks some and takes it to Oedipus. He accepts and shares it with her, chewing carefully, as she has always seen him do, like someone who knows that food is in short supply and must be rationed.

She goes back for more and is in the process of picking the fruit when she hears a shout behind her. She turns, it is the farmer, furious at seeing her thieving. She does not know what to do or how to justify what she is doing. At that moment

Oedipus's tall frame appears behind her. As the man nears them, he sees Oedipus is blind. He says: 'I didn't know, take what you want!'

With horror, Antigone sees Oedipus kneel, stretch out his arms towards the man and say, like a real beggar: 'Give a little bread to the blind, as you would to Zeus and the great gods, protectors of Thebes.'

Nervously, the man asks: 'Are you Oedipus, the old king?'

'I am a blind man, a supplicant. Don't come near me but give us a little bread to see us through the day.'

Terror-stricken, the man rushes away. Antigone thinks he is fleeing and will not return. She is horrified by what she has just witnessed; never did she imagine that her father could kneel and ask for bread. He stands up and she implores him: 'Why do you humiliate yourself like this?'

The reply is not the one she dreads. He does not say: 'For you,' but: 'I ask for bread and say how things are.'

The farmer returns. Keeping a safe distance, he leaves a piece of bread and a small pitcher on the ground and hurries off. Antigone goes to take the bread, picks up the pitcher that contains a little wine and pours it into the gourd. In silence, they eat half the bread and Antigone puts the rest in the bag with the fruit.

He stands: 'You saw what happened, worse incidents could occur on the road and I am in no position to protect you. Return to Thebes, Antigone; I am not ordering you, since you no longer wish to obey me, but I do beseech you to.'

She does not protest for she is frightened he might kneel at her feet to make her consent. She agrees.

They return to the road. He kisses her and they part, each in their own direction, he to the east and she to the west – towards Thebes, the city with its seven gates closed to Oedipus.

She has walked for a long time, oblivious of the wind, the sun burning her, the length of her journey. Her heart is heavy but continues to draw her back to Thebes, as if there she might find peace and the answer to her questions. Overwhelmed by fatigue, her body no longer responding, she cannot help but slow down. With the last of her strength, she reaches the well where she met Ilyssa the previous day.

She lowers the bucket but is too tired to raise it. Afraid she will faint she is forced to lie down, and with the last vestiges of her strength, she calls Ilyssa. She must have sounded in great distress for Ilyssa comes running.

Ilyssa gives her a drink, washes her face and hands, and tells her to eat. She opens Antigone's bag and gives her the farmer's bread. Seeing it, Antigone thinks: 'Oedipus has nothing, he is on the road with nothing.' She grabs the bag and wants to run off in pursuit. Ilyssa restrains her: 'Eat and rest first and wait for the heat of the day to pass.' Like a little girl, Antigone sobs in Ilyssa's arms; she is consoled and led to the shade of a tree. Ilyssa gives her bread and biscuits. As the sun begins to go down and the road becomes shadier, she accompanies her part of the way: 'Don't hurry. As my mother used to say: work needs time. The blind man cannot go fast, you will catch up with him – but be careful, they say the bandit Clius is in the area. He is handsome and irresistible to women. Later he kills them.'

Ilyssa can go no further for she cannot leave her children. They embrace and Antigone, turning her back on Thebes, leaves to follow Oedipus. She walks slowly, stopping as Ilyssa advised her to, to rest and nibble at the bread. The weightiest and most secret part of her being has successfully tipped the balance and is pulling her towards the dark abyss over which Oedipus is leaning, and into which she will have to follow him.

By dusk, she can see her father in the distance; walking is an effort for him, he stops often and sometimes falls; his silhouette has changed. She would like to run and catch up with him but she remembers Ilyssa's advice and saves her strength. When she is nearer she sees that he is wearing a straw hat for protection. Someone must have given it to him, for he was not wearing it before. He can go no further and leaves the road to collapse at the foot of a tree. He has drunk all the water in the gourd and walked all day without food. He does not object when she raises to his lips the leather bottle that Ilyssa gave her. He drinks, incoherently muttering words in the Corinthian dialect which she does not understand. No doubt he has the beginnings of sunstroke, it is fortunate that he has the hat. Who gave it to him? 'A man,' he replies, 'who came like a hunter without making a sound and then left without saying a word.'

Oedipus does not seem surprised, not at feeling her close, nor at the food she brings. She thinks that perhaps he does not know who she is. She stays near him until he falls asleep, before finding herself some kind of shelter in a field.

II

CLIUS

Next morning Oedipus seems better. They share what is left of the water, the last of Ilyssa's biscuits, and the fruit. Antigone is anxious, afraid there will be no water along a track as remote as this one.

Oedipus has already set off. She follows a little way behind. The track takes them through a forest where the shade is pleasant and soothing. She delights in the beauty of the foliage and the sun filtering through the lower branches, but an inexplicable, deep-seated anxiety leaves her feeling uneasy. She does not know if it is the sound of the wind rustling in the trees, or the impression she has had since the morning that they are being stalked and spied on. Through the branches she notices a stream flowing not far from the path. She shouts to her father that she is going to fetch some water. She hopes he will stop. She gets to the stream, kneels at the edge and dips her face into the water. Raising her face, she catches sight of the reflection of a man. She turns abruptly. He is standing behind her; she cannot understand why she did not hear him approach. He is young and has a smiling face; although he does not look evil, there is something wild and bitter in his expression that frightens and intimidates her. He says: 'You're beautiful and your fear makes you even more beautiful.'

She tenses because she knows this is not so, especially when she is afraid, and because she is capable of uttering no more than a feeble: 'Who are you?'

He does not bother to reply, but says, as if it were his responsibility: 'You won't find any more water for a long time. Give the blind man a drink, then come back and fill your gourd and water-bottle.' Adding, still in his alarmingly self-assured manner: 'I'll make a pool for you so that you can wash – him too. You certainly need one.' And he disappears, soundlessly, towards the path.

She finds Oedipus seated on a stone: 'He told me to wait for you here.'

'Who?'

'The man who walks noiselessly.'

When she returns to the stream, the man has gone. She is relieved and a little disappointed. She sees he has built a dam of stones in the middle of the stream creating a shallow pool, where, after two torrid days on the road and two nights of sleeping on the ground, she will be able to bathe. But perhaps he is hiding in the undergrowth, waiting to spy on her? She inspects the surroundings. There is no one. She undresses, takes great delight in bathing and dresses hurriedly. She fills the water-bottles and returns to the path. Oedipus must have heard her coming for he is already standing. She has barely taken a few steps when the man emerges from a thicket. She thinks he is going to speak but no, he walks beside her in silence. She cannot stop herself from looking at him. How handsome he is, his dark curly hair tumbling over his high forehead, his superb mouth forming a sardonic smile. His eyes seem to challenge both heaven and earth with irony for – ah! how moving – he has nothing to gain, nothing to lose. Eyes that see right through you, poor girl, and which see so easily what is going on in your thin body and half-formed soul. Yes, without your realizing, he has understood what you desire. As you walk next to him he takes your hand in his, and though you know you should withdraw it instantly, you do not have the will. You walk, completely dependent on that hand that slides up to your wrist, moves up your forearm. When it is near your shoulder you, Iocasta's daughter, realizing what is happening, come out of your trance and move away swiftly. A look of impatience and cruelty flashes across his features and suddenly, with all his strength, he strikes her across the face. He is ready to hit her again but the pain angers her: 'So, that's your game, we'll see about that!' She leaps back, taking out her dagger as she does so, and, by skilfully escaping a second blow, throws him off balance. She could stab him but cannot bring herself to damage so beautiful a body. She is content to keep him at bay by threatening him with her weapon. He backs away and laughs, exclaiming: 'What a girl!' He has a weapon at his side but she would strike before he had time to draw it. Despite his fury he is laughing. She revels in this, enjoying herself despite her fear, which is why he catches her off guard. He raises his leg, very high. She thinks: 'A dancer's leg.' With the full force of his foot, he hits her forearm. She feels terrible pain and thinks: 'He's broken my arm,' as the dagger slips from her hand. She falls. He is already on her but instinctively, relaxing her body, she lands in the position Polynices taught her, and with her feet and knees knocks him over. She hears him say: 'Well defended!'

Once more they are face to face, but now he holds the dagger while she, breathless and without a weapon, has lost the use of her arm. Slowly he circles around her shouting: 'I'll get you yet!' and hits her again, harder than the first time. Her mouth fills with blood which spills down her lip. Pain and shame reduce her to tears. She no longer has any means of defending herself, whereas he is dancing around her, waiting for the right moment, for his choice is not yet made: should he rape or kill her? She thinks: 'It's him, it's Clius the Bandit,' and absurdly, as if he were still able to protect her, she shouts as loud as she can: 'Father, help me!'

The man takes a few steps back, draws his sword and laughs. She looks round. Oedipus is there clutching his pitiful wooden lance. The bandit circles around him, laughing wildly, but her father is also turning on the spot, holding up his lance, in true Theban technique fashion. She thinks: he is lost. Unarmed as she is, she does the only thing she can and lunges at the bandit's legs to throw him off balance. Her right arm still useless, all she can do is grab hold of his left leg. He does not fall, but she sinks her teeth into him as hard as she can, whereupon he, with one kick, sends her rolling along the ground. She hears Oedipus's calm voice saying: 'Don't move Antigone. Leave him to me!'

The bandit turns this way and that, leaping unpredictably around his adversary but with every move he is confronted by the twirling staff. He says: 'So you're not blind, you're only pretending.' Several times, he tries to get Oedipus to drop his guard, and Antigone sees with mounting apprehension that he is enjoying himself more and more, happy to find his opponent a worthy match. He says: 'The Theban Defence. The secret defence. We'll see about that.' He glides full-length along the ground and lunges at Oedipus. There are cries of pain; Oedipus is wounded, but only in the leg since he retreated in time, and his parry has landed heavily on the bandit's left arm making him drop Polynices's dagger. The arm hangs loose and Antigone hopes yet fears it might be broken. She grabs the weapon and realizes that even though the man is still laughing, his circling of Oedipus and his pain have tired him. Saving his strength, Oedipus is happy to swivel on the spot presenting his opponent with a constantly moving wall. The man's movements grow heavy. The leg Antigone bit is bothering him. Oedipus takes a step forward, then another to the side; his adversary thinks it is a break in his defence and sees an opportunity to attack.

Antigone recognizes the move and waits for the incredible reverse-twirl to take place at the chosen moment. The sword is snatched from the bandit and a second blow, aimed very low, catches his legs, making him fall. She admires that faultless manoeuvre which Polynices taught her, but she could never have executed it so fast nor with such confidence. The bandit is on the ground, dazed. Antigone has seized his sword; Oedipus, foot on his throat, raises his lance. He is about to bring it down on the man's head and smash his face. She shouts: 'Father, don't kill him!' He stops mid-movement, apparently surprised by what he was about to do. He lowers the lance, withdraws his foot, stoops over his opponent and helps him up. Antigone sees that the man's arm is not broken and that his supercilious smile is gone. He appears amazed, overcome by what has just happened. Head hanging, he looks at Oedipus and it is with a weak voice that he asks: 'Are you really blind?'

'Yes,' says Oedipus.

The man finds this difficult to believe but sees from Antigone's eyes that it is true.

'What's your name?' asks Oedipus.

'Clius. In this country they call me Clius the Bandit.' Oedipus returns his sword. 'Take it and go.'

Once again Clius's face expresses surprise. He takes his weapon and begins to walk away.

Having taken a few steps, he returns to Antigone: 'Take these leaves and this clay, put them on your wounds. Here is some bread, you'll need it.'

He bends down to examine his leg then looks at Antigone: 'You bit me like a bitch!' The vicious mocking smile returns to his lips: 'You did well.' Soundlessly, he plunges into the trees.

Oedipus is suffering from his wound and she is too shaken to continue. He allows her to guide him to the clearing where Clius built the dam. They sit down by the stream where the water babbles over the stones like the sound of clear voices. He does not reproach her for what has happened, does not ask her to return to Thebes. He says: 'As we have bread, let's eat.' They ration the bread but drink their fill; after days of thirst it is a great relief. She helps him to soak his feet and legs in the water of the shallow pool. To the wound, she applies the leaves and clay, the healing properties of which are known to her father. She prepares a bed of bracken and helps him lie down. He thanks her with a smile and she thinks: 'How handsome he is.' Not the venomous, sombre good-looks of Clius the Bandit, but a once laughing beauty, now serious and reserved.

She dares ask: 'Father, how did you overpower him without being able to see?'

'I don't know. I could sense each of his movements, everything he was about to do. For a few moments I was elated, then my melancholy returned.'

She sees he is not happy talking of the incident, but carries on none the less. 'Is he a skilful warrior?'

'Yes, skilful, very skilful but he doesn't know the secret Defence of Thebes. And he has become smug, deluded by pride and presumptuousness.'

There is an amused silence between them. 'Is Clius really as handsome as you find him, daughter?'

With a little laugh: 'Yes, too handsome, much too handsome . . .'

They are both lying down. The oppressiveness of the day has been dissolved by the coolness of the stream. The crescent moon is rising.

She wonders if he is asleep, but then hears him murmur quietly, as if he were a little ashamed: 'Antigone, I'm glad you are here.' At this, she too feels elated. She hears his regular breathing, he has fallen into his deep sailor's sleep. Why a sailor's? From far away an old expression of her mother's comes to her: 'You must never forget, my darling, that your father is first and foremost a sailor.' Yes, it was all very well for Iocasta to say that, but how can I, a little town-dweller from Thebes who has never been to sea, understand.

The following morning, Oedipus's wound is still painful but he assures her he can walk. He is in no hurry. After their meal, she offers to help him wash but he does not answer. It is as if he were waiting – but for what? Clius maybe, for here he is, with his weapons and face gleaming. Were it not for the stiffness of his arm and the wound on his leg, it would be difficult to believe that the previous day's events had taken place.

He places his javelin and sword at Oedipus's feet and kneels. Seizing him by the knees he says: 'Do not spurn me Oedipus, I come to you as a supplicant. I, Clius the Bandit, who wanted to add to my crimes a felony more monstrous and, to my eyes of yesterday, more attractive than previous ones: to seduce a young girl, a naïve and fearless princess, to defeat her and have her at my mercy in the presence of her blind father. Then to kill you both, and leave your bodies unburied and your souls to roam in this forest. That is what I had wanted to do.'

'But you didn't,' says Oedipus.

'You prevented me and this morning, on waking, it seemed to me that someone was summoning me. All my people are dead, no one can call me. You were the one I could hear.'

Oedipus takes Clius's hands in his and makes him stand. 'When I had power, I never turned away a supplicant and I will not do so today, though I have no more to give. Forget and go in peace.'

'Go where?'

'You are free.'

'Free to steal, to rape, to kill? Are you free when you have killed your father and married your mother?'

Oedipus sighs and does not answer. Clius continues: 'This morning when you summoned me, I felt that you were my last hope.'

'I did not summon you. I am no one's hope. I call no one.'

Then Antigone says: 'You summoned him as you did me in Thebes. In your heart, you are calling him, you don't realize this because you don't know what is in your own heart.'

A smile of grief and uncertainty crosses Oedipus's lips: 'All right, tell me what you want, you, whom I have summoned unknowingly?'

'I want to go with you and do what you do.'

'I am a man whose eyes and actions are blind.'

'I shall serve that blind man; with him I shall protect Antigone. In the past it was not women who served you but men. I know what to do. I shall look after you as a king, albeit dethroned and in exile, should be looked after. I can begin now.'

Oedipus does not reply. Antigone is happy and says: 'Begin!' She withdraws and Clius leads Oedipus to the stream where, with extreme care, he washes him, dresses his wound, cleans his clothes and untangles his thick, tawny hair.

Clius suggests they spend another day on the banks of the stream. Antigone objects as they have no food, but he hands her a brace of partridge he caught at the edge of the forest. Out of earth and stones he builds a small enclosure for the fire. They eat. The birds are not very fleshy but they taste good and he has brought what is left of his bread.

Oedipus remarks: 'You are a very resourceful man.'

He replies: 'Before we were struck by disaster, my father was a stockman and farmer. He was also a good hunter. In our mountains you had to be able to do everything.' Antigone realizes that a catastrophe must have befallen him, the traces of which can be seen on his sharp and often gloomy features. But she does not have the courage to ask him about it.

In the evening he makes a bed of bracken for Oedipus and another for himself close by, so that he can respond to the slightest call. A little way off, he builds a roof of leaves to shelter and protect her. That night she has strange dreams about him and is not surprised to see him rekindling the embers of the fire in the morning.

The men have washed and Clius is now preparing a herb soup into which they drop what is left of their bread. He says to Antigone: 'We must leave as we have nothing left to eat, you will have to beg.'

'Will you help me?'

'No, people will run away if they see me.'

'I'll go with you,' says Oedipus.

'If they recognize you,' said Clius, 'they will stone you.'

They leave. Antigone hopes Clius will take the lead. He does not. Wanting to help her father, she takes his arm, he disengages himself angrily and says: 'I have to make my way alone.' He sets off with that faltering, hurried step; she feels better not watching him for it makes her uneasy. She lets him go first. She thinks

Clius will join her but he walks behind. The road curves and the sound of an approaching cart is heard in the distance. Oedipus hides behind some bushes, followed by Clius. The cart is pulled by two young men, a woman trails some way behind. On it are sacks of wheat.

Antigone stands in their path: 'My father is blind, give us some grain.' They look unsure as to whether to do so, no doubt they are waiting for their mother to make the decision; laughing as though she were not there, they tell one another what they would like to do to her.

The woman has caught up with them and says: 'Those sons of mine, take no notice of them. The fields haven't yielded much this year as you can see. The drought again. Open the sacks you two and give her three good handfuls, we can't spare any more. What are you going to grind it with girl?'

'Stones.'

'Choose good flat ones and take your time. That lost cost us dear this year.'

Antigone recites one of the Theban blessings. Laughing as they go, the two sons set off again followed by the dark, thin woman.

That evening Antigone finds some flat stones and patiently grinds the grain. Clius builds two improvised shelters while she cooks a broth to which she adds herbs.

During the night a storm breaks. In her dreams Antigone hears the rain falling into the courtyards and on to the rooftops of the palace at Thebes. She is a young child again. Anaïs, her nurse and Ismene's, is sitting at their bedside reciting ritual prayers to protect the city from being struck by lightning. She wakes to find herself in the leafy hut. She is well protected and hopes that her father and Clius are too. She would like to go and see, but dares not: the thunder, the rain, the darkness frightens her. She thinks: 'I can stay under shelter. They are adults, but me, I am too young. Fourteen is not so old.' She puts her arm over her face as if to shield herself.

In the morning when she emerges from the hut, Clius is busy

in front of the fire. He is half naked, Oedipus too. The ground is scattered with pools of water, steaming after the storm. The sun reappears. She sees their clothes drying on the roof of her hut.

They move on with nothing left to eat. At the end of the day they come up to a village and Antigone wants to beg alone, but Oedipus decides he wants to accompany her. His being there makes her nervous. The village is poor, she hears exclamations of: 'Not more beggars!' She stands in front of each door, asking for help for her and her blind father. He stands behind her, silent. Doors slam in their faces, others are not opened. One woman gives her a piece of bread, two others some vegetables. A little hope returns.

She stops in front of another door, a woman calls out: 'Coming!' A man's voice cuts in: 'No. There's too many of them. It's easier than working.'

The woman appears in the upper opening of the door. She looks kind. Surreptitiously she slips Antigone a piece of bread but for her husband to hear, says: 'I can't give you anything, go and ask the rich.'

Antigone asks: 'Where are the rich?'

The man appears, his features thickset but not mean, and answers: 'Not here, girl, in Thebes maybe, the famous ramparts of which I worked behind for so long.' Then to his wife: 'Give them something, it pains me to see that blind man kneeling.'

Antigone turns round, her father is kneeling, reciting a prayer. A man appears who used to be a soldier in Thebes, he recognizes Oedipus and says to the others: 'It's the old tyrant, the one who killed his father and built up the ramparts.'

Then to Oedipus: 'Go away! You will bring us bad luck.' He throws some earth in front of him, it is obvious he does not want to hurt him. Oedipus is still on his knees, Antigone is trying to drag him away.

More men arrive, they also throw earth, not to hit him but as a gesture of purification. The women join in as they shout: 'Go away! Go away!' A younger boy throws manure at Oedipus and bursts out laughing when it strikes him in the face.

With one bound Oedipus is up, looming over them, he looks every inch a king. Astounded they fall silent. He shouts: 'Men without pity, houses without welcome for a blind man and a supplicant, I curse you. May the misfortunes that have befallen me come down upon your heads.'

Fearful, then angry, they pick up stones and begin to throw them at the pair. Antigone is hit, she is bleeding, she screams and grabs Oedipus by the hand. They flee in the direction of a haystack from behind which Clius appears. Their assailants pursue them, throwing stones and rubbish. Those nearest are stopped by a shower of stones aimed with deadly accuracy. Antigone takes advantage of this to reach the shelter of the haystack but Clius shouts to her to carry on running. He soon catches up with them, seizes Oedipus's other hand and their pace accelerates. Now only a handful of men are chasing them. Clius turns and faces them. Seeing that he is armed, they stop, confer, then return to the village.

Clius joins the others: 'They have gone to get scythes and clubs. They'll be back, we must leave immediately and get as far away as possible.' He leads the way. They both take Oedipus by the hand and hurry despite their exhaustion. Clius keeps looking back over his shoulder. There is no one. It is the middle of the night when they come to the edge of a stream. Antigone takes from her bag what she has been able to salvage, a few pieces of bread and some vegetables which they eat raw since a fire would give them away.

As they eat Antigone asks Oedipus: 'The one who recognized you talked of you raising the height of the walls of Thebes as if you had done something wrong. Iocasta used to say it was the most glorious thing you had ever done.'

'I used to think so.'

'Who paid?' He does not reply.

Clius laughs: 'It's the same old story, the poor paid for the walls of Thebes and built them and it's the rich they protect.'

Antigone is disconcerted: 'Is that true?'

'It is. I was thinking of Thebes not of the peasants.'

Clius's wicked laugh echoes out: 'The ramparts completed, the rich chase you out of Thebes and your daughter has to go and beg from peasants.'

Antigone stops him, she sees that Oedipus is in anguish. She asks her father if she can beg alone in future. He agrees and says that not only is he blind but also a fool.

'Such magnificent folly,' says Clius, 'that of a real king of Thebes; we could have stayed there the three of us.'

The night passes, Oedipus and Clius taking it in turns to keep watch. If they are pursued they will have the advantage. To preserve it, they leave early, having shared the little bread that is left. Oedipus leads, going straight ahead as usual. Clius thinks it is perhaps the best way to outwit any pursuers but that it will take them into increasingly arid territory. All they see are flocks of goats or sheep and wild-looking shepherds who move away as soon as they come near.

The three of them are hungry, they are drained by the events of the previous day and the short night. Oedipus moves slowly, struggling against a feeling of vertigo and a secret desire to collapse. He is oblivious to the presence of the other two, obstinately insisting on taking the lead and refusing to stop. By midday the heat is intolerable. Clius thinks it is essential to find some shade and rest, for Antigone is having difficulty keeping up. Everything around her becomes blurred, icy sweat pours down her face and back, she stumbles over a stone, her legs give way and she doubled up groaning, falling down unconscious.

The two men lean over her. 'Your daughter is dying of exhaustion and hunger. What do you intend to do in this desert?' Oedipus does not reply. He hands his staff to Clius, takes Antigone in his arms, and makes his way to a huge oak growing on a hillock they passed earlier. His vertigo seems to have vanished as, without faltering, he goes straight to the tree. He lays Antigone down where the shade is deepest. Clius hands him the gourd, Oedipus gently pours a little water between her lips, moistens her face and hands. She has a fever. He removes her sandals, massages her feet, her legs. She sighs deeply and Clius gives her some more water. 'She'll come round soon, it's the effect of fatigue, heat and emotion. She needs to eat, have we nothing left?'

'Nothing.'

'The first flock you come to, ask the shepherd for a lamb, some milk and some bread. In exchange give him this necklace that Iocasta gave me.'

'And if he refuses?'

'Then take what we need by force but don't kill him. Drink before you go.'

Clius is impressed by the curt voice, the authority and assurance of its tone, but his anger has not subsided: 'If I have to use force Oedipus, be prepared to see a band of shepherds come down here and for us to be pursued yet again by the love of your former subjects.'

Oedipus does not reply. He waits a moment and says: 'My friend, she must eat. Then, if necessary, we will fight together.'

As he walks Clius mulls over Oedipus's words. He is no longer alone, alone against the world. He has a friend who is also the father of that fearless girl who trusts him and whom he must save.

Antigone's breathing eases. She is asleep. Feeling the ground, Oedipus gathers wood to make a fire. He concentrates his thoughts on Antigone and Clius. It is his powerlessness that sustains them, her in her sleep and him in his action. He is sitting against a tree trunk and, opening her eyes after a bad dream, Antigone sees him next to her. He smiles, she will never know to whom nor why but it is of no consequence, since the smile permits her to go back to sleep reassured.

Although Oedipus has not heard Clius return, he is suddenly aware of his presence. He has brought back a lamb, chopped into pieces, some dry wheat biscuits and a flask of ewe's milk. The shepherd turned down the proposed exchange; Clius was forced to kill the dog, overpower the man and take the victuals by force. The shepherd is not hurt and Clius left him the necklace, but they should be ready for the clan to retaliate. He lights the fire; the smell of the roasting meat wakes Antigone. She is delighted by the milk; she drinks, eats and goes back to sleep.

The following day she takes Oedipus's hand in hers: 'Yesterday, when you were carrying me half-conscious, I thought: In Thebes, there would have been no one to carry me like this. I was happy and this morning I am even happier.' Her fever gone, she is hungry but too weak to stand. She eats, and worries when she sees that Clius is not there. 'Has he left us?'

'He has only gone to the river to get some water, it's a long way.'

He returns, she is happy, ecstatic even to see him and wants to tell him but does not dare. She smiles, grimacing the way she used to at her brothers. He responds as they used to.

In the middle of the day ten shepherds with big black dogs appear. They circle the tree under which Antigone is lying. Standing, Oedipus and Clius are waiting for them. They have openly laid Clius's sword and spear in front of the tree, rather than hold them in their hands.

Oedipus says: 'If you are here to talk, let us be seated.' With great dignity, they all sit where they are. The dogs stretch out nearby. Their silence is not hostile, it is the silence of men who do not have much use for speech but who, when they do talk, do so with the reserve and sobriety characteristic of their lives.

'My name is Selenus, I am the leader of this particular clan, which has cross-border links with shepherd clans from here to the sea. Yesterday your companion attacked one of ours. His act was attributed to hunger. By way of compensation the shepherd was given a necklace worth a thousand times what was taken from us. We cannot accept this discrepancy and hereby return the necklace. When a flock is repeatedly attacked by a wolf, we consider that either the flock or the wolf must perish. Our clan and the shepherds and labourers of this country are being persistently persecuted by a man who is far more dangerous than a wolf. This man, Menes, robs us of the fruits of our labours and we think that your companion Clius could deliver us from him.'

'What has this man done to you?'

'With the help of the soldiers in Thebes who are in his pay, he has had us barred from all the markets except the one at Goria, in the district he governs. At this market, no one would risk outbidding him, for his brother commands the town garrison and his uncle is president of the tribunal. He is the only buyer; he fixes the prices to the detriment of us all. He buys our goods at a derisory price and resells them for much more, especially in Thebes.'

'Do you want Clius to kill him?'

Selenus answers 'yes' and his companions nod in agreement.

'Another will take his place,' points out Oedipus.

'Not easily but in any case we will have been avenged!' Selenus's tone is abrupt, full of such startling hatred that silence ensues. Antigone, who is still lying next to Oedipus, whispers: 'Father, I should not like Clius to have to kill someone because I am ill.' Clius, untouched by the scrutiny of the shepherds, hears her and the elation he feels reminds him of the euphoria which comes with rain after a long drought.

'I must confer with Clius before I give you my decision,' says Oedipus. 'To stop Menes there is perhaps an alternative to murder. I suggest we meet tomorrow to discuss it.'

Selenus stands; the shepherds do likewise: 'We will not reject an alternative but we doubt there is one. You, your daughter and your companion the dangerous bandit, now know of our desire to be rid of Menes. We cannot afford this secret to be known. We shall not return tomorrow but tonight. Do not move from here, we are many and you are surrounded. If you do not deliver us of Menes, we shall be obliged to kill all three of you.'

Oedipus stands tall in front of him: 'It seems to me that you are offering us a contract: Menes's death or our own. And if we rid you of him what will you do for us?'

'From Thebes to the Eastern Sea, you will be like brothers to all the shepherd clans. We might be poor but we are numerous.'

'Does Menes,' Oedipus asks, 'give those to whom he sells or from whom he buys, a writing tablet which bears his seal?'

'Not to us of course,' says an old shepherd, 'but when I take the animals he buys from us to Thebes, the big merchants of the town have been given a tablet stamped with his seal and I bring it back to him with the seal of the purchaser.'

The shepherds leave.

Oedipus asks Antigone: 'If they were dictated to you, would you be capable of writing down Menes's crimes in the Phoenician script, for him to acknowledge with his seal?'

'Yes. Is that the alternative?'

'That's it,' says Clius. 'All we have to do is bring Menes here and get the shepherds to agree to our plan. It will not be easy.'

At sunset the shepherds return. There are no longer ten but thirty of them, each accompanied by one of those terrifying black dogs from the High Mountains who do not bark but pounce silently on their master's enemies. Oedipus explains that if Menes were killed, the soldiers would swoop down on them and wreak revenge. This can be avoided by forcing Menes to acknowledge his crimes in writing. The tablets, authenticated by his seal, would be kept hidden in a place designated by Selenus. They would constitute for Menes and his accomplices a permanent threat and this would destroy their power.

'How will you get him to come here?'

'By offering him the possibility of buying, at a very low price, the necklace Iocasta gave me. He is only too well aware that Creon or my sons would pay him handsomely for it.'

'Who will bring him?'

'I will,' says Antigone, 'he will suspect nothing if it is me.'

The shepherds confer and decide to accept. 'When will you go?' asks Selenus.

'In three days, when Antigone has recovered.'

'Right. We shall bring you provisions and water. Oedipus, you were a king who was often misunderstood but who tried to be fair. We are depending on you to rid us of Menes.'

'Get some writing tablets and a stylet. Set up a tribunal amongst yourselves, he will have to be put on trial.'

Three days later, escorted by a young shepherd, Antigone

accosts Menes in the square at Goria. He does not look like a rapacious man but more like one of the many dignitaries she has seen at the Palace, dulled and bloated by good living. The type whose shady dealings are not executed by them but by their underlings. When she tells him her name and that she is Oedipus's daughter and Creon's niece, he understands immediately that this is an affair of some importance that could have political consequences. This tall, thin girl, despite her dirty, darned dress has the air and language of the court. The segment of the necklace she shows him is of gold and precious stones of great value. Moreover, she gives him to understand that a price could be agreed with her father, which must mean the latter is in difficulties. He only met Oedipus once when he was king. His victories were being celebrated and the Theban army was already the best, but he did not benefit from his triumphs as much as he could have done. He was a man observing events from afar and from on high, which prevented him from seeing what was going on right under his nose. All that, only to end up putting out his own eyes and allowing himself to be dethroned, while his brother-in-law, without even having to raise his little finger, finds himself in power!

His mule follows the young girl's but when the road widens, he moves next to her and tries to engage her in conversation; but her replies are monosyllabic. Impossible to fathom this girl from the court; is it because she is shy or because she is clever? When he asks her why her father wants the sale to be officially recorded and stamped with his seal, she says it is to protect the purchaser from any dispute with Polynices and Eteocles.

The countryside gradually becomes wilder, there are no more houses. He asks where her father is living. She replies that he has no home, that he is camping under an oak tree.

'Why didn't he come to Goria, he could have had a house?'

'My father is outlawed, he has been cursed. You will have to purify yourself when you have seen him.'

Menes thinks that under these circumstances, he will have no problem getting him to reduce the price considerably. 'Does he wish to return to Thebes?'

'Perhaps, if he is summoned.'

Menes feels that this marks the beginning of negotiations and that it is for this reason as much as for the necklace that Oedipus has sent for him.

They arrive at the foot of a hillock at the summit of which a large oak is visible. The young girl dismounts, he does the same and tells his guard to keep an eye on the animals. After the glaring light on the road, his eyes are bothered by the intense shade of the tree. A young man greets him, smiling. Oedipus is waiting for him at the foot of the oak. Menes did not remember him being so tall. He has lost weight, his face is becoming lined. He still has a thick tawny mane and, below his brow, a black band covers the place where his eyes once were.

Menes remembers the king's piercing gaze and is disturbed by the unexpected deep blackness which now confronts him. Despite his obvious poverty, Oedipus still has the presence and urbanity of a king.

They greet one another and, after a few preliminaries, Menes announces that the price of the necklace is too high. 'No,' replies Oedipus. Menes is taken aback by so short a reply and the ensuing silence. He has the feeling that this blind Oedipus is more dangerous and can see better than the one of old. He offers a quarter of the asking price, which in his eyes signals the beginning of the inevitable process of bartering.

Oedipus half smiles as he says: 'So you want to rob me the way you rob these people?'

Menes turns – around the tree are about fifteen shepherds with their dogs. He wants to call his guard, but with a disconcerting laugh the young man who greeted him points to where his man is being carried away at a gallop, tied up on his mule.

Things move quickly. Three shepherds make up the tribunal, they call the others, one after another, as witnesses. Each in turn accuses him of a crime or of a theft committed against him or the State. Menes does not say a word, he does not know what game Oedipus is playing. Does he still take himself to be king? The tribunal passes sentence: death. What is the significance of this pitiful farce? They know very well – for it is the only answer he has given to their questions – that his brother, who commands the garrison, and his uncle, the judge, know about his trip and that if he is not back by evening, they will send soldiers. If the shepherds kill him or harm him in any way, the soldiers will massacre them and confiscate their flocks. Oedipus's daughter who fetched him would be regarded as an accomplice to their crimes.

Selenus raises his voice: 'Your threats don't bother us; we're ready to submit to anything to be rid of you. There is one way, one only, to avoid death, and that is to admit to your thefts and other crimes. The catalogue will be consigned to tablets and you will append your seal by way of confirmation.'

Menes refuses.

'So, over to us, Clius,' says Selenus. The handsome young man and a shepherd bring a container full of water. Without further ado, Clius plunges Menes's head into the water. When he feels that the man is beginning to drown, he relaxes his pressure. Menes lifts his head only to feel the sharp point of Selenus's knife at the nape of his neck. The more he lifts his head, the more the knife sinks in. If he lowers it he chokes. Selenus allows him to draw breath a little, once, twice. After the third time, Clius keeps up the pressure until Menes faints.

When he comes round, he knows he is beaten and is ready to confess. Antigone appears with her tablets and stylet. Selenus forces Menes to dictate his principal thefts and crimes, committed by hired assassins. Antigone finds it difficult to keep up; he still has Selenus's knife in the nape of his neck and if he stops or hesitates the point of the weapon sinks further into his flesh.

When Oedipus and Selenus decide he has said enough, Antigone re-reads the summary she has made of his avowals. At the dictation of her father, she adds: 'I, Menes, confess to all the aforementioned acts. In testimony of this I append my seal and imprint it with my right thumb.'

At the moment of execution, Menes hesitates but, like a scream of hate, the order: 'Do it!' bursts from the mouths of the shepherds, and the blade of the knife sinks once more into his flesh. Terrified he resists no more and appends his seal and imprint to the tablet.

Bewildered, he looks at the two tablets which for the moment would serve no purpose in Goria, where everything is under his control, but which, in Thebes, could have him immediately committed for trial. Three shepherds prepare to carry them to an unknown destination where they will remain, a perpetual reminder of the sentence hanging over him. His power over the shepherds and peasants, his monopoly of purchase in the market and all the systems of usury they engender, have been destroyed. He will have to accept the inevitable; after all it is only one of his sources of income. When Clius and Selenus were holding him between the threat of suffocation and of the knife, he thought his death was nigh. He now feels light-headed. Do they not have a little wine? A shepherd hands him a gourd, the wine is mediocre but he knocks back half of it. He is beginning to feel better, he is a little drunk. He is alive. He has riches on both sides of the border, more than these poor people could ever imagine. He drinks again and empties the gourd, his confidence has returned and with it a curious need to tell them of the other exploits that those present know nothing about and therefore could not make him confess to. All his villainous tricks – the oldest, the worst, those of his youth when he had, at all costs, to escape poverty – come pouring out, interspersed with gales of uncontrollable laughter. His rapaciousness, his guile towards the weak, permeate his account, together with the vanity and incompetence of those in high office who themselves often ended up becoming his victims. Antigone witnesses this scene with amazement and at first without understanding, but suddenly she grasps that the game unfolding before her is, in a more cynical and shameless way, the same as the one she watched unfold in Thebes without being able, beneath its respectable exterior, to make sense of it. She suddenly sees the awful yet funny side of the sinister games played by the powerful and what a relief it is when, like today, it is others, like the shepherds, who win the game. A silvery laugh breaks from her, a laugh of triumph, for with a few characters on a tablet, she has beaten one of those monsters and no matter how much it might amuse him to recount his crimes, he is after all nothing more than a loser laughing at his own defeat. She laughs with such glee that Oedipus laughs and the shepherds also; at the unbelievable cunning of this serpent who, not so long ago, was crushing them but whose venom has now been neutralized with the help of a blind man and his lanky daughter. Menes, increasingly drunk, might have believed, from this merriment, in a general reconciliation, but there is one who is not laughing.

Clius suddenly grabs Menes by the collar, kicks him down the hill and plants him firmly on his mule, which he sends galloping off across country at full tilt. He returns, sits by the others and looking at them with a dark smile, says: 'To have had his blood on our hands would have given us even greater satisfaction.'

The shepherds stand. It is obvious that many agree with him. They deposit small gifts at Antigone's feet and leave.

Next day, as Antigone wakes up, Clius is returning with the gourds he has filled at the river. She runs to him, dancing and shouting: 'We're going to eat. Then we're going to leave.'

Taken aback, he asks: 'Does Oedipus want to go already?'

'No, I do. I've had enough of this place, of being ill, of listening to the disgusting stories of that old man Menes and of knowing that all you think about is spilling his horrible blood.'

He laughs: 'All right, let's go; but first we must eat.'

After their meal of delicious things left by the shepherds, Clius approaches Oedipus: 'Allow us to guide you. Ploughing through everything the way you do, you are tiring yourself and, even worse, you are tiring Antigone who doesn't have your stamina. She's been very ill, we must look after her.'

Oedipus is troubled, he looks anguished: 'I have to find out where I am going, and to discover it almost with each step I take. To be able to proceed I had to lose my sight. Since then,

I have had to follow my vertigo which leads me anywhere. If Antigone is tired, tell me and I'll stop.' He turns and sets off alone.

They follow him. Antigone wonders why she is so happy and realizes that it is because Clius is looking after Oedipus so well. Not as a servant but as a son; a friend. He is not doing him a favour but accomplishing a ritual. And Oedipus, who during that terrible year of waiting in the anteroom of the palace became angry whenever his sons or daughters wanted to do anything for him or see to his clothes, lets him get on with it. There is no devotion to the task on Clius's part, no gratitude due on Oedipus's. How did he know that that was the only approach her father could accept? She is so delighted that she has to tell him. She grabs his hand and kisses it, saying in a little girl's voice: 'I'm happy because you're looking after him so well.' He is surprised and touched. She blushes, ashamed of having kissed his hand.

They walk behind Oedipus, but this time he stops frequently, inviting Antigone to sit or lie down. In the afternoon he hears the sounds of a village. He tells Antigone: 'Go alone, Clius will not be far. I'll stay here. If they turn you away, come back immediately. Don't take any risks.'

Antigone is frightened, frightened of being alone, frightened of threatening faces and shouts and even more of stones. She wants to run away but inside she hears Polynices's voice saying, as he used to when they first started to train with real weapons: 'You're weakening little girl, but you'll get there.' She knows Clius can see her and that helps her stand tall and walk with determination. In fact he is watching her, hidden behind a tree, and when Oedipus joins him and asks: 'Is she frightened?' he answers: 'Who wouldn't be in her place? She's still going though!'

Antigone is in the village. She has decided not to speak of her blind father any more but to stop in front of doorways, like a beggar from the countryside, and recite a prayer learned in her childhood:

33

Inhabitant of this house, if you want to be at peace with Zeus,
Smiling yet terrible Master of Heaven and Earth,
Protect and feed this beggar tried and tested by the road
For none knows whether it is not some radiant god or goddess
That you see before you at your door,
Begging, clothed in misfortune,
With neither fire nor resting-place.

In a low voice, she sings her supplication at the first house she comes to and soon a child brings her some bread. She advances and in the upper openings of the doors women appear, some of them carrying babies. Her bag is soon filled with vegetables and bread. A woman comes out to meet her, and gives her a pitcher full of delicious smelling soup. 'Take it to your father. I've been expecting you.'

'How do you know who I am?'

'My husband and his brother are shepherds.' She smiles: 'Come back and spend the night with us.'

Children walk with her and a little girl holds her hand as far as the outskirts of the village, then they run back as fast as their legs will carry them. She is surprised at having seen no men; not wanting her to be frightened the shepherds must have spoken about her. By the time she rejoins the other two, Clius has been to draw water and is lighting a fire. She sees from the relief on their faces that they had been worried.

'The shepherds are true to their word,' says Oedipus. 'Go and stay there the night.'

The woman, called Clea, is waiting for her with her young children at the entrance to the village. Doors open revealing inquisitive faces but this time the men show themselves. The house is not large, and has a fire in the centre, surrounded by a sheep-pen. 'In winter the animals heat the house,' says Clea. From every direction come strong earthy smells; the house, all white inside, has only the barest of necessities but nothing is lacking.

For the first time since she left Thebes, Antigone finds herself in a bed. It is hard, with its mattress of straw placed on a board – bed-linen is unknown in this house. Clea coming to tuck her up and kiss her goodnight gives her a feeling of well-being. In the middle of the night she wakes to the sound of two mice scampering over the beaten-earth floor around the hopper. She falls asleep again cradled by the regular breathing of the other sleepers.

Antigone gets up and eats with them. She would like to give them something but has nothing; now she can only receive. She tells them but they seem so pleased to have had her to stay that by the time she leaves, she too is elated. Clea accompanies her to the outskirts of the village and asks her where she is going. Antigone indicates she does not know. Clea folds her hands over her stomach and begins to cry.

It is no easy task to follow Oedipus, day after day, in his relentless walk. He takes account of neither road nor obstacles. He goes through thickets, woods, ploughed fields. He climbs hills and rocks unnecessarily, plunges perilously into ravines, climbing out and up their vertical slopes, crosses streams, torrents, rivers, holding on to anything he can. He is torn by brambles and branches and is covered in scars from his falls.

He continues through everything, following an invisible road, which, by the end of the day, turns out to have been a straight line. By the evening he always manages to end up not far from a house or a village where his daughter can beg and find refuge for the night. The ordeal is making Antigone healthier and tougher, but the road is so hard it is wearing her out. Clius watches this with mounting anger, for Oedipus does not seem to be aware of how exhausted she is; she who, alone, takes on the responsibility of feeding them and the humiliation of begging.

One evening, after a gruelling day's march, Oedipus stops in the clearing of an olive grove. He asks Antigone if there is a track going up the side of the plantation, then another bearing right. Surprised, she says yes. 'Right. We've arrived. Follow these paths and you will come to a house where you can rest for a few days or stay longer if you wish. Go with her Clius. A woman is waiting. Ask her permission to build a hut and make a fire nearby.'

'Who is this woman?' asks Clius.

'I don't know. I only know that, like us, she is part of the alliance between Selenus and the shepherds. I trust her.'

Antigone and Clius skirt the plantation. At the end of the path there is a long white house surrounded by trees and flowers. In front of the door there is a grey-haired woman who, smiling and motionless, watches them approach. When Antigone is in front of her, she says: 'I have been expecting you. I am Diotima.' Clius is standing a little behind. Antigone feels great respect for this woman, still beautiful despite the ravages of time. Hair unkempt, dirty as she is in her dusty dress, she performs without faltering the regal curtsey of Thebes.

Diotima takes her hands: 'You are indeed the one I have seen in my dream, the dream in which Selenus announces your arrival and that of your father. Who is this with you?'

Clius advances: 'I am Clius, once called the Bandit. I did a great wrong to Antigone and her father. They have forgotten it and since then I do all I can to protect them. Grant Oedipus and myself the right to build a refuge near the olive grove. Give us a little food and I will work all the time that we are here.'

'In the name of Narses my son,' says Diotima, 'and of our ally Selenus, I welcome you. You shall have all that you ask for.'

She invites them into a room, all white, where a young girl who is preparing the meal fills Clius's sack; he thanks her and leaves.

The young girl brings the food and Diotima seats Antigone next to her. She can hardly eat she is so tired and moved to find herself in a house, which for the first time since she left Thebes, reminds her of that city and of the time when she was a young girl, with a mother and father, a little different from those of others, part queen, part king, but, all things considered, parents like any others, parents who loved her.

Diotima and the young girl seem to understand what is going on inside her. They know that if she opened her mouth to talk she would cry, so, in a gentle manner they remain quiet. They lead her to a room where a bed, also all white, has been made up for her. The young girl, who is called Larissa, brings her a large bowl of warm water. She helps her wash and gives her a sweet smelling linen robe for the night.

Next day Diotima asks Antigone what she can do. She has learned how to carry out household chores, to dance the way they do in Thebes, to play a little music. She can weave but not very well, it is Ismene who excels in that. Her father wanted her to learn to mould clay and sculpt like him.

'What else can you do?'

Antigone laughs: 'Fight my brothers with weapons. That's what I was best at; I can handle the pike, spear and shield very well, the sword less well. I'm not very good with a bow.'

Diotima is astounded: 'Who taught you all that?'

'My brothers, especially Polynices; it amused them. Oedipus liked to watch us when we were training together.'

'In my dream, I saw you with a spear like Athenae, and a tablet covered in characters.'

'I learned to write – my mother wanted me to.'

'Today you will spin with Larissa and continue to rest. Tomorrow you will help her write. Tell Clius to come and see me, I want to know what he can do. Here, so that everyone can eat, everyone must work.'

The following morning Clius works in the garden, then he sees to some repairs in the house. Antigone copies on to tablets the inventory of a ship's cargo that Narses is sending to Asia. Larissa dictates; she can read but cannot write yet and she watches Antigone admiringly. In Thebes, apart from her parents and a few priests, no one was interested in Antigone's scribblings and her brothers teased her constantly. Here, on the other hand, everyone considers it to be very important. During the evening meal, Diotima tells her that though her handwriting is good and legible, she makes too many mistakes. Narses's inventories are evidence against possible disputes with the purchaser, or damage sustained during the voyage. They must not contain a single mistake. Antigone is not absolutely sure what Diotima is trying to say but she understands that what she writes must be perfect, if not she is of no value.

Of Clius, Diotima says: 'He has a hand of gold, for he can turn it to anything. If you all return for the winter Narses will find you work. In that way you will earn your keep and that of your father and you will not need to beg any more. Ares, my husband and the chief of our clan, died at sea. Like him, Narses is a shipowner and sailor. He sails during the good season and runs our pottery during the winter. He will teach Clius his craft, so that he can rebuild his house and reconstitute his flock.'

Antigone says that she does not know what her father wants to do; she thinks he will want to leave once she has recovered.

'Where does he want to go?'

'He doesn't know, something he says anywhere, sometimes nowhere, but he walks and walks all day. Always straight ahead.'

'It's a good sign if he wants to go nowhere and yet still walks.'

Antigone is on the verge of tears but she holds them back; for Diotima, for no apparent reason, is smiling at her with that gentleness and firmness she has grown to love.

The next day it is Antigone who takes Oedipus his midday meal. She is pleased to see him eat with a healthy appetite, in his well-arranged hut, his clothes washed and repaired by Clius. Does he want, as Diotima proposes, to stay here for the winter? Perhaps, but they must leave first.

'Towards the sea?'

'Yes, towards the sea. That is why it's better for you to stay here. Autumn is approaching, the journey will be more arduous. Don't stop us from going, we will return.'

'Who will beg for you?'

A radiant smile lights up his face: 'The heavens have provided up until now.'

Overjoyed, she asks: 'Do you mean that the heavens are me?'

'In a way, Antigone.'

She feels recompensed for her suffering and torment.

'If, in a small way I am heaven to you, surely you cannot

imagine I would give that up. Let me rest for another two days and I will come with you.'

Silence. Then he says: 'Tell Diotima that we shall be back for winter.'

Antigone reports their conversation; Diotima says nothing, showing neither approval nor disapproval. She only says: 'When you return, there will be work for Clius and for you. Oedipus will also find something to do.'

On the eve of their departure, as night falls, Antigone is seized by fear. After the contentment of the last few days she is not prepared for it. She can no longer help Larissa, who is also downcast, so she makes her sit by the fire. She wants to cry but has no tears. She realizes that she is terrified at the prospect of having to beg again; of oppressive days of sun, wind and rain; of the pity of women, the curiosity of children and of being the butt of men's jokes. Of setting out with Oedipus who remains silent. Of Clius and his desire, his hate of nearly everything and the intimidating bitterness in his face. She would like to remain here, in soothing occupation, bathed in Larissa's cheerfulness and Diotima's calm. Yet she knows she must leave.

It is the evening meal. She thinks she will not be able to eat but Diotima, with a few simple gestures, restores her courage. Antigone is hungry, ravenous, and is beginning to feel better.

At the end of the meal Diotima goes out and returns with a superb blue coat. 'You left Thebes with nothing, you will need a coat. This one was woven here, I dyed it myself with Larissa. Try it on and if it fits it's yours.'

Antigone puts it on; it is warm, supple, magnificent. All she can say is: 'It's a colour that won't show the dirt!' They burst out laughing: 'You'd think it had been made for you; with you so tall, it hangs beautifully!' exclaims Larissa.

They sit down around the fire and sing. Diotima tells her she has an excellent voice: 'Does your father sing too?'

'When we were little he used to sing with us. Since then, I have never heard him.'

'He should. Through his father he belongs to the line of the

Clearsingers. Those who have received the gift cannot keep it to themselves.' Antigone is amazed for she knows nothing of Oedipus's lineage.

She is exhausted. Larissa leads her to her bed, telling her she looks queenly in the blue coat. It is because she has never seen a real queen, a queen like Iocasta, who is radiant without trying and who dies unflinching. Whereas she, little Antigone, she flinches beneath the storm like her father, but she does not crack. Not yet. She is glad to have sung, happy that she looks radiant in her blue coat. Larissa helps her into bed and tucks her up. Antigone would have preferred it to have been Diotima but Diotima did not come; she would only come to her in her dreams, with her gentle grey hair and her peaceful presence.

Their farewells are brief. Diotima shows Antigone how to wrap the coat around her for maximum warmth; how best to hitch it up if there is mud or if she has to cross a ford or water. She instructs her just as Iocasta once did, except that with her it is advice and with Iocasta it was an order. She kisses her tenderly and quickly, gives her a sack of provisions saying: 'See you in the winter,' and is gone.

Larissa accompanies her as far as the end of the vineyard, to the corner of the olive grove where Clius is waiting. She kisses her hurriedly and runs off, no doubt so that Clius will not see that she is crying, and because she is frightened of seeing Oedipus. Antigone wonders whom Larissa is crying for. Because of her or – ah! this is not a pleasant thought – because Larissa is in love with Clius. The latter is in a bad mood, she realizes it too late. She cannot stop herself from asking him why Larissa was so sad.

'Because she is in love with me.'

'But Narses loves Larissa, she talks about him incessantly, they're going to be married.'

'That doesn't stop her from being in love with me, like the rest of you.'

Antigone is horrified: 'So you think that I, I am in love with you too?'

'It's obvious, no?'

'It's obvious!' Antigone is mortified: 'Whereas you, of course . . .'

He stops, turns to face her, with that dark little smile she adores, and cuts in: 'Me, I only desire, I no longer love.'

Oedipus, who is a little way ahead, stops: 'Really?'

That one word provokes a spurt of anger in Clius and he rushes at Oedipus. Antigone thinks he is going to punch him and runs to them thinking: 'That! That I will never allow!' while realizing, with a certain bitterness, that were Clius going to hit her, she would no doubt allow him to, even desire it. Clius does not punch Oedipus, his fist drops and he contents himself with stamping with rage like a little boy who, thinking he was very angry, discovers he no longer is.

He shouts: 'I have only loved once, a boy and that was by accident, yes, and it was by accident I killed him.'

'Who loved the most, who loved the least,' asks Oedipus, 'him or you?'

Clius is thrown by the question. Antigone sees his beloved yet infuriating face contract. The bitter, insulting smile disappears, all that is left is a young man, a child, overwhelmed by sorrow, whom she would like to take in her arms. Once more, he tries to shout: 'Him, he loved the most. Much more and much better.'

And Oedipus: 'Well then, don't be so sad, the one who is happiest is always the one who loves the best. Come Clius, we must make a start, we have a long way to go, a very long way.'

They leave, but instead of bringing up the rear as usual, Clius walks alongside Oedipus. He points out obstacles to him and this time Oedipus does not object. Clius warns him: 'There is a large muddy puddle here, so go round it; some big grey rocks there, let's cut through the middle.' He describes the colour of the stubble-field they are crossing in which there are still a few ears of corn to be gleaned: 'The field is the colour of a lion. At the edges are a few poppies missed by the reapers.'

At midday they stop by a stream. Antigone makes Oedipus

feel the softness of the material of her coat, the perfection of the weave. Admiring it, he asks: 'In that colour, are you beautiful?'

With Clius watching her, she dares not answer and it is he who says: 'She is beautiful. It is a heavy blue, deep, that looks as though it were made for her.' She is surprised at his way of seeing the colour – they are reconciled. Antigone turns to Oedipus: 'Diotima often sings. Yesterday we sang together and my feelings of sadness went away. She says that through Laius you are descended from a line of Clearsingers and that you should sing.'

Oedipus's face clouds over: 'Let me tell you how I met my father. He appeared at a crossroads in a chariot drawn by horses covered in foam. He ordered me to move aside. I too was leading horses but they were not harnessed. First, I would have to pull them in, then back them out of the way. Out of respect for his age I was about to do this, when suddenly he began to insult me and hit me in the face with his whip. Surprised and angered by the onslaught, I killed him without realizing who he was. I know nothing more about him, I have no idea if he was a Clearsinger or whether I inherited the gift from him. When I lived in Corinth I loved singing. In Thebes I sang for you sometimes when you were small. Your mother did not like it. Because of Laius, maybe; or because of some idea she had about royal dignity. I'd like to sing, but something prevents me.'

In the days that follow, Clius, when Oedipus allows him to, places himself at his side and tries to make the journey easier by pointing out what lies ahead. It is difficult to tell whether Oedipus, who continues to move forward tapping the ground in front of him with his stick, is listening to him or not. Sometimes he skilfully avoids the obstacles that lie in his path and at other times stumbles up against them, as if nothing had been said. Clius is not discouraged, he varies his warnings and perfects them, describing configurations, colours, changes of light.

He describes memories evoked by what he sees: 'To the right, there's a spring of clear water, can you hear it? It's not as full as the one at the bottom of the orchard where I used to draw water with my mother.' On describing a garden they pass enclosed by a low wall, with its patch of onions, vegetables and fruit trees, Antigone learns that he grew up in a house run by a conscientious mother who grew vegetables and tended an orchard and a beautiful olive grove. One day he describes, with obvious delight, a field in the distance on the rounded curve of a mountain, overhung by a thin rocky needle: 'It's up a mountain like that one that my father would send me in summer with our ram, the ewes and their lambs, as soon as they were strong enough. I would stay there for six suns, then my father would relieve me for two days, and later I would climb back up. This went on until winter if the snow did not come sooner. How long and balmy those days were, and how interminable the autumn.' His sorrow was evident. Once more, he points out the mountain to Antigone: 'The wolves would sometimes come out in the autumn. The first time I saw one I was still very young and did not know what it was. I saw a beast with a long tail attacking one of our ewes. I hit it with my stick and as it wouldn't release its hold, I grabbed it by the tail and pulled with all my might. It turned round and bit my leg. I hit it again and as our dogs began to attack it from the side, it ran away. I managed to reach home with the flock. When my father saw the wound, he said: 'That's a wolf-bite!' and he kissed it.'

'My father never did that,' says Oedipus.

A light mist rises from the ground, a huge red sun sinks below the horizon. Oedipus stops. they see a solitary house, surrounded by well-tended fields and a few trees; Antigone goes towards it. A peasant and his wife, forewarned perhaps by the shepherds, come out to meet her and take her in. Soon the chimney is smoking, they have revived the fire, she is safe.

Clius prepared a fire and the bivouac. He and Oedipus eat silently. In the flickering light Clius's sharp face is seen clearly, leaning over the flames. Anxious, he is watching Oedipus whose features, gaunt through fatigue, seem to have been stilled by the absence of sight. Tonight, Clius would like to talk of him of what he has never wanted to tell anyone. Oedipus's silence exacerbates his awkwardness and it is with trepidation that he hears himself say: 'I'd like to tell you about when I was young, and about my friend.'

There are a few moments of silence into which he plunges as on a chilly day, then Oedipus's voice commanding him to begin.

III

ALCYON

Every summer, there was another shepherd who would take an even bigger flock than mine up the mountain opposite ours. He was a little older than me, and as I watched him across the narrow valley that separated us, I thought how handsome he was with his sensitive, cheerful face. I particularly liked the way he walked, the way he moved, his smile; there was an ethereal quality about him I have never found in anyone else. Sometimes as we were making our way up our respective mountains or accompanying our flocks into the afternoon shade, we would find ourselves quite close but neither spoke nor made any kind of signal, though we would often hide in the bushes to observe one another. Since time immemorial, there had been a blood feud between our two families. Its origin had long been forgotten but with each succeeding generation, it had been fuelled by new disagreements, clashes, injuries and murders. He was the second son of Atus, chief of the enemy clan. His name was Alcyon, and as the descendants of Orpheus his was the clan of the song.

Ours was the clan of the dance. In the evenings we would

dance in the house or garden and in summer on the mountain. My father was the best and had even been known to dance while he was working. My mother usually accompanied him, and as a small child I would join them whenever I could.

All through the summer the sounds of Alcyon playing the flute or singing would drift over and I would hide so that I could listen to him. As the years went by, his music became more exquisite. One day I could contain myself no longer. I left the high grass where I had been hiding, climbed on to the flat rock that overlooked the ravine through which the stream separating our mountains flowed, and began to dance. At first, familiar clan dances, then unknown ones, inspired by the sounds of his flute; finally I plunged into a trance-dance and collapsed.

When I came round I saw him up a tree, stretched out along a branch, watching me anxiously. Dazed, I stood up; perhaps his staring at me had prevented me from staying too long in the sun on that burning stone. With an almost imperceptible gesture he indicated that I should move into the shade and drink. I answered in the same way. We could do no more than that, for a fast flowing river of blood separated our two families. Next day, I went down the mountain, back home, where I asked my father whether he would mind lending me his flute. He tied a cord to it so that I could hang it round my neck and showed me how to play it, saying: 'Be careful, we are the clan of the dance, not of the song. Although we are neighbours, there will never be peace between us.'

Despite his warning I could see he regretted the situation. Whenever he had taken my place on the mountain, he had heard Alcyon play and had experienced the extraordinary power of his music. He was in no doubt that it was because of him and for him that I wanted to learn. Despite that he still gave it to me for he realized that germinating within me there was a happiness that I would not readily relinquish. Once back on our mountain Alcyon drew from his flute sounds of pleasure and of pain such as I had never heard before. He was not only revealing the beauty of his friendship for me but also its fragility, the impossibility even of this unspoken intimacy. By way of an answer and to show him I had understood, I embarked on a dance inspired by his music. When he saw me slip into the trance-dance, he slowed the rhythm and intensity of his playing and ended on a softer note. He knew the trance-dance should only be done at night so that if you fall the enemy cannot know you are at his mercy.

The mountain stream that flows between our mountains widens at the base of the gorge and its current slows before reaching the waterfall, which plunges into the valley a little farther on. It is the only place where the flocks can drink in safety. We could have easily crossed the ford in summer had a harsh directive not forbidden us to do so. On either side, tracks zigzagged down to the water. My father had told me that by virtue of a secular agreement between our two clans, dating from before the hostilities, I had the right at the end of the day to be the first to take the animals to drink. Only when he heard us climbing back up, did Alcyon and his flock take the path to the ford that came out downstream from ours.

A clump of hawthorn bushes grew near the cabin where I sheltered at night. Exhilarated and inspired by the music I had just heard and by the revelation of Alcyon's friendship for me, I remembered the hawthorn blossom. My euphoria drove me to make him a wonderful spray. I took it with me when I led the flock to the ford and while the animals were drinking, I constructed a small raft with two logs and plaited rushes. From where I was standing, a light current drifted over to Alcyon's side. I began to take the animals back up but halfway I ordered the dogs to continue moving them on. Taking care to keep out of sight, I made my way back. Screened by the rushes at the water's edge, I waited a while for Alcyon to start calling his animals out of the water before releasing my raft. He could not miss my craft as it glided towards him with its white bouquet, like the dress of one of those goddesses my mother often talked of, who come out to dance in the moonlight. He saw it and ran to take it from the water. He clasped it in his arms, then raising it above his head, offered it up to the sun. Fortunately he did not call me or try to signal. He knew I could not be far away, but like me he feared we might be watched and severely punished if caught. Following his flock up the track, he thrust his face once or twice into the blossom before shouldering it and bursting into song. As I recall my emotions at that moment, it seems to me – though I was not much more than an inexperienced child – that he was singing a song of glory. I was so inflamed by these new sensations racing through me, that to calm myself I plunged my head into the water and kept it there for as long as I could. When I stood up again, dripping and out of breath I did not recognize myself. I had become someone more handsome, freer, yet with an intensity of joy in his eyes and a sorrow I had never seen before.

That night was the happiest of my life. I dreamed of stars and when the brightest fell in a great blaze of light, I did not think on waking that it could herald anything other than absolute bliss.

All morning we were busy tending our respective flocks, following the sheep and goats to where the grass was at its most succulent. When the animals had settled in the shade I did not wait for him to start playing but took out my flute and blew a few clumsy notes. Hidden amongst the leaves, he repeated the notes one by one carefully focusing on my mistakes. I practised them until I could reproduce them more or less accurately. He stood at the edge of the ravine opposite the rock where I had danced and tentatively tried out a few steps. So limpid and ethereal when he played and sang, he now betrayed his heavy, clumsy, drab side as I had done with my music. Carefully I scrutinized the mountain slopes and when I had ascertained that only the eagles gliding high overhead could see us, I climbed on to the big rock and meticulously went through each movement correcting his steps as he had done with my notes and showed him some exercises that would help him progress. That afternoon marked the beginning of an enchanting period in our lives. At the first opportunity, he would play a simple tune that I would then endeavour to reproduce, or I would dance and he would attempt with growing dexterity to copy my movements and follow my rhythm. Correcting each other in this way, we progressed not only in one another's art but also in getting to know each other. With each day that passed my playing improved and I gained a deeper understanding of music, although I realized I would never be an inspired musician.

It seemed to me in the course of those days of mutual revelation that my friendship for Alcyon was somewhat lacking in comparison to his. Dancing was forcing him not only to use his body but was also leading him to a greater inner understanding. Without being aware of it, I was helping him reach the zenith of his music.

The needs of our flocks often kept us apart. As soon as he knew I could no longer hear his flute he would send me wordless messages with his powerful voice, in which I discovered, not without shame for having allowed myself to forget it, what a presence, a miracle I was in his life. Out of caution I would allow some time to elapse before acknowledging these gifts that the heavens were sending me across the mountains. Then I would release the call of the shepherds of our clan which struck me as somewhat mediocre compared to his.

Alcyon's perception of our situation was better than mine, he knew just how vulnerable it was. We could love one another and try through our music and dancing to get to know one another better but only in the strictest privation and secrecy. Never would we cross the frontier of the mountain stream that separated us, never would our hands touch nor our mouths speak to one another. He was ready to accept what destiny had unexpectedly brought us; to be satisfied to see me, hear me and exchange the inner words that we spoke to one another. His music gave me the impression that to him, loving through seeing and hearing was the most perfect form of love. But it was not what I aspired to. I felt that an actual encounter – a bringing together of bodies, glances, words – would produce a more intense spark, a revelation in the relationship that had only just begun. Aware of the changes taking place in our clans he was in a better position than me to weigh up the reality of the situation;

he knew that if I broke their laws I would have to pay for it with my life. It was a risk I was ready to take. He was not.

Until I met you Oedipus, I had thought he was wrong, that it would have been better if I had died there and then in that glory, or dream of glory, which I was experiencing so intensely.

The return of my uncle, the head of our clan, turned our world upside down. For many years he had been in the service of a great foreign king, first as a soldier then as a commanding officer. He was a seasoned warrior, exceptionally strong and highly skilled in his handling of weapons. He had been generously rewarded for his exploits by the king. Some of his gifts had been entrusted to my father who had bought land for my uncle and a share in our flock.

Upon the death of his wife, men from the enemy clan had seized what was left of his goods. Learning of the pillage on his return to Greece, he fell into a terrible rage; pledging the annihilation of our enemies, he began to prepare the men of our clan.

Alerted by a series of punitive measures my uncle had taken, the enemy prepared for an attack. That was when Alcyon sent me his first wordless message. I felt its impact without being able to understand it. As usual, I had gone to the place where we spoke with our flutes, but this time received no answer. That evening I noticed that a huge fire was burning in front of his cabin and I could hear the sounds of feasting. He had been joined by some of his clansmen. First they sang, then played their flutes. I had no difficulty in identifying the purer sound of Alcyon's playing. The others stopped to listen but I knew he was playing for me. Across the night sky that I had been gazing at so intently, came his solemn warning. An increasingly perilous time was approaching, but no one bar ourselves and nothing save our impatience, our mistakes, could prevent our friendship from continuing to grow.

That night he appeared in a dream. I was in a state of blissful peace; he was talking to me, speaking of things of great beauty. On waking all I could remember were his last few words: 'The loving invention of one another.' He faded and I found myself alone, repeating this phrase which seemed on the one hand to be opening up limitless horizons while on the other sounding like a farewell.

The next day he was back with his flute. At the end of our lesson and exchange I heard my father's voice calling me in the distance. Alycon hastily clambered down from the great tree from where, standing on a branch amongst the leaves, he had been able to watch how I handled my flute. I hurried down the mountain. My mother, who rarely had time to spare, was with my father. I understood that if both were there they must have something of great importance to tell me. But first I was so pleased to see them after such a long absence that I rushed down the slopes shouting excitedly. My mother looked at me as though she were seeing me for the first time. While she was resting in my cabin my father examined each of our animals one by one. He declared himself satisfied with the state of the flock and the grazing. I was becoming an accomplished shepherd, which was just as well, given that this year he would not be able to relieve me on the mountain as was his custom, for he was needed by the clan. He could not have given me better news but I refrained from telling him so. His other news foreshadowed major upheavals in our lives and seemed to contain an invidious fore-boding. In order to finance the purchase of weapons my uncle had decided to sell his part of the flock. As his house had been burned down at the time of the plunder that had followed the death of his wife, he was moving in with us and would be personally responsible for training me in the use of arms when I returned with the animals for the winter. Full-scale war between the two clans was unavoidable and it was my uncle's intention to lead us to total victory. The battle would soon take place. But only the adults would participate. The younger sons of the chief of the enemy clan and myself would be excluded.

The meal was coming to an end and by way of a distraction from the news, my mother asked me, with a smile, if I was making any progress with the flute.

'A little,' I replied, 'I practise every day, though I'll never be a great musician.'

'Unlike our neighbour?' As I did not reply she asked me to play. I launched into one of the tunes Alcyon had taught me and performed it fairly well.

My mother thought I had made astonishing progress. She smiled again and asked: 'Has the shepherd opposite made as much progress with his dancing?'

Her question made me blush, but I had the courage to say: 'Why do you ask?'

She hugged me with that same tenderness which had brightened my childhood years and said: 'The boy who set off up the mountain in spring was still just a child. The one I find today is nearly a man. Your father and I sense enormous perils hanging over our clan. Dreams and presentiments I have had confirm this. Do not aggravate them by being imprudent. You must master the force which is overflowing inside you. This is not a virtue that comes naturally to you but you will need it in the days to come, not only for yourself but for the one who, at great personal risk, has become your friend.'

She kissed me but I disengaged myself to ask: 'What risk? Who is threatening him?'

'He is and you are,' my father said. 'Alcyon has been endowed with the gift of music. Last winter he performed at all his clan's gatherings and at a few festivals. All those who heard him were transported. In the evenings when he played in his parents' house, people would flock to hear him, sitting around in a circle, having braved the darkness and the cold. Many villages have asked him to perform at their festivals. Two kings have invited him to their courts. Since the spring he has turned everything down saying he is a simple shepherd and that only in the air of these mountains can he find inspiration. We are frightened that this inspiration, which has plumbed new depths and passions this last year, comes from his friendship with you. Don't give in to it, it would mean your downfall.'

'He has never come near me, we have never so much as spoken to one another.'

'You have acted wisely,' said my father.

'Do you love him?' my mother asked.

I was on the point of saying: 'Yes.' But at that moment, lurking behind that assent, I glimpsed an avalanche of suffering and distress hurtling towards us. My mother could not see it. I felt invaded by a terrible chill and began to tremble. I could not lie to my parents, but neither could I find the words to describe the revelations that had come to me through music and dancing. I was on the verge of tears and don't know what would have happened had Alcyon, almost as if he had heard us talking, not embarked on a tune, there in his usual place in the big tree on the other side of the mountain stream.

The melody seemed to rise from the earth itself, taking with it the grass, flowers and mountains in its care, up into the air, uniting in space to create something that was beyond words. Consequently it became necessary to love without reserve the gift of life and the highs and lows and risks that emanate from its immensity. At that moment I saw my father stand and collect some of the torches I had prepared to use in my spare time through the dark months. He placed seven of them in the clearing in front of my cabin and as he lit them, he marked out a circle of light around us. Alcyon's flute went quiet, he was singing, his song had no words. It started with an 'a' and, like the majestic flight of a bird, slowly ran through the rest of the vowels. Without ever enunciating it, the song spoke my name, uniting it to his in a vast parallel flight. Our two names were face to face, in intense confrontation, never merging – an indefinite self-denial, prolonging our love; one that I, while lost in admiration, was none the less unable to prevent myself from hating.

Tears ran down my mother's lovely gentle face. She was not weeping for herself but for Alcyon and me and the impossibility of our friendship. Alcyon returned to his flute and my father, leaping into the circle of light, began to dance. The exquisite dancer that he was, my father, touched to the very core of his being by the music, surpassed himself that day. Never had I seen a body so gracefully in accord with the lightness of the air, nor the rapture of existence revealing itself with such perfect movements.

When Alcyon stopped, my father placed himself between my mother and me, an arm around each of us. I could feel his strength and his fearlessness penetrating and filling me – just as they had in my early childhood – with the certainty that he was the strongest man in the world, capable of protecting me whatever the situation. I was gratified that from his branch in the tree Alcyon had been able to admire him, as magnificent when he danced as Alcyon was when he played. When my father started up again my mother could not resist his entreaties to join him in the clearing. It was to be the last time these two superb dancers would face one another, each encouraging and inspiring the other. It was through dancing that my parents had met, from her had come the ardent love they bore one another, in her and in me it had grown in strength.

I was lost in contemplation of these two dazzling figures and the perfection of their movements when my mother beckoned me to join them. It was my turn to leap into the clearing. I felt that something in their attitude to me and the space I occupied had changed. Up until then I had danced around them, I was the hope they nurtured with their warmth. I coiled and uncoiled my body on the periphery of the beautiful oval they formed as they moved tenderly towards and away from each other. This time, not only were they drawing me into their affection but into the very centre of their love; into the actual trunk and roots of the infinite tree of dance. In the circle of light created by my father, they made a place for me equal to theirs, and my gestures, my bounding and swooping, were in no way poorer than theirs. I admired them, felt passionately at one with them; they felt it too and together we found an equality we did not know existed.

We were swept along by Alcyon's music, lifted out of ourselves. With our bodies we brought him back to earth, from where he wanted at once to soar again like a bird into the sky. Mingled with the pleasure and enthusiasm for movement, there was a kind of contest taking place between Alcyon and ourselves. We the three dancers, my mother the central and primordial image, were also seeking the path of love but it was not the one that Alcyon's music wanted to lead us to. Through us the dance was imploring him not to forget the law of the body, the striking fidelity of its geometry nor the unyielding demands of its weight. It was requesting him not to push the movement's developing potential to the extreme, to the edge of madness; with timeless elation, my mother circled around us twice and then stopped like a doe after a leap. My father followed suit signalling me to continue alone. Alcyon abandoned his flute returning to his wordless hymn where the 'a' like the primary utterance of a being seemed to rouse and guide the luminous and terrible course of the vowels. His voice glided but I knew the movements I was making on the ground and in the air were in no way secondary to it. My dance, despite what united us, was in conflict with his music. I sensed the suffering in his voice, the sadness at the segregation imposed on us. I accepted the suffering but would not agree to renounce it. I wanted to continue my journey along the road of discovery and mutual wonder that our meeting had brought about.

My mother stood. I thought she was going to start prophesying as she sometimes did. And so, exhausted by the dance, I dropped to the ground. She said nothing but joined her pure soft voice to Alcyon's high ardent one and guided it, to bring him back from the endless reaches of divine despair to the more measured spaces of hope and earthly sorrow.

When the song was over my father rose and with great solemnity bowed to my mother and then to Alcyon, the way the members of our clan bow to that solitary disc when it appears in the course of the year at the zenith of its strength or the nadir of its exile. The torches were burning out and the full moon would soon disappear behind the mountain. Already I could no longer see its light clearly, for in my eyes it merged with the light radiating from my mother. My father at her side was like the evocation of the rising sun. I could picture their union, like the meeting of two heavenly bodies at that precise moment when the night begins to lean towards the day. I beat a hasty retreat, leaving them the hut, and went to sleep with the flock. It took me a long time to settle, for my thoughts, after such an extraordinary evening, were battling with the too ethereal image of Alcyon. Before dropping off, I sent him my first mind message which consisted of just one word: happiness. At the moment of waking, as I half-dozed, there were two words on my lips: despite everything. I felt certain that these words, bursting with courage and optimism, were his reply. Refusing to feel dejected, I got up and gathered the half of the flock that my uncle intended to sell and drove the animals down to the hut where I rekindled the embers of the fire and prepared a meal. When my father appeared he saw that everything was ready and I knew he was pleased. The three of us ate in silence, my parents gazing with obvious regret at the animals we had grown fond of that were about to be delivered into the hands of strangers. I had to voice my concerns: 'Do we have to involve ourselves in this pointless conflict with our neighbours? Why do we have to submit to my uncle? He's a warrior, not a man who works the earth. When we have returned the animals and land he left in our charge, could we not leave the clan and escape his madness?'

As she heard my words my mother winced and my father's face clouded over. 'When you are born into a clan,' she said, 'you do not leave it without bringing dishonour on to yourself. Without the clan, we would – like so many others – have fallen prey to the soldiers, judges and priests of foreign kings and cities. It is thanks to the clan that we are free and we must remain loyal to it. And that includes you, Clius.' It was the first time she had ever spoken to me in this way. I was thrown as much by her tone as by her words. I could see that my father agreed with everything she had said.

The cloud that hung over us soon dispersed for she could see I had understood. When we kissed goodbye, we were confident that we would soon be together again. Despite the dangers which lurked around us, we were still under the influence of the

previous night's enchantment. I watched my carefree father drive
the flock down the mountain; he radiated life, happiness and
strength. I remember thinking how he was like a great tree. It
was the last time I saw him alive.

Alcyon led his flock further afield. I did the same. Sometimes,
after a long interval we would send out a call from a rock or the
top of some crag – as confirmation that we were still there and
had not forgotten. During those frequently anguished days
and nights of solitude and of receiving no news from the valley,
I was beginning to hope that there would be no battle. On the
seventh evening when, having spent some time nursing a sick
ewe, I was getting ready to go to sleep, my body and mind were
suddenly alerted by an abrupt message: Go down! I did not
doubt for one moment that it came from Alcyon who must have
received news before me of a serious incident. I tore down the
mountainside faster than ever before. Just before I reached home
I caught sight of my uncle, still armed, kneeling behind a tree
and staring into the darkness. As I approached he stood up, huge
in his leather breastplate. He was wounded; his wild, desperate
face was that of a madman. 'We will be avenged!' he roared and
I knew that something terrible had happened. As if he were a
mere obstacle, I ran round him and towards the house. As I went
in I distinguished two pale shapes stretched out on the ground:
my father's badly lacerated body and my mother beside him.
Tearless and speechless she clasped me in her arms and I felt as
though I were embracing nothing more than a shadow.

At sunrise she pulled herself together. Refusing offers of help,
she set off alone to ask our enemies to suspend hostilities so that
the two clans could take time to honour their dead. She spoke
to the head of the rival clan without referring the matter to my
uncle. No one knows what transpired between them but a forty-
eight-hour truce was agreed. The one as much afflicted as the
other – our enemy, Atus, had lost his oldest son in the battle –
the two negotiators hoped, I think, that this would lead to a
more lasting and secure peace. But my uncle's insanity prevented
it. This was the last of my mother's actions that reflected her true

nature. Tragedy was to engulf her with such ferocity that from then on she would be able to do no more than survive.

The battle's disastrous outcome had been entirely my uncle's fault. We were four; the other clan seven. There was still time to turn back but my uncle would not hear of it. The enemies' tactics took him by surprise. Three of theirs went for three of ours while the other four took on my uncle. Seeing he was wounded and trapped, my father – having despatched his opponent – ran to my uncle's assistance. In the terrible fray that followed, my uncle – with a supreme effort – slew one of his assailants but the other three, their strength united against him, dealt my father a mortal blow. Bellowing with rage and grief, my uncle threw him over his shoulder and charged at the enemy with such force that they were unable to stand up to him. He thought he had saved him but when he arrived home, my father was dead. The last of our men to survive also got away. Each side had lost two men.

In the evening of that fatal day I went back up the mountain to see to the flock. As the moon rose I heard coming from the other side of the mountain stream the sound of Alcyon's flute. With his help I managed – for a few minutes, hours even – to escape time, my grief and my anger against my uncle. Rising above us, sombre yet luminous, I saw an edifice of music, as Alcyon with just the air from his lungs and the movement of his fingers raised a monument to my father worthy of him.

The next day I went home. We built a funeral pyre for my father and his fellow clansman. My mother did not have the strength to sing as she had intended, but around the bodies she performed a ritual dance of a harsh yet stately splendour. It struck me at the time that it would be the last time she would dance. I was not mistaken.

After that I no longer went up the mountain regularly. My uncle insisted I devote as much time as possible to being trained by him to use weapons. He was in no way conscious of having been the cause of my father's death, it had only exacerbated to the point of madness his desire for war and vengeance. When I did go up Alcyon would make sure he was far away. Sometimes he would invade my dreams or thoughts to remind me of his presence, his hopes and the need to be on my guard always. He was right, for one day I caught sight of my uncle spying on me from the branches of a tree. I pretended not to have seen him and suddenly he disappeared as only he could.

My uncle had moved into our house with the surviving members of our family. They had suggested getting my mother a slave but she refused and ended up being treated as their servant. Totally preoccupied with their training or incursions into enemy territory none of them did any work. I helped her as best I could but my uncle's demands on me grew as he insisted he would make an accomplished warrior of me, daring to add: worthy of my father. He was a remarkable combatant and despite his savage temper, an able and patient instructor. In spite of my inner resistance, not only did he initiate me in the use of weapons but also in the wild pleasures of combat, blood and metals.

As I was bringing the flock down one day, my mother announced that my uncle — being a widower — had claimed the right given him by the laws of the clan to marry the widow of his brother. She had told him that such a prospect and so soon after my father's death filled her with disgust. He had nevertheless demanded what he saw as his right and had already determined the date.

I carefully weighed up the odds and told my mother there was only one course of action left — to flee. Engrossed in his blood feud as he was he would be too busy to give chase. She refused. As a woman of the clan she would continue to stand by its laws whatever the consequences.

I immediately went in search of my uncle and punched him in the face, screaming that he had murdered my father and that he could not force my mother to marry him. Stunned and furious, for he had loved his brother, he turned on me. We fought. He had no difficulty keeping me at bay, then when he was ready he knocked me out with a single blow. He needed me for his war and had no wish to kill me. Life with my parents had often been hard but never devoid of affection. My uncle never forgave me and I never sought his forgiveness. He enforced the law and married my mother; from that moment he lived under a cloud of hate.

My uncle rode my mother every night so that she would give him a son. I couldn't stand it so I built myself a cabin and moved out. She became pregnant. I was so sickened by her condition that I could not bring myself to look at her. We grew ashamed of one another.

A second skirmish took place during one of my uncle's pillaging expeditions. My uncle killed one of our enemies and wounded another but one of our clansmen also died. That left them with four men and our side with only my uncle and me. Now I was even more indispensable to him. I asked him why he did not regard Alcyon as an enemy. He replied that as Alcyon was seen as a priest of Orpheus his clan did not want him to take part in any fighting. He added: 'When we have slaughtered the others he will be our slave. He can play and sing for us.'

My uncle became increasingly impatient for me to attain manhood. It was winter so I could no longer go up into the mountains. I spent all my time with him training with the sword, pike and bow. He taught me to exercise like a soldier and as he was also an experienced huntsman, I learned to crawl and move soundlessly through any terrain. All of this later helped me survive. As our swords crossed, he was fully aware of my desire to kill him. Never dropping his guard for a moment, the hate he read in my eyes warmed him. He would say: 'You must become even more cruel, ferocious like a pack of wolves.' There was no time to work and I had lost my appetite for it. We were eating our way through the sheep faster than they were being replaced by lambs. The greater part of our fields had gone to waste. Only the garden my mother tended was looked after as it had been in my father's day. We were becoming progressively poorer. Unperturbed my uncle would say: 'It doesn't matter. When we've destroyed them we'll take their possessions, their women and children.' I refrained from pointing out that by the end of the war they would no doubt be as poor as us.

One day I wounded him as we were practising together. He roared out: 'Now you're as skilled as me. Soon you'll be able to avenge your father's death and we shall rid the earth of our foe.'

In spring he gave me leave to spend a few days on the mountain with what remained of our meagre flock. As I had hoped Alcyon was waiting for me hidden in his tree on the other side of the mountain stream. I could not see him but as dusk fell he began to play. His music was sublime and yet so melancholic that I did not have the heart to dance. The whole of that night and the next day I was in a state of ecstasy and anguish. The last few months had been dominated by my uncle. I had had to harden myself and become like him – closed off in order to survive. My mother was all that remained of the sunshine of our former life but she was now a desperate woman and an infinite source of grief. Reaching behind the inner barricade within which I had shut myself, Alcyon's music put me back in touch with the truth I had lost. When evening came he was not in his tree. With a few notes I called him and he answered from far away, high up on the mountain, with a few bars of his song without words. Then, nothing more. In the morning I awoke to these words: Be on your guard! I knew they came from him but I was past wanting to be on my guard. I could see his animals on the slopes on the other side of the ravine and hoped he would play or send me some sign. Nothing. So at midday I climbed on to the big rock and danced as I had never danced before. I danced his and my desire, and my despair at the world of metal and violence that had become mine. I had decided that if he did not respond I would cross the stream and climb his mountain in violation of the laws of our clans. I did not care if his people imprisoned or killed me. I felt sure he was watching but he remained hidden. His answer came in two notes: one very low like a lover's murmur, the other screeching a warning. Something compelled me to turn round and I saw my uncle approaching, huge and menacing, blocking my access to the valley. While I had been dancing he had hidden my weapons and was now coming towards me armed with a cudgel. I could have fled further up the mountain but I did not even consider it for I felt powerful, receptive once more to love and capable of dealing with my uncle. He had told me I was as strong as him but this had been to give me a false sense of security. Not once during our training sessions had he betrayed the extent of his strength and speed. I went for him with my shepherd's crook but with a few unanticipated moves he made me realize I had no hope. Like you, Oedipus, he just snatched the weapon from my hands. Under the barrage of his blows I shouted out in anger and pain then fear. My strength sapped; he grabbed me by the hair and threw me repeatedly to the ground the way men breaking in bulls seize them by the horns and topple them in the fields.

My defeat, my humiliation and shame took place in full view of Alcyon but with the vestiges of heart and spirit left to me I prayed he would not try to intervene. He was not a man of blood and my uncle would have killed him. When I was beyond being able to defend myself, my uncle continued to hit me for a long time with unrelenting precision. I was howling and blubbering like a child but I would not beg for mercy. When I fainted he abandoned what he called his work. He did not want to kill me but to bind me to him for ever through the obedience that is born of fear and hate. In my stupor, I felt the sun disappear and the cool of the night fall. I was aware of a beneficial presence close by. Was it him, the music of his flute or only his thoughts? I shall never know.

My uncle expected my mother to give him a son. She gave birth to a daughter. He fell into a frightful rage, a girl was useless to him. He grabbed hold of her to take her into the sun and leave her to die. With what little strength she had left my mother tried to save her child, grabbing hold of a knife she even managed to injure him but he pushed her to the ground and kicked her repeatedly. I could hear her screams. I was armed but he had had time to seize his weapons. I fought, yes, I fought for my mother, but I had not recovered from my injuries and the humiliating defeat he had inflicted on me. I fought knowing I could not win and with a few well aimed blows he had me down by my mother's side. He exposed the child. She only survived for a few hours. The next day my mother was dead.

I was chained to my uncle by fear, hate and a desire constantly rekindled by him to wreak revenge on our enemies for my father's death. I could not even think about Alcyon or believe in the existence of music. Dance itself had become something grotesque, for we only danced on moonless nights. We would drink heavily before launching into movements of such barbarity that soon we were plunged into a trance-dance black as the blackest of nights, which lured us into a frothing fall down a kind of horribly delectable abyss.

I stopped going up the mountain and stopped working in the fields; we ate what remained of our flock one by one. All I had any respect for was my mother's garden over which I had scattered her ashes and those of my sister. Right up to the end I tended the vegetables and flowers she had loved. My time was taken up in training with my uncle – hunting, spying on the foe, plundering what we could. There were four of them and two of us. Our only hope was to take them by surprise. Pretending to be running away, injured, I lured one of them out of his hiding place. My uncle wounded him and I finished him off. As a sign that the war was a fight to the kill, my uncle disrespectfully cut the head off the corpse, taking it with him as a trophy. He wanted to nail it to our door but as I refused to go into the house if he did, he eventually allowed me to leave it near a spring where our enemies could find it and bury it in accordance with their rites.

My uncle had his spies and informed me that for his safety Alcyon had been brought down from the mountain. Our two mountains were now deserted. Although he was a priest of Orpheus, Alcyon relieved his companions on guard duty and no longer had the time nor the heart to play or compose. I had resolved that should we come face to face I would defend him. And each time we undertook an expedition I would send him, with all the strength I had, a signal warning him to be careful.

Soon, there was no let-up in the fighting between the two families. Night marches, surprise attacks, pillaging and fires succeeded one another unrelentingly. At first, thanks to my uncle's skill, we had the advantage. We set fire to one of their sheeppens and stole some of their animals. One evening, thinking he had sent them off on a false trail, my uncle set out to burn down one of their isolated farms. They had seen through our plan and were lying in wait near the farm. Just as we were about to enter the barn where, with the help of others, they intended to burn us alive, I heard a stifled note and every bit of my body knew it must flee. I shouted a warning to my uncle and ran as fast as I could dropping my bow and sword, keeping only my pike as my father had taught me to do. Running in front of me my uncle was hit in the stomach by one of our foes posted to intercept him. I struck the man down and continued to flee. My uncle managed to escape but the effort of running aggravated his injury. Knowing their main adversary had been badly hurt, the enemy decided to wait until morning before killing him, rather than engage him there and then in a fight to the death.

When my uncle arrived at our hideout he had lost a lot of blood and was having difficulty dragging himself along. He had had to abandon his weapons and his breathing was laboured. The desire to assuage my hate and kill him was overwhelming. He read my thoughts and giving me a wry smile said: 'Tomorrow you will be the head of the clan.' I was struck by the absurdity of the idea but when I returned to my hate so that I could be done with him, it had disappeared. I tended his wound as best I could but, choking on a sudden rush of blood, he died as violently as he had lived. I took the food that was left in his bag, placed some wood under his enormous body and after having lit the pyre fled into the mountains.

Next day they found my uncle's ashes and burned down our house. From up on the big rock I could see the fire and realized it was their way of telling me they were determined to destroy me, to be finished with the blood feud for always.

After that they hunted me like a wild animal. I ate whatever

I could catch or steal. Each night I had a different hideout. Bent on surviving and avenging my father and the clan, I spoke to no one, my mind devoid of thought. Twice they attacked me on the mountain but I escaped for I had assembled rocks and tree trunks ready to roll down on them. Alcyon was there no doubt as they tried to trap me but he was too far away for me to see him. Spying on them constantly to see what they were doing was fruitless. I never heard him play or sing again.

My resilience and determination had grown. My uncle's strength, his cunning and cruelty had reincarnated in me. Although I often woke at night sobbing after having dreamed of my parents, Alcyon or the charred remains of our house, as soon as I was conscious in the mornings I would find myself once more infused with hatred. I thought only of eating, hiding and waiting for an opportunity to loot or injure the enemy. They were planning to capture me the moment the snow forced me down the mountain. Taking advantage of a moonless night I escaped and went far away.

Arriving in a town intent on becoming a soldier, I presented myself to a king. I was dishevelled, my clothes in tatters; he looked me up and down doubtfully. Guessing that behind my wild exterior there lurked a hidden strength he said: 'Go and wash. Come back to the palaestra tomorrow.' Next day I returned accompanied by his guards. 'Run,' he said. I outran his men effortlessly. 'Throw your javelin.' I threw it further than any of them. Then he said, 'Defend yourself against this man.' Using the techniques I had learned from my uncle I soon vanquished him. The king appointed me to his guard and I helped him win a war and take a city. That was where I learned to rape women in their homes, to kill old men and reduce the survivors to slavery. As a reward for what he called my bravery the king presented me with gold embossed armour. The armour pleased me but I did not like the king. He had the same mentality as my uncle without having his valour. He never fought on the front line.

On our return I said: 'Sire, spring has come. I have to leave you.'

'Stay,' he said, 'I need you. I will give you a house, a necklace of gold, a beautiful slave and put fifty men under your command.'

I told him I had a blood feud to settle.

He was familiar with our mountains and knew I had to honour it.

'When the blood has been appeased come back. We will take another city and you will be its governor.' As I took my leave of him I did not kneel as was customary in that diffident land. I took great pleasure in watching him restrain his anger. I frightened him but his desire for me to return was great, for without me he had no chance of ever becoming petty tyrant over three miserable cities.

Each day the trio makes its way to the sea and every evening Antigone leaves them in order to beg and find shelter for the night. When she has left, Clius lights the fire, sees to Oedipus and after they have eaten continues with the story he had abandoned the evening before. Oedipus listens without interrupting, without saying a word, totally absorbed. It is thanks to this absorption that Clius finds the courage to return to the darkest or brightest, most hidden recesses of his past. Had he done so alone it would have been to discover nothing save the ruins left behind. When he stops Oedipus is there; Oedipus whose soul he has invaded and whose memory he has impregnated with the misadventures and images of a life he will never erase. He plunges into Oedipus's consciousness and penetrates it as though it were a cave or thick forest, at the end of which he can just glimpse the ambivalent glimmer of freedom.

He has been recounting his story each evening for a day, two days, several days at Oedipus's request to continue. Antigone finds it distressing for she can sense there is an exchange taking place between the two men; a discovery that excludes her. They walk farther than usual that day. Towards evening she distinguishes a distant rumbling above the myriad of murmurs. It is the culmination of an event she had already come across in her dreams. Night has fallen when they arrive at the rocky cliff. The broken light of the moon through the clouds illuminates the sea and the waves breaking and foaming on the reefs beyond the headland.

In the rock Clius finds a shallow cave sheltered from the wind. As it is too late to find refuge elsewhere Antigone decides to spend the night there. The men agree. She prepares a meal while Clius makes her a bed of bracken in the cave. At the end of the meal with the fire uniting them in its circle of warmth, Oedipus turns to Clius with his usual evening request to continue with his story.

Clius hesitates for Antigone has missed the beginning; but Oedipus give her a brief summary and Clius continues: I had expected my return to the mountains to take the enemy by surprise. I was mistaken. They had been waiting for me for some time and had made elaborate preparations to destroy me. I thought I would be safe wearing the king's armour. Imprudently crossing a wood I was hit by an arrow. My aggressor ran off. Clad in armour it was impossible for me to give chase so I abandoned it and took up the life of the vigilant wild animal again. Although it was summer it was difficult to find food. On our lands everything had been burned and razed to the ground. On theirs, flocks and families had regrouped and moved to a few easily defended spots. With the help of decoys gradually they pushed me up our mountain. I was surrounded. I presumed they planned to starve me out but it was worse. As I climbed the slopes I loved so much, I noticed that wood had been stacked at different levels almost as far as the summit. I did not understand the nature of the trap and could not have avoided it – hunted on all sides as I was. I was alone, all I had were my weapons and, to quench my thirst, water from a spring spouting out of the stones a little way down from the peak.

When my food ran out I resolved I would go down the next day for the final confrontation while I still had the strength. If Alcyon was there I would refuse to fight him. I tried to convey that to him with my flute but he did not answer. I woke up in the middle of the night. The water from the spring was flowing past my head. The wind had changed direction and the sky was overcast. I looked back over my life so lamentably begun. Buried in that time before the beginning of those tragic events I rediscovered the image of Alcyon and the love, the hope which perhaps he had imparted to me and which were now lost.

In the morning I woke to the smell of smoke. They had lit the stacks of wood I had seen on the slopes and the wind – they had been waiting patiently for it to change – was already chasing the flames towards the summit where other piles of logs and branches were waiting to feed the fire. The situation looked hopeless; the ground was covered in scrub and grass already dried by the heat. Stampeding animals were fleeing to the top of the mountain, only the birds had any chance of escaping the great flames advancing towards me with their terrifying din. There was a sheer rock face to the north of me where the flames would not take hold but I could see the glint of enemy weapons coming from that direction; there – facing the rock – I could have climbed down, but only slowly. I had gone through every eventuality if I lost: injury, death, enslavement even – but not fire. My fear, my horror of fire was overwhelming me. Shaking, yelling in rage I backed away before it. When I reached the top I could see that at a certain point and probably not many minutes since, the fire had abated. Perhaps I could cross it, in any case it was my only hope. I went back to the spring and the fast approaching flames and soaked my clothes and hair. I covered my face with a piece of damp cloth and ran down the slope as fast as I could holding my pike with both hands. Approaching the fire I shouted. Yes, I remember, I gave a cry of warning. I leaped as far as I could. Surrounded, blinded by the flames, I took another leap and rushed headlong into Alcyon whom I had not seen. He was standing unarmed in front of me. Carried by the momentum there was no way I could avoid him. My pike went straight through him and we both rolled on the ground. Panicked by the fire I carried on running but he did not move. He had died instantly. It was only later in the night; miserable, crouching beneath a rock that I understood what had happened. I thought he had murmured my name as he went down. I shall never know whether I really heard it or only imagined it.

The following day I came out of hiding and went to look for the two surviving members of the enemy clan ready for the final battle. I was weak with hunger and from my burns. I could not forgive myself for having killed Alcyon. I wanted to die and that is what saved me. The struggle was long, unpredictable. But as well as wanting to strike me they fought to protect themselves. I was not interested in defending myself. I no longer wanted victory but longed for death and a conclusive end to my barbaric adventure. I was hit several times. But with a blow dealt with the remnants of my strength I mortally wounded their best fighter. Injured in the thigh, the other, realizing he had been left to confront me alone, threw down his weapons and fled. It would have been so easy to strike him down but not in the back. He turned suddenly and dropped to his knees calling out: 'Spare me for my son Alcyon loved you. I am the head and the last of my clan as you are the last of yours. Let us end this tragedy.'

I discarded my weapons and took Atus in my arms. We both wept at the misery and folly of our existence. I dressed his injuries. He tended my burns and wounds and gave me food. That night we slept in the same cabin. Following the customary rites, we attended to the funerals of the dead. He placed Alcyon's flute in his right hand and I put mine in his left. As we stood before their pyres we solemnly pledged that the blood feud between our two clans was over for ever. Dead, Alcyon looked as handsome and ethereal as he had in those early days on the mountain. Unfortunately my soul was inert, rotten, infected as it is still and I could draw no hope of rebirth, no hope of a real life from what I saw on his face that day.

The following day Atus came to me with a strange proposition: 'For the last few years we have been raising a fiancée for Alcyon. We adopted her when her parents died. Her name is Io. She's only five. I will help you rebuild your house and plough your land. In a few years you can take her as your wife. You will be our children, your children will be the children of one single clan that we shall found together.'

While I found his offer touching and disturbing I was too sick at heart and sick of soul. I told him that first I wanted to see the world so that I could put these catastrophic events behind me. He replied: 'My offer will hold until our daughter's fourteenth year.' With that he left but I soon realized that I had lost all incentive to rebuild the house, plough the fields or reconstitute the flock. My uncle had infected my spirit. I had become a man of blood, war and destruction. I considered returning to the life of a soldier but I was incapable of following orders. I had measured my strength against that of other men and discovered my power over women. I set off across Greece leaving behind the ruins of my house, our mountain and the tombs of my people. Until I met you I lived off seduction, theft and plunder. I nourished my hate and my shame with increasingly useless crimes.

No one says a word. The sea breaks across the reefs and slaps against the cliff. Inland is heard the cry of a screech owl. Antigone weeps on Oedipus's shoulder. Clius is touched by her emotion and asks: 'Why are you crying?'

In a broken voice she replies: 'Because of your little fiancée.'

'I have no fiancée.'

'Yes you have. A real one. One that Alcyon gave you. How old is she now?'

'Seven I think.'

'There is still time for you to learn to be happy with her, to have children.'

'Don't cry Antigone, don't be sad.'

'I'm not crying now. I have a right to be sad and a right to be happy, because of Io your little fiancée.'

Oedipus stands: 'It's been a long day. Come, we must let her sleep.' They leave the cave and stretch out near the fire each enveloped in the other's silence – thinking of Alcyon, Iocasta, music reverberating through the mountains, enigmas, oracles and life. Life that invites you to begin and then resists the invitation.

IV

ANTIGONE'S DENIAL

They leave the headland a few days later. Autumn is well advanced and shedding its colours. With each day that passes the snow gradually appears further down the slopes of the mountains. The journey is long. They follow Oedipus as he leads them a different way back to the house set among the vines where Diotima greets Antigone as though she had only left the day before. 'You will spend the winter with us,' she says. 'Clius can build a hut for your father and himself, on the hill where the great oak tree stands. No one will disturb them there.'

Clius finds stones, wood and tools near the oak. He lights a fire. A fine rain begins to fall. At the sound of the soft music he feels an undefined regret stir deep within him. Oedipus breaks the silence: 'Clius, you need a flute and it's time you took up dancing again.' Clius is so taken aback he does not reply. Darkness has fallen, the night will be cold. They lie down near the fire huddled together.

The hut finished, Clius starts out for the nearest town to buy himself a flute. Left alone, Oedipus sits in front of the great oak

71

tree and tries to visualize it in his mind bearing its burden of dead branches and its underground crown of roots. Sometimes as he captures it, Oedipus can discern the inner tree surviving despite everything. More often than not there is only the wind and the rain; time that has become infinite to the blinded man and the tragedy he had sought maybe or, inexorable thought, which had been sought by no one.

Clius returns. On his way, he had hunted in the forest and exchanged his prey against two flutes which he brings back. The more beautiful of the two he gives to Oedipus, who is filled with apprehension, wondering whether he can still play. He decides to try and music floods the hut where Clius, who thought he would never dance again, once more allows himself to be transported.

Oedipus sets out at dawn the next day followed by an anxious Clius. After walking for some time they hear a low rumbling in the distance. Oedipus makes his way towards it. He reaches the edge of a river which, following a storm, has burst its banks. Debris, tree trunks, dead animals are swept along in its plummeting descent. Oedipus is moved by the turbulence and violence of its waters. Removing all his clothes, he plunges into the river. He is carried away by the current, submerged by the waves, grazed by the tree trunks that rush past him. He stays afloat, but Clius, running along the bank calling his name, thinks he is unconscious. Oedipus is borne along by the flood towards the spur of a small rocky island. Just as he is about to smash into it, he manages to pull himself up on to a rock. Standing unsteadily on the slippery stone, he is elated, overwhelmed by the intensity and fury of the elements. The waves rise up and break against his knees; he is surrounded by movement, squalls, an unrivalled frenzy. A vortex, black and enticing, forms around him. It is his destiny to allow himself to slide into it and its unfathomable depths. Clius sees him fall. He runs downstream and throws himself into the water to intercept Oedipus. The current carries the body towards Clius. He grabs it and, holding it up, attempts to swim towards the shore. Oedipus appears to be unconscious

– the bank is close, Clius focuses his attention on it. At that moment a tree trunk strikes him violently on the head. He releases the body and sinks.

Clius comes round. He is lying on the shore and a man of remarkable strength is kneading his chest, forcing him to vomit up all the water he has swallowed. Oedipus, for he is this man, rubs him down, warms him up, forces him to stand and make his way through the rain back to the hut. Blind, how could he have pulled him out of the water and brought him back to the river bank? Clius asks him. Oedipus looks surprised. In his unique way, he says: 'Here we are.' When – and not without great effort – they reach the hut where Antigone is waiting for them ready to bandage their wounds, Clius realizes he will never know.

Through the winter months Antigone works with Larissa and Narses teaches Clius the craft of the potter at which he proves to be very competent. In the evenings Clius brings Oedipus his flute and he draws from it a wild music quite different from Alcyon's. Clius likes it however, and dances in the restricted space of the hut by the light of the feeble embers of the fire. Performed virtually on the spot, it is an intense dance. He does not abandon himself to it but seems to be carving and digging into a substance that cannot be seen. Clius sometimes brings back some clay from the workshop to mould and shape into objects or animals. Oedipus helps him. He thought he had lost this ability and soon realizes he was mistaken. Clius finds a black stone in a waterfall. Oedipus gives it a mouth and the beginnings of a smile. Antigone presents it to Diotima who names it: 'The stone's first smile'.

A few days later, Diotima hands Antigone an olive branch requesting that Oedipus carve it. He hesitates before accepting, feels it with his hands, his whole body seeking to discover what it conceals. When it is finished, Clius feels uplifted, as though summer had already arrived with the coolness of its waters and the pleasure of its shade. Antigone asks Oedipus for the name of the sculpture. All he says is: 'There is a spring.' Antigone hears the sound of rushing water emanating from the supple lines and angles of the wood. She cannot see the spring and Oedipus offers no explanation. Clius carries the piece to Diotima's garden. She is delighted with it and shows Antigone how the spring emerges at the top of the carving. It is possible to imagine a sigh which is the spring and to distinguish the sound of the water meandering beneath the grass, and then leaping over stones to escape. Antigone recognizes the stream and the spring whose babbling waters stir the sand a little before moving on. She and Ismene used to play there sometimes at the edge of a wood near Thebes, at a time when her life was predictable and clearly laid out before her. Contrary to all expectations, here she is, a beggar now, soon to set forth once more with that vertiginous blind man who has just made her this beautiful object which she can contemplate with her eyes, touch with her hands and listen to with her heart without ever growing weary of it.

It is the night of the Black Moon. Clius can feel it through the violent certainty, the necessity to dance that has taken hold of him. Thinking Oedipus is asleep, he leaves the hut and goes down to a lonely dell. He waits for the phenomenon that is approaching, the one that occurred each year when the clan still existed.

He notices that Oedipus has followed him but it is too late to do anything about it. The clouds close over the sky, darkness is complete and already the dance has taken possession of him. No longer are his steps, his movements, under his control. There is no alternative but to plunge into and lose yourself in the Divine Woman; the way she loses herself in you. You are obliged to spin round and round and yield to the rotation of the world which, the moment you tilt your head, tips itself savagely on to you. In the midst of the frantic racing of the clouds and the fleeting appearance of a star, a strange exhilaration takes hold of you. As though on the cutting edge of a knife you move in the most dangerous of directions, perhaps that of thought – if what you name as such has not lost contact with the Mother. For here she is – fragrant, her flesh fiery, her skeleton powerful. Will you survive? Is it the same for Oedipus? Maybe, for you see him, huge, whirling like a mountain, lifting his visionary's face towards the sky and its millions of blind stars. You spin on the trembling edge of pleasure and both of you discover the rapture of no longer being either the meaning or the centre of yourselves. You are at the end of time, it brings you down and throws you on to the ground, anywhere, anyhow.

When Oedipus comes round, the sun is already high in the sky. He has no idea where he is and has lost his staff. Antigone appears. She has brought cool water. 'What a state you've got yourself into!' she says, just as Merope used to when he was a boy. The words bring to mind the smile he so cherished. Antigone gives him a drink. He is covered in mud – she wipes it off, finds his staff and sees to Clius who is also awake. She climbs back up the slope out of the dell. They follow her like two children. Her fear that they will go mad has receded for she has discussed it with Diotima who said: 'They mustn't suppress their sorrow, it's better for them to live it. Your father has at last found something he can do. People love his little statues.'

They set off again in spring and end up at the headland where they were the previous autumn. Clius finds work with a potter in the small port nearby, and Antigone has no need to beg for a woman who knows Diotima has invited her to help weave cloth for the Athenian merchants. Clius arranges the small cave above the headland to accommodate Oedipus and himself. Antigone finds lodgings in the village but visits her father each day. As Oedipus is left alone practically all day, he goes down to the end of the headland and sits on a rock overhanging the sea to work on his sculptures.

In a dream one night he experiences an intense delight which disappears on waking. When the day is at its hottest, he goes down to the sea and into the water. Sinking into a semi-conscious state, he recalls the threads of his dreams. There was a door he could not bring himself to knock at. It was opened by a woman of a bygone age. She was beautiful, with white hair. She gazed at him in admiration as if he were in the process of accomplishing some great task. On the wall of the passageway, which looked

75

like the entrance to a cave, were green symbols which he could have deciphered had he known the language.

He had been ridiculed by oracles and pythonesses. They had lost him the kingdom of Thebes and his sight. But this sibyl – he feels sure – will not mislead him. On the contrary she is opening the door of her home to him.

Over the next few days Oedipus continues as before, installing himself at the top of the headland to work on his sculptures. He listens to the waves crashing against the cliffs and the cry of the seabirds. Everything is as it was and yet everything has changed. Clius brings him stones or pieces of driftwood. It is in vain, for Oedipus works on them less and less. His hands have become inactive for his mind has turned away from them to cross the threshold of dreams and become absorbed in the sea – in its great expanse, its monotony and stinging salt. Perhaps he had not appreciated it when he had eyes. Today something has begun to open up inside him and periodically the sea appears in all its fullness, yearning for him to abandon himself to it or be consumed by it.

Often unable to reach it, he falls back into darkness – that of his blindness cut off from the dazzling mass – that of his deafness which no longer hears the shrill voice. There are days when he feels vacant, rejected, forsaken; but the days when, exhilarated, he can bound out of himself to become benevolent husband or beloved wife to the sea, become more frequent. And the times he is able to escape, to grow sublimely or fade away into space, become longer. It is only a question of time – soon they will last for ever. All that matters now is the time spent in unconditional hope, all that is important is the time spent lost in contemplation. He will never forget the day when, having gone further, deeper than usual into that limitless vision, it suddenly disintegrated with the tearing sensation of a rejection that was beyond his comprehension.

The door had been opened, he had been seized by the light, overwhelmed by it. Now, he is back, lying in the place he thought he had left for ever. It is night – the weak light of a fire glows next to him. Antigone – dear, distant, alas, intractable Antigone – is stooping over him. What has he done to her poor, tender anguish, he who understands the vanity of all grief? Antigone's voice reverberates unrelentingly. Does she not know that he cannot hear her? That he can listen to no one? Can only gaze perpetually at the great luminous spaces that have opened up before him. Why can Antigone and Clius not allow him to return to that place of ecstasy and appeasement he has just left? Why is she crying, why can he not blot out her entreaties? 'Don't leave us. You have been away two days and two nights. Eaten nothing. Not known who we were. This is worse than your madness, worse than your vertigo. Am I dead to you? Does Clius no longer exist? What are we doing here if you are not with us? Am I really of no use to you? Am I in the way?' She shakes him, shouting: 'Oedipus! You cannot die! Before – yes! In Thebes . . . But here you no longer have that right!' She straightens up, shrieks like a pythoness: 'You no longer have that right! I deny you that right, because . . . because of me, Antigone!'

Oedipus hears Clius calming her, making her kneel down next to him. He knows he cannot defy her legitimate, terrible denial. Because it is what she wants, he drinks, compels himself to eat, allows forces other than those of the light to re-enter him. He is vaguely aware of Antigone's dreadful voice muttering: 'What are we . . . what are we doing here, if you . . . you leave?'

And Clius saying to her: 'Leave him, you can see he's suffering. You can see he's coming back.'

He is coming back since that is what they want, he feels the pain of returning to that opaque instrument – his body, and to a world enslaved by gravity. He feels Antigone's tender touch, she who has placed his head on her knees, making him eat slowly and sip his drink. Clius takes his hands and warms them in his. Then, taking out his flute, he plays him one of Alcyon's tunes. A poor tune compared to the music he might have heard but which nevertheless unexpectedly touches a corner of his heart that is so sensitive; he feels rising within him something closely resembling tears. 'Don't cry,' says Antigone, 'you can go back if you want, but not so far and not for so long. Not to that terrifying bliss, without us, without anyone. Do you understand?'

Alas, he understands only too well. With obvious distress yet strangely relieved, he becomes conscious once more of his heaviness, his blindness, his lack of definition – there, where he is on the road.

The following day, he asks Clius: 'Why were you so frightened?'

'It lasted so long, each time it was longer. That expression of utter bliss of your face, your body inert. We were used to the relentlessness of your walking, your hands and thoughts constantly on the move. Everything you call your vertigo that disappears whenever you cross into the unknown.'

'I won't go any more.'

He sees that Clius, who is preparing to go down to the village, does not believe him. After Clius has left, he picks up a stone and works on it once more, remembering the dream of the sibyl, the door she was holding open, which did not lead to infinity, but to the place where she lived.

That evening Clius informs him that an envoy from Ismene came to see Antigone. Ismene is in contact with Theseus, King of Athens. The latter is willing to receive Oedipus in Athens. Ismene sent Antigone some gold which she would not accept, but she sent back the messenger with news of them. She has also learned that King Theseus is due to sail past the coast with the Athenian fleet on its yearly journey to Thrace.

A few days later, Antigone hears that Theseus's fleet is approaching. Together they go up to the headland. Clius describes the scene to Oedipus: 'There are seven ships in all. As there is insufficient wind they are having to row around the headland. The oarsmen are singing. The sides of the ships, oars and sails are purple.' Clius and Antigone are enthralled, for through the rhythm of the songs and sharp lines of the ships, they discover the freedom of adventure of a seafaring nation.

King Theseus is at the centre of the fourth ship, in his usual place – at the helm. His eyes are fixed on the headland. He knows – for he knows everything that takes place on these shores – that Oedipus, the former king, has taken refuge here with one of his daughters. The other has become an ally and keeps him informed of events in Thebes.

Theseus hugs the shoreline. As he rounds the headland he sees Oedipus at close range, standing tall at the top of the cliff, his face cruelly cut by the black band that covers his eyes. Theseus with a magnanimous gesture salutes him with his sceptre. Without his companions needing to tell him, Oedipus returns the salute.

The headland rounded, the wind rises and swells the sails. Theseus give the orders, the sailors rouse themselves and the fleet moves off rapidly. When the king looks back Oedipus is standing in the same place: that of a sacred individual.

V

THE WAVE

A narrow path runs below an over-hanging rock on the northern side of the headland. It is a place where feral goats can often be found sheltering. Battered by waves during storms, the great dark rock-face beneath the overhang plunges abruptly and precipitously into the sea. Oedipus and Clius have come to examine the cliff-face which Oedipus has carved in his dreams. Oedipus runs his hands over the stone, heaves himself precariously up on to the rock-face. Pressing against the roughness of the stone, he examines it, explores it with slow heavy movements like a half-submerged swimmer. Clius declares: 'The rock looks like an enormous wave rising up, ready to engulf everything as it falls.'

Oedipus is satisfied. 'The wave is there, we must somehow prevent it from sweeping us away. One man can't do this on his own, we'll need a ship and oarsmen.'

Searching with his body in the intrinsic complexity of the cliff for the position of the oarsmen and the boat he feels should be there, he suddenly finds it – he becomes the boat – using his body he outlines it in the stone. He wants to sculpt it. Clius

80

wants to know why. Because of his dream, because of the three of them, swept away by the sea. Clius cannot see how it is possible to escape the wave.

'We must fashion the cliff,' Oedipus says, 'and uncover what it is trying to reveal.'

'That's an enormous undertaking!'

'We must begin right away. Get some tools. Antigone can help us, she creates excellent bodies and faces.'

Exhilarated by the project Clius goes down to the village to find Antigone and ask the fishermen for some tools. Left alone Oedipus continues to explore the rock, to familiarize himself with the wave. Sometimes he slips and cuts his hands. It is almost a pleasure to mark the cliff with his blood for the wave is there as well as within him; just as the sea was, when he was lost, contemplating it. But the sea was compliant as he gazed at it contentedly; immersed in its featureless immensity. Not so here where everything is hard, unequivocal, like the fishermen of Corinth he loved so much when he was a boy.

Remembering his early childhood, he sees himself in the port amongst the giant-like sailors and enormous ships. Queen Merope holds his hand as they go to the quay to buy fish. When she comes to a ship whose mast has been ripped off in a storm, she stops. The fishermen had managed to bring the ship back, the catch intact, for the fish glisten in the hold. Merope is horrified when she sees the damage inflicted by the sea, but the master of the vessel has survived many storms and demonstrates how he steered her through the swell. Up, down, constantly on the lookout for the next wave and, more importantly, keeping a cool head. He laughs in a self-assured manner and today Oedipus finds comfort in the recollection of his merry laughter and steadfastness.

Their first obstacle is Antigone who refuses to help them. She finds the project – so attractive to the two men – absurd, preposterous. She is not prepared to give up her work in the village to return to her life as a beggar. The next day Clius goes down to the port and Oedipus begins the task of carving the wave alone.

Antigone has a dream where she sees a child standing at the foot of the immense cliff, his diminutive tools in his hands. It is Oedipus, full of confidence, calling to someone. Despite the howling wind she eventually catches his cries: sister, sister! She wakes in tears. It is the middle of the night. She opens the door, the moon is bright. Dressing hurriedly she runs to the headland. She longs to throw herself into Oedipus's arms, but he and Clius are asleep and she does not want to wake them. Instead she lies down next to them, thinking that she can refuse her father's request to contribute to this colossal task, but how can she do that to her brother, a brother struck down by misfortune, whom she followed, pursued, when he left Thebes?

The men wake up to find Antigone preparing a meal. Without any explanation, Clius hands her some tools. When they attain the foot of the rock Oedipus shows her what to do. It soon becomes apparent that Antigone is the most skilled at doing detailed work. She will not need to beg, for when the villagers hear about Oedipus's project, they offer to feed them while the work is in progress in the belief that the wave will protect their ships.

From morning to night they hew the cliffs, only pausing at midday to bathe and eat. The stone is hard but as their arms and hands strengthen, Oedipus has to warn them not to strain the rock. The wave exists. It is just a question of helping it to emerge. Although Clius and Antigone cannot see it yet with their eyes they feel its presence beneath their hands. Whenever they lose confidence, they call Oedipus over. He permits his hands to glide over the stone. He listens to it, tastes it with his lips and tongue, flattens his body against it. 'Let yourselves be guided, transported by it.' Then they are reassured that the wave exists. It has entered their lives with a vengeance, submerged them, might submerge them again, but the knowledge does not prevent them from feeling alive.

They begin to feel the wave, but not the ship. Oedipus has

located its position, but dares not attempt to give it a shape. Storms and erosion have blackened the stone. As they dig into it, it becomes white and the foaming outline of the wave emerges bright on the dark background of the cliff-face.

While he is working, Oedipus sometimes releases two or three melodious notes. The other two hope he is about to sing, but no, and this saddens Antigone. So she stops working and launches into a sea shanty she was in the habit of singing in Thebes, a time so remote it is hard to believe it ever existed. When they hear her, Clius's hands and feet dance on the narrow path and Oedipus takes out his flute and plays. There should be a song to follow on but either Oedipus cannot or is reluctant to sing and they become dejected.

Leaving the other two to work on the wave, Oedipus marks the outline of the ship in the rock, its slender stem pointing towards the yawning chasm. Already the wave is beginning to curve back over the poop. The boat takes its rhythm from the exertions of the three oarsmen. There is a man standing behind them at the rudder. The ship plunges into the depths. As her prow begins to right itself she skips under the wave. It is a breath-taking spectacle and only when it is certain she will overcome the obstacle does relief set in. The wave looks invincible but the more subtle craft uses its adversary's incredible strength to elude it.

The outline is done. Oedipus asks Antigone to concentrate on the oarsmen and the man at the helm, as her hands are delicate enough to do this without disturbing the natural lines of the stone. Oedipus will fashion the boat to resemble either those he knew in Corinth which sailed the high seas, or those from here described to him by Clius. But this one will be sharper, similar to those first shapes which emerged one day from the sea. As he sculpts his thoughts are on the Sphinx who, like the wave, was infinitely more powerful than him. He used her strength to dispose of her, plunging the knife of his replies into her abstruseness. The Sphinx faded in the same way that waves do. He accepted responsibility, embraced his victory, the queen and the kingship; oblivious to the fact that another wave, this one much higher, was already rising up in front of him ready to sweep him away. Not so these oarsmen. They will know that this is not the only wave, that it is not solely a question of conquering it but that the full force of the storm with its succession of waves will have to be faced before they reach port.

For a while Antigone scrutinizes the oarsmen and pilot Oedipus has outlined and then gets down to work. Something is troubling her, she feels Oedipus has made a mistake, that he has not followed the invisible line of the rock. She calls him over, makes him touch the stone and feel the real position of the oarsmen. They are not pitched forwards, their heads bowing beneath the spray. They are at the apex of their effort, bodies and heads pulled back, exhaling the air from their lungs, eyes fixed on the enormity of the wave before them and the pilot, his valour, skill, his voice even, an inspiration to them.

At dusk, Oedipus tells his companions to go and rest, but he works on for several more long hours and it is already night when he joins them. White, slim, graceful, the stone ship has emerged triumphant, projected forwards by the wave like an arrow.

Antigone focuses on the three sailors. With powerful strokes, they row; preserving their energy, for they still have a long struggle ahead of them. These oarsmen, she thinks, are the three of us, battling to help the cliff bring the wave into the world; as Oedipus says: helping the cliff in its act of creation. The first is Clius: handsome, intent, but without that ferocious expression, that cruel hunted smile which appears all too frequently. With those magnificent eyes, his mouth forming a smile of defiance, he watches the pilot and not the wave as he gives rhythm to this dance in the storm. The androgenous body of Antigone sits behind him, the natural lines of the rock creating a head of foaming hair that floats in the wind. Her face she cannot do, for she is unaware of who she is or what the rock wants. Oedipus can do it if he can. Oedipus who in a dream compelled her against her will to join them on this cliff, calling her: my sister, in that harrowing way. Unable to bear it any longer, she picks up her tools and runs off.

Oedipus, who has been smoothing over the front of the boat, stops and for some time explores the face of the first oarsman with his hands. He calls Clius over. Clius is overwhelmed, at once full of admiration and fear. So this is how Antigone sees him, how she wants to see him. Angry, he says: 'This is what she wants me to be like.'

'She has made you as you are,' declares Oedipus. They return to their work – Clius, rejecting the statement and yet deeply moved by it. Oedipus moves on to the second oarsman. He feels the stone, examines it and with light blows begins to chisel the face. By the time evening falls, Clius cannot see well enough to continue. He calls Oedipus, goes over to him, speaks; but Oedipus is so absorbed in his work he does not hear, just as he did not on the headland when he was lost in contemplation of the sea.

Exhausted, Clius leaves. He lights the fire and prepares a meal. As Oedipus does not return, he lies down and falls asleep. At dawn he opens his eyes long enough to see blind Apollo glowing above him. The light radiating from the god is weak, for he is broken by his night's work. Dropping off again, Clius feels him lie down next to him.

Two days spent resting in the village and Antigone is pleased to return to the headland. The sun has dispersed the mist; the fishermen, with their red sails billowing in the head wind, have set out to sea. Before joining the men, Antigone goes to lay flowers at the statue of the local god – protector of the village. The statue has been marked by time and rain; it is rubbed smooth by the many hands that have touched it, of people hoping for protection or a cure. She can just make out a head rising delicately from the plinth which she presumes represents the trough between two waves or the furrow of a field. The head is faceless and yet there is the hint of a smile in its shape – humble, self-contained like the village. This eternal little rustic god will always exist. The place where he stands will still be sacred long after the wave, through the action of the weather and storms, has crumbled into the sea, as Oedipus knows it will. As she knows Oedipus wants it to.

The onset of autumn is beginning to colour the leaves, recent rains have turned the fields and hills green again. From the cliff, they can hear shepherds calling and dogs barking. Antigone can feel the earthenware jar pressing on her neck and shoulders as she ascends the coastal path. It weighs down on her, giving her strength while at the same time helping her keep her balance. She knows how her body must respond beneath its burden, she feels it guiding her, encouraging her. She thinks: my body is made to carry, one day it will carry a child, and she smiles to herself. Placing her pitcher at the entrance to the cave, she sees Oedipus steadily and confidently walking into the setting sun. As he reaches the edge of the void, she is about to shout a warning when he stops, offering up his body and face to the rays. He is practically naked, still young, still handsome, bearing the invisible yet ever-present scars of misfortune and exhaustion. She admires his strong, lean body, but has difficulty connecting this picture to the wonderful mental image she has of him as a child, when laughter, speech and ever-changing expressions constantly animated his face.

He has heard her and half turns the way he used to when she came into his room in Thebes. She is a small girl running towards him. Kneeling to be the height she once was, she clasps him around the knees and waist as she kisses him. She snuggles up to him, she must for it is the other one, Ismene – who is always petted without seeking to be. Antigone has to do something, ask before she is noticed. Ismene just waits. Maybe she does call out, does ask – but who knows since even she does not know why it happens. Ismene may be the more skilled, but it was she, Antigone, that he summoned with his heart in Thebes, it was she who heard him. She buries her young girl's head in the hollow of Oedipus's hip. He catches her by the waist and with amazing strength and ease lifts her in his outstretched arms. Head and torso arched back, he raises her above him. To Antigone's astonishment and shame, she hears herself gurgling with delight like a small child. How could she be so self-indulgent? Oblivious to this, Oedipus twists her round and presents her to the sun dedicating her to him. Unable now to look at her as he used to, he entrusts her to the gaze of this other living body. Once he has set her down, she tries to recapture the feeling of her tiny hand slipping into the great warmth of his. But her hand has grown, her lips too: she is tall. With agonizing regret, she kisses the scarred, callused hand which has shrunk in relation to hers and which will never again be the giant hand she loved. He strokes her hair and looking up, she receives full face the imperious glare of the sun as if it were his.

She moves down into the shade and cool light of the cliff. She sees the brilliant white ship emerging from the gigantic rock and how, over the last two days and nights, Oedipus has personified his daughter Antigone in the stone. Around her forehead and long hair, whipped by the wind, the line of the stone has formed a crown of foam. So this is how Oedipus sees her, how he wants her to see herself, infused with a beauty quite unlike Iocasta's or Ismene's. A vibrant, determined beauty, suffused with confidence. Although this face understands the power of the wave's crushing weight, it remains undaunted. The stone wanted it to look enlightened and solid, like the body she herself had carved and is astounded to discover. Oedipus has accentuated the bold outline of the body which could belong to a strong boy or a slim young girl, more intrepid than the young girls of Thebes. Their bodies united in their efforts to survive, her body adds its muscle to that of the other two oarsmen. Oedipus has achieved this effect through the amazing, unsmiling face he has sculpted, in which everything is concentrating on physical exertion and correct breathing. And yet, like the village's little worn god, her whole head and body have been imbued with a smile, the transparent light of which emanates directly from the stone. What she finds so striking and what moves her more than anything else in this outline born of Oedipus's vision, is its clarity. And this is how – through her confusion, her uncertainty – he has loved her with his soul and with his hands. She embraces the hidden smile he has given her, here in the stone. She feels more reconciled to herself, feels that maybe one day, as Diotima has told her, she will at last truly become Antigone.

Oedipus and Clius advance down the path together. Oedipus is looking tired and thinner. But he refuses to rest, despite the colossal work he has just completed. He pauses in front of the second oarsman and runs his hand over his work as far as the curve of the brow. With a brief smile, he says: 'It's good.' He looks dazed, as though, having just woken up, he is still attempting to separate what the day has in store from what belongs to the subterranean world of sleep.

Antigone leans over, takes his hands and kissing them says: 'Thank you.'

A tender, teasing expression appears on Oedipus's face: 'Now you have found the shapeless little god's smile.' She is speechless. How does he know? He chuckles as though he were saying: I know, I know who you are, much better than you ever will.

They resume their work. Oedipus finishes the boat which bounds upwards, propelled more by the booming trough of the waves than by the oarsmen. Clius works on the crest of the wave that must turn and fall back into the depths. The ladder he made is not high enough, so he brings a ship's rope from the port, attaches it to a protruding rock and lowers himself to within reach of his work. Antigone is frightened when she sees him swinging above the void. Sometimes, when she raises her head, she sees him watching her with that strange smile – part tender, part ironic – on his lips. The smile of a man who knows all there is to know about women and what they are really like when they give themselves to a man who loves or desires them, as Clius has so often done, and still does – for they have told her so in the village. He knows everything she does not know. What Iocasta knew so well, as each one of her movements revealed. It gave them their warmth, their essence and that unusual majestic quality. She is not like that and never will be. She is just tall, thin Antigone who that man up there on his rock – with his handsome, anxious face and dancer's body – respects and desires with an unwieldy longing. She begins to sculpt the third oarsman, aware of Clius's gaze following each of her body's movements beneath its dusty, worn clothes. When the sensation ceases, she raises her eyes and sees he is absorbed in his work, no longer preoccupied by her. Relieved at first, she feels a dull penetrating grief the longer it continues. Then, she too becomes engrossed in the shapes her chisel is creating. The third oarsman is Oedipus, not the one she once knew – Zeus incarnate to the citizens of Thebes and to Iocasta's eyes and body. She wants to carve him as he was before that time, the savage boy – conqueror and victor – who beat the Sphinx with his sharp but youthful intelligence, who rode the first wave only to fall at the next. He who, with the help of the others, must now avoid being drowned.

She is oblivious to the passing of time, only half-aware that evening is approaching, when she hears a shout. Clius has detached himself, slid down the rope and is dangling high above her; he drops without losing his balance, audaciously and effortlessly landing next to her on the narrow path. Examining her work, he bursts out laughing: 'Still the little girl in love with the once handsome Oedipus!'

She is offended: 'Is he not still handsome?'

'Yes. In a way. But he's not as you see him, any more than you are still how he's represented you.'

He pulls on a tear in her dress, making it worse; as Ismene used to whenever she was caught in the kitchen helping the servants.

'Look at you! Filthy, dusty, scruffy! Covered in fleas no doubt. The village is crawling with them!'

'And what about you! Aren't you dirty at the end of a day's work?'

'Yes, but I do as I'm told, especially when the master is his usual silent self, but you are his daughter, his younger sister!' Then instantly: 'In a way, Antigone, you are beautiful, unique, fortunately you are quite unaware of it. Maybe I'm in love with you, sometimes I think I am, but that's not what we're here for.

Come, you need food and rest. Leave the old fool to kill himself if that's what he wants. He'll find his own way back.'

She follows him, so upset that she leaves her tools behind. She turns back and sees the one he called the old fool bent over his work, completely absorbed in it.

She runs and catches up with Clius. The evening is no different from any other. He lights the fire, she prepares the meal and washes as best she can, for there is very little water. She changes into her other patched and darned dress which is relatively clean. It is late, too late she feels to go back to the village, so Clius rearranges the cave for her. Oedipus returns. The moon is high and casts a diffuse light over his tall frame and dusty clothes and hair. He is tired and preoccupied. Never has he seemed so tall or so noble as today, in his poverty and weariness. How could Clius have had the gall to call him an old fool.

She tries to eat but suddenly disheartened and overcome by an unexpected rush of nausea, in full view of the two men, she leaps up and filled with shame at her groans, vomits behind a rock.

She returns to the fire. How magnificent, how complete – like the rocks – they are. She is acutely conscious of her fragility, her pain, her vulnerability. How she wishes Iocasta were there so that she could rest her cheek against her beautiful shoulder. If only Ismene were not so far away, or that she could be in the safety of Diotima's company. But first they must finish the wave, and that is difficult, too difficult for someone like her as soft and malleable as the earth itself. She is weeping, shedding bitter tears of exhaustion, then honeyed tears, as they put their arms about her and lay her down in the cave.

When she wakes, the fire is lit and the food ready. Clius appears and today he is in a good mood: 'Come on. We have a surprise for you.' Like an excited child she rushes out. Oedipus is mixing flowers and herbs into two pitchers that Clius has filled with water from the spring. The water smells exquisite, its fragrance familiar. It is what Iocasta used to call her enchanted water. So many plants were needed for its preparation and an expert hand to pick them, that she rarely used it. But whenever she did, she would feel invigorated and attractive. As a treat the little girls would be given a few drops in their cupped hands to pat over their faces and necks. So it was Oedipus who prepared the enchanted water, but this time he has done it for her. The men leave. Very slowly, she pours the contents of the pitchers over her head, as she had watched Iocasta do, and massages the streaming water into her whole body, starting and jumping and squealing with pleasure as she did when she was young. Then, shivering, she stretches out in the sun totally relaxed, looking up at the sky, losing herself in it, the aroma permeating her whole being.

She stands up and dresses, experiencing a sensation of lightness, the like of which she has not felt for a long time. She joins the others; the meal is ready and tastes good. She eats with a hearty appetite. To have picked so many plants, Oedipus and Clius must have set out before dawn. After a hard day and a short night, the one guiding the other, they had carried out this difficult task to assuage that moment of incomprehensible pain she had experienced the previous evening. Clius is watching her. With an almost imperceptible gesture he apologizes, indicating that that is how he is as she knows only too well. They consider the work to be done over the next few days; Oedipus asks her to concentrate on the master of the boat. 'Do the outline and I'll carve the rest. When you've done the pilot, the third oarsman will be easier.' She is reluctant to abandon the third oarsman, but realizes they have already discussed it between themselves, man to man. Why? Why not? She agrees – she will do the master next. She can sense they are pleased. They must have debated at length.

They return to their work. Antigone searches to find the pilot's position. Suspended from his rope, Clius becomes increasingly frustrated with the crest. He loses his grip then his footing. The rope swings him vertiginously along the cliff-face and he lets out a fearful laugh. Antigone shouts up to him to climb back up and rest. Instead he climbs down, lands near her and sits down exhausted. Oedipus joins them, picks up his flute and plays an ancient tune which at one time could be heard on feast days throughout the poorer districts of Thebes. The enchanted water is taking effect, Antigone feels carefree, scented and confident; she sings and Clius periodically joins his voice to hers. He leaves, no doubt going back to the cave to sleep, and this gratifying moment comes to an abrupt end.

Antigone scans the stone where the pilot will surface. She was right, the outline marked out by Oedipus is not large enough, it is out of proportion in relation to the oarsmen. The stone cries out for different dimensions. He had not detected the majestic sweep that leads up towards the top, he could not see the shadow where the rock straightens, nor the expression of hope on the faces of the oarsmen enlarging it. But to where? Confronted by the stone she is alarmed to discover that even her new delineation is too restrained. The master of this craft must be tall, extremely tall. The discovery of this lack of moderation scares her. She runs over to Oedipus: 'The stone is turning the pilot into a giant!'

'Well then, the stone must be right.'

She is on the verge of tears: 'But I've never seen a giant.'

'Yes you have. Think back, everyone was a giant to you when you were small.'

She works on the contours and proportions of the body. Once again the enchanted water works its magic making her lighthearted and self-assured. The outline begins to take shape. The pilot seen in profile will be tall but not too tall – like Oedipus and Iocasta were in the sacred kingdom of Thebes. She is satisfied but it is time she returned to the village. The fire in front of the cave has gone out. Clius is waiting for her: 'I'll walk down with you.' He looks preoccupied.

Half-hidden behind the clouds, the sun casts an uneven light over the coastline. Boats are returning to port, their sails hoisted, the sailors resting on their oars. Clius holds her back: 'I have to talk to you.' A thrill of anticipation and wild hope races through her. He goes on: 'I can't do the crest, I'll never manage it.' She cannot disguise her deep disappointment. Fortunately, Clius has not understood. Angry, he grabs her roughly by the arm, hurting and alarming her: 'That wave is Oedipus's folly and mine. I've managed to make it rise, but it must turn and fall back into the sea. But I can't, there is no way I can hold it back. Do you understand? It will crash on to the headland and drown us all.'

'But Clius, it's made of stone.'

'That's what you think Antigone — but let me tell you, the wave's impossible to control. Completely impossible.'

She is appalled when she sees the full implication of what he has said. They must find an immediate solution. Disengaging her arm she asks: 'Do you want me to take over?'

'You, hanging from a rope! Never, never!'

Delighted she murmurs: 'Why?'

'For my sake,' he replies.

She is conscious of her blushes as elation replaces delight. Then the significance of Clius's words hits her: 'You want Oedipus to finish the wave?'

Decisively he replies: 'Yes.'

'My blind father hanging from a rope!'

'He must. Otherwise the wave will engulf us all. You must tell him!'

This last directive fills her with dread and she protests: 'Why me?'

With a smug yet disarming grin he adds: 'For my sake.' He has turned and left, bounding up the slope like a goat or the dancer he is. He returns to the headland, lights a fire, gives Oedipus his food and sees to his needs as he does every night; dances perhaps, if the stars are auspicious.

At the port all the villagers are there. The fishermen are bringing in their catch and sorting out their nets; the women are calling in their children for the evening meal. They have seen Antigone returning from the headland and greet her. Many have already taken her into their homes but tonight it is Chloe's turn. She is the wife of an old fisherman; she lost a son at sea and two newborn babies. Her face is serene and dignified; she was obviously a girl and then a woman who enjoyed a good laugh and who still does when the mood of the sea allows her to.

Antigone asks an old sailor: 'What's it like in a storm?'

He finds the question amusing and scratching his head replies: 'Difficult to say when you're in it rather than on the outside.'

Chloe has made room in her bed for Antigone who falls asleep in the warm, strong, reassuring presence of her body. Next day, when the men have left, Chloe gives her a basket filled with flowers, fruit and three fish wrapped up in leaves. 'I'll take back the basket when you've finished with it.' Antigone thanks her and bending her knee gives her the curtsey of a Theban princess. Chloe beams and a network of delicate wrinkles flickers across her face. She goes into her house and watches Antigone climb the hill, her basket on her head, agile, barefoot, her sandals in her hand.

When Antigone arrives at the cave Oedipus is seated at the top of the headland, his face to the sun and sea. She remembers how it was there that she had shattered that unbearable state of ecstasy he had plunged into.

As she approaches him, he says without needing to turn round: 'Antigone'; just that: 'Antigone.' It is enough, for in the syllables of her name she senses that he understands and loves her for what she is. Returning from the poverty of the village, her clothes are impregnated with the scent of Chloe's flowers and the smell of fried fish.

She sits next to him: 'Clius can't finish the wave, he says he won't be able to make it curve back and fall into the sea.'

'I know.'

She is greatly relieved at not having to elaborate. He is covering up his eyes with the large white band he wears to protect them while he is working. When he has finished, he says: 'Tell Clius to prepare the rope.'

Clius appears and helps Oedipus into his working clothes. Antigone heats up the fish. The men eat; she had thought she would not be able to swallow a thing but on an order from her father, she forces herself and feels better. Clius wraps a sheepskin around Oedipus's waist to soften the contact with the rope and binds the knot with cloth. He did not go to these lengths for himself. Antigone checks the knots. She wants to help him but Oedipus tells her to carry on as usual. The moment she has gone, he starts to shake and his teeth to chatter.

Clius is concerned: 'Will you be all right going down?'

'Yes. It's nerves. The void. Vertigo! You understand.'

He understands. Slowly, he lowers Oedipus.

Oedipus searches for footholds in the cliff. Antigone can hear him cutting into the rock in front of where the wave must begin to unfurl. She listens to the normal, regular beat of Oedipus's hammer and feels half-reassured. Up above, Clius calls out his instructions. Suddenly she hears the notes of the flute demanding: Bring me back up! Oedipus clambers along the rock-face. A piercing shout! He has slipped and fallen before Clius could take up the slack. He swings across the cliff-face, his body smashing into the protruding rocks. He is still clutching his tools and making vain attempts to find a hold in the ridge; but each time he is frustrated by the overhang. He cries out, howls in anger, just as he must have done when he killed Laius and his guards. Clius will never be able to bring him back up alone, she must go and help. She passes beneath Oedipus, now groaning even though the slack of the rope has improved. She turns and stops, stunned. Writhing at the end of the rope, shouting between each spasm, Oedipus is sick several times. He has given up trying to find a foothold, he just dangles miserably from the rope like a stained object. His vomit runs down the stone and falls on to the path. She flees, too petrified to look round. As she runs up the slope, she hears that his groans have turned to shouts of rage. He still has not found a foothold but at least Clius has managed to help him right himself. Breathless and overwhelmed by the sounds coming from Oedipus, she stops and realizes they are different again – more like those he used to make when he was out training with his guards in the courtyard of the palace, when Iocasta, as she watched him from the balcony, would chase away her daughters if she surprised them trying to catch a glimpse of him in the frenzy of the fight.

Antigone has reached the headland; Oedipus is silent. It is not yet night but the sky is jet black. She rushes over to Clius who, having secured the rope around a rock, is flat on his stomach on the ground. Leaning over the void totally engrossed, he does not see her approaching. He does not look anxious, not even concerned – she has never seen him look like this. He seems drunk. She touches his shoulder, he turns and shouts: 'He's done it!' She does not understand what he means, she has come to help but he does not need it. Then she also leans over and sees that Oedipus has cleared the protruding rock and found himself some deep footholds. His back against the overhang, he is chiselling with rapid powerful strokes. 'Everything is fine,' says Clius. 'Go and take shelter. A storm is on the way.'

She does not want to take refuge. Like him she wants to watch, she wants to know: 'How did he do it?'

'He turned on the offensive and that was it.'

'I saw him being sick.'

'There was a sudden change,' says Clius, 'and now nothing can stand in his way. Listen. It's as though the wave itself were carving.'

It is true, the rhythm of his blows is not patient and restrained but relentless, sending chunks of stone flying out in all directions, as though the sea had unleashed its energy or the storm were hurtling towards them. In the distance – the rumble of thunder and now the first drops of rain. The storm breaks. The waves roar up to the cliff and crash down again. Sheets of rain hammer down. Frightened, Antigone shouts: 'Come up, come up quickly!' Oedipus's cries of elation ring out to be answered by Clius's ecstatic laughter. Then he roars out between two claps of thunder: 'The wave's rising! It's rising! He's going to force it, turn it!' Oedipus pulls himself up on to the end of the rock and sits astride it, both hands free to wield his enormous tools. Blinded by the rain and lightning, Antigone can still hear the rock shattering beneath the frantic blows of chisel and hammer.

He is like a giant striking, moulding, the cliff. Clius laughs, yelling out messages as he regularly adjusts the tension of the rope. Oedipus's jubilant peals of laughter rise in reply. Antigone feels crushed by the torrential rain, wind and crashing thunder. Lightning flashes, will it strike Oedipus? No – it hits an enormous tree on the shore that burst into flames – the eye of the storm has not yet come.

Clius hollers into her ear: 'He's done it, the wave's fallen back!' Afraid and chilled to the bone she does not understand. Clius is now virtually naked, whooping with glee as he continues to manoeuvre the rope. Antigone knows the sea will have washed away Oedipus's vomit, it will have gone, leaving no trace of that terrible moment which she alone experienced.

A few rays of hazy sunlight pierce the retreating clouds but already a second squall is on its way. Another clap of thunder, but at least the rain no longer blinds her. She leans over to warn Oedipus. Sparks shoot out around the massive shoulders and head with its shrouded eyes. With deadly accuracy, he is striking into the base of the overhanging rock, forcibly wrenching out the wave, turning it under him and sending it back, furious and foaming, to unfurl into the sea. Can Clius see this? He does not seem to find it alarming, quite the opposite; he is flushed, elated, and when Oedipus calls out in his deep resonant voice, he echoes him with all the power of his own lungs. He turns towards her, compelling her to look, to understand, to copy him and lend the full power of her own voice to what is taking place. She cannot refuse. Sibyl or pythoness, reduced to being no more than a voice forcing from her body her loudest cries, she screams back in response to Oedipus, or Zeus, as he and the sea roar out together. And in the meantime with his hallowed tools and remarkable shoulder he makes the cliff quake.

The rain increases, flashes rend the sky, bolts strike in several places. Trees burn on the cliff and she thinks: 'Let's hope the fishermen are back.' She has become disorientated by the turbulence of the elements.

All of a sudden, Clius strains at the rope and shouts: 'All is well; he's coming back up.'

Two massive hands grip the edge of the cliff, brace themselves and instantly the giant is there, still surrounded by sparks. Laughing, he snaps the rope attached to his waist and with one superb movement he is up, towering above her. Handsome, blind, radiant, exuberant even. How he glows, viridescent, as with a sweeping and careless gesture he throws his enormous tools into the sea.

Standing before her with arms open wide, his mouth, brow and − concealed behind their white band − eyes, radiate his consummate goodness. She runs to him, wraps her arms around his leg, then rests her forehead against his mighty knee, level with her mouth. Cheerful or tearful, what bliss to sink to your knees, to catch hold of and kiss those ankles and bare, wounded feet. Will this giant grow any more? Leap into the sea, be taken up into the sky by a blazing chariot drawn by fiery horses?

The rain is still falling and she is cold. We need a fire, she thinks, they must be as frozen as me. Perhaps the body she no longer dares look at is by now lost high up in the clouds. She turns and takes off through the torrential rain like a hunted animal. She gets back to the cave and tries to revive the fire. It is not easy and the billowing clouds of smoke sting her eyes. At last a flame. Frantically she starts throwing on to it all the wood Clius has stored. The torrents of rain make the fire sizzle, but nevertheless it springs to life. The wind drives the flames into the shallow cave. She flattens herself against the rock convinced she will burn to death. She is so numbed by fear she cannot even scream. All is well, Clius is there. Leaping over the flames, he kicks back the fire and rolls the logs out of the cave. She thinks he is going to pick her up and carry her but all he does is clear a path and lead her out, helping her jump over the embers. He tries to make her rest on a tree stump but she refuses. After what she has just been through she must have fire, more fire with its incredible light. She picks up the logs Clius rolled out to save her and throws them into the flames. Stunned at first,

Clius is seized with the same impulse, the same ebullient rage. They throw on to the blazing pile all the wood so carefully amassed since they have sheltered there. The heat and great flames feed their exuberance and shield them from the sea mist creeping along the headland.

Had Oedipus not taken over, thinks Antigone, the uncontrollable wave would now be engulfing us, separating us. Through the thickening smoke and mist she can just make out Oedipus. Now his normal height, he is standing a short distance away in his rain-soaked clothes. He looks exhausted and yet she can still detect in his features traces of his giant's gentleness and euphoria. He stands there, silent. She would like to run over to him but like Clius she feels she must respect his need for solitude. She takes a few logs from the fire and starts to prepare some food; for whatever the heart might feel the body continues to make its unrelenting demands.

Oedipus draws nearer, picks up his flute and plays one of those simple, elementary tunes he is so fond of, reminiscent of the sea. Then his voice rises; weak, timid, shaky, like that of a child's. On hearing it, Clius weaves around singer and fire the exquisite movements of one of his dances. Antigone understands neither words nor phrases in Oedipus's song, but she senses a feeling of jubilation beyond its actual meaning. She would like to glorify it like Clius but alas, she is not lithe, she is earthbound. Neither does she have his passionate nature nor his ability to improvise movements; so she goes and stands next to her father and is content to follow the inflections of his voice that seem as though rusted after a long winter.

Oedipus falls silent. Clius, swept along by his enthusiasm, yells: 'You turned it, you bent it back!' Oedipus chuckles and Clius rushes at him, embraces him, swamps him with whoops of glee and they end up collapsed on the ground with Clius repeating: 'You did it! You saved us!' and Oedipus, the blind man, the supplicant, responds with a mute yet noisy laugh that is new to Antigone. Experiencing a pang of jealousy, she is drawn into their exhilaration, this mad yet sober intoxication. She throws herself on to them, hugs and kisses them in turn, shouting ecstatic, jubilant. She hears their voices, their laughter resonate in the distance with the thunder, while deep inside her a hushed rather nebulous voice whispers: Yes, we have all been saved, just a little – a tiny bit saved.

Antigone insists that Oedipus sit by the fire on the tree stump. He is shivering, his teeth chatter, he has cramp in his hands and feet, he has reverted to the human condition. Gently but firmly Clius removes his wet clothes, dries him, rubs him down, puts dry clothes on him and massages his hands while Antigone busies herself with the meal. Clius may look after him but it is she who gives him the hot drink and biscuits she has cooked on the embers. As they eat, Clius looks first at Antigone then at Oedipus: 'Your daughter looked very beautiful when she was overcome by it all. Rolling on the ground, smelling of fire and smoke, shouting and kissing us the way boys in the stadium or soldiers after a victory do. How lovely she was, slightly burned, slightly singed by the blaze!'

Suddenly conscious of how tired she is and how painful her burns are, Antigone stands and leaves their comforting warmth and ring of light. As she nears the village, she turns. Their stockpile, used up in one go, still illuminates the headland with its flames. She pictures Clius having settled Oedipus, circling around it, dancing.

By the time Antigone reaches the village the fog has cleared. She is relieved; the ships are all back in port, without the storm having claimed any lives. The fishermen and many of the sailors' wives are there. They have obviously been waiting for her. To her amazement they come and thank her for the fire. 'In that storm, we couldn't even see the ends of our oars the wind and fog were so bad. It's thanks to the fire that we all got back.'

Chloe asks: 'How on earth did you make such a huge blaze in that terrible storm?'

'I was careless. I lit it in the cave and almost caught fire myself with the wind blowing as it was.'

A young woman touches her head: 'Your hair's singed. You're

lucky it was raining. Come to my house, I'll tend your burns and see to your hair. My name's Isis and I cut the hair of the loveliest women in the village.' Antigone follows her. Some of the women are astonished, for Isis is a young widow with a bad reputation. She is considered to be a bit of a sorceress and since her husband disappeared sailors and shepherds have often visited her, some have fought – and even died – for her. As she walks into the house Antigone breaks into an icy sweat and is on the point of collapsing.

Isis lies her down, warms her and removes her clothes. 'I thought as much, you've burned your legs, arms and shoulders. All your lovely hair could have gone up in flames.' She washes her very gently. 'You're lucky, it's not too serious, I'm going to apply clay, herbs and Egyptian ointments. My mother was Egyptian, my father a pirate. He kidnapped her. He was a real tyrant but he did love her. He really did! Just like your Clius!' Although thrilled beyond belief when she hears this, Antigone realizes Clius has been a regular visitor.

She rests for three days while Isis and Chloe take it in turns to look after her. They have patched and washed her scorched dress.

On the morning of the fourth day, after they have eaten, she tells Isis she is going back up to the headland. Isis informs her that Clius, who has come each day for news of her, is waiting outside.

There he is, covered in dressings, head practically shaved, giving him an even wilder look. He laughs unkindly when he sees Antigone's singed strands of hair that Isis has not completely disguised. Despite her protestations he heaves a large bundle of wood on to his back and sets off in front of her, his body bent beneath its weight like a tree in a storm.

As they reach the headland, Antigone hears the regular rhythm of Oedipus's hammer and chisel. At last Clius speaks: 'All the time you and I have been ill, he's continued working. The wave's coming along well.' She is cross when she sees the load has dislodged and soiled his dressings. She insists he sit down so that she can attend to them. She notices that the cave has been restocked with wood and provisions and that half-burned logs smoulder on the fire. There is nothing left to remind them of the events of the storm save the rope, lying at the edge of the void, which was attached to Oedipus as he harnessed the wave. It is still there, not cut but visibly broken by some giant force. Taking an axe, Clius severs the fragment that is left.

They go down the path. Arriving at the place where the wave rises, Antigone is suddenly anxious. On the overhanging rock the wave curves back, twisting under the pressure of its own weight and falls, as Oedipus wanted it to, plunging back into the sea.

Next day, Clius works on linking the section of the wave that rises up with that which is breaking. Oedipus carves the body of the third oarsman. Antigone is struck by the control and delicacy of his movements – so unlike the violence and fury of the blows made by he who forced back the wave. For the first time she notices that his wonderful head of chestnut hair is turning grey. He turns his face with its bandaged eyes towards her, on his lips the smile that once conquered all hearts.

She says: 'I'm slowing you down.'

He replies: 'You've got plenty of time.'

She feels that despite the onset of autumn and winter, he is giving her a vast stretch of time, telling her that it is vital not to hurry. She settles herself in front of the outline she has marked out for the pilot and is momentarily daunted by the amount of work still left to be done. Because Oedipus is allowing her to take time, she stares at the stone, loses herself in it, rests her face on it, runs her hands across it. Beneath her forehead she feels a centre of calm. Finding inspiration there, she slowly draws it into her whole being and sets to work. By midday, the foot, ankle and leg are delineated.

With wood and ropes Clius builds her some scaffolding, enabling her to move easily along the giant body. First she works on the shape, the body's general stance, then Oedipus accentuates the relief, he smooths and polishes the stone emphasizing the shadows and angles. They hardly speak but when he senses she is tired he tells her to sit and draws from his flute tunes and sounds that come from a long time ago, a period predating Thebes, Zeus and Prometheus; predating the discovery of fire, when men and women were like the eagle, in their original state of innocence and ferocity.

Clius completes the wave then turns to the rudder. To take the pressure off Antigone he takes charge of the cooking. He has moved some logs down to the path and builds a fire at the base of the scaffolding so the others can warm themselves whenever it rains or the wind blows cold.

In the evenings she goes down to Chloe's or Isis's where there is always a fire and a hot meal waiting for her. The two women talk of the giant pilot as though he were a sea god. Antigone is preoccupied, for although the body is almost finished, she still has to do the head. She says to Isis: 'Up until now my hands and eyes have known what they were doing but I have no idea what the head should look like.'

'Don't worry,' Isis replies, 'you're not alone.'

What does she mean? She decides not to ask for an explanation. Indeed, tonight she is not alone in this restful house where, after Isis has massaged and bathed her, she is tucked into bed.

She has a dream that night that she is communicating with people who have taken refuge underground to escape annihilation by those living above. Endurance has become a skill and they move freely through rock, water and earth, surviving on infinitesimal amounts of food. As they adapt to this subterranean existence, their minds unite, enriching and improving the quality of their lives. Love is paramount and spreads beyond their world to the outside. From them comes man's craving for all that is beautiful and sacred. At one with matter, sight has become redundant, they no longer use their eyes and people might think they are blind. A perceptive inner vision has inspired them with a greater sense of justice and strength. It would appear that they have overcome death and if, like those who live above ground, they have their problems, then they are those of a higher plane.

Antigone wakes unable to decide whether it was a dream of something she experienced in a semi-conscious state. It leaves her with the impression that these subterranean people are encouraging the three of them because they understand, perhaps because they are waiting for them.

Oedipus is already busy when she arrives at the headland. Clius looks at her with admiration: 'Last night after you'd gone, we both spent a long time examining your sculpting with our hands, for by that time it was dark for both of us. Oedipus said: "Antigone's inspired." '

Despite her pleasure at hearing this, she says, 'It's not me – it's my hands that are inspired.'

'You are your hands,' says Clius, 'your hands are you. Oedipus also said: "Antigone is no longer conceiving the stone, the stone is conceiving her. Her pilot is worthy to look out to sea." '

She would like to tell him of her dream but she is frightened of undermining him by forcing him into the ambivalent fabric of words; apart from which she must get working. They both walk down the path and find Oedipus kneeling on the scaffolding already hard at it. She kneels in front of him. Taking his face in her hands, she feels how thin and gaunt he has become since he has been working so relentlessly. Running his hand down the back he is polishing he says: 'A man with victory in his spine.'

All three are on the scaffolding. The north wind blows harder, biting into them. Clius lights the fire and when Antigone is too cold to hold her implements she goes down and warms herself while the other two sit nearby with hot drinks. The two men eat but she is incapable of swallowing anything. Occasionally she examines her hands, chapped and callused despite Isis's efforts to care for them. She surveys her patched clothes, conscious of her dusty face and body. Clius has stopped taunting her and calling her grubby and dishevelled. On the contrary he now often suggests she go and relax in the cave but she always declines.

The brow and windswept hair are almost finished. She moulds

into the stone that lofty figure so familiar to her when she was a child. She searches and recalls her father's former radiant good looks. But she cannot ignore the bitter creases left on his face by the plague, his father's murder and Iocasta's death, nor the scars of that long introspective road leading nowhere, and worse still, the loss of the vertiginous rapture he had found while contemplating the sea – that happiness which he had relinquished because she could not bear what she considered to be an escape, an evasion, but which might have been no more than the crossing of the abyss. She does not regret what she did. She demanded from him, and was granted by him, a different fate. But what right did she have? Could one still talk of such a right? She was the strongest and summoned him to a different destiny, the one that led him to spend months sculpting the cliff, displaying the strength of a god and the tenacity of a labourer. The same fate which demanded that today she create on this faceless victorious frame a giant representation of him gazing out to sea.

One day, one evening, several evenings, Clius helps her clamber up the cliff then down to the village as far as Isis's door where he entrusts her to the care of the young woman, and that of the old woman as well, for come nightfall Chloe is there, ready to look after her too. Antigone is exhausted. She allows him to kiss her hand or shoulder before he bounds away as usual. Every evening, she promises her friends she will take a day off but by sunrise she is up, ready to resume her work. Clius is outside, waiting for her in the half-light. They go up the path in silence watching the sun rise gradually from the sea. In front of the cave, there is but the fire, for Oedipus is already on the cliff. They eat and as soon as it is light, make their way down the path together. As she pulls herself up the scaffolding, Oedipus turns and gives her one of his confident, shrewd smiles; one that understands the terrible power of the sea, and of fate, and which knows they can be vanquished. It is that fleeting, elusive smile that she must capture and extract from the cliff. She touches the stone, strokes it for a long time the way Oedipus does. She stares at it and receives a reply – trembling with new questions. Could it be a message from the rock-dwellers who appeared in her dream last night? She sees a smile, or could it be a mouth, emerging from among the shadows and indistinct signs occupying the space where the face should be? All she has to do is let it happen, by carefully moulding the stone. Determined, magnificent, the laughing mouth is taking shape, asking to be restrained, controlled, so that it can confront tremendous unleashed forces. All day she is absorbed in it; a whole day with the wind biting through her. Though cold and hungry she cannot pull herself away from her place on the scaffolding. When the men call her down she answers but does not move. Clius brings her soup and hot stones so that she can warm herself. Only when the face that will be is brightened by the laughing mouth, the smile; only when she is certain she can see it and hear it, does she decide to come down. Unable to descend on her own, she calls to Clius for help. In the light of the dying day, he looks at what she has accomplished: 'That's the most exquisite thing you've ever done.'

'It wasn't me, it was them!' Utterly exhausted, her voice is aggressive, hard, as though he had upset her. He guides her down; she feels heavy as if she were about to faint. He helps her get warm then accompanies her to Isis's house. She is so tired she has to keep stopping. He feels that part of her would like him to take her in his arms while the other would never forgive him if he did. As they stand in front of Isis's door she says: 'I still have to do the eyes but I can't visualize them!' Taken aback, he remarks casually: 'Never mind. Tomorrow you will.'

She replies coldly: 'No,' and slams the door in his face.

Later, attending to Oedipus, Clius relates that although Antigone is pleased with what she has achieved, she is worried about the eyes as she cannot visualize them. Oedipus lies down, makes himself comfortable and stretches several times, as he often does before falling asleep: 'If there are no eyes that is what will be depicted.'

On her way to the headland with Clius in the half-light of the dawning day. Antigone is no longer preoccupied with the eyes. She consoles herself with the image of the gigantic face of the father of the sea. Just as she is about to go down to the cliff, Clius repeats what Oedipus said the previous night: 'If there are no eyes, that is what will be depicted.' Astounded she steps on to the path echoing: 'If there are no eyes, no eyes . . .'

Oedipus has accomplished his work on the giant. Everything behind the pilot is finished. He is now turning his attention to the third oarsman. They are waiting for Antigone to complete the master of the ship. She goes up to Oedipus, takes him in her arms and blinds herself by pressing her eyes against her father's face. Indeed there are no eyes – that is what is so painful when the memory of what he used to look like returns. However, and she goes over it in her mind with the fragment of his phrase, perhaps he sees more now. Like that small invisible community of rock-dwellers, he continually watches you with his inner eye, and so envelops you with a more perceptive organ. Closing her eyes, she spreads her hands over Oedipus's face. She feels the band that Clius carefully ties over his sockets each morning. She sees him every day and thought she knew him but it is only now, through her hands, that she feels him and knows him, as her father. Why didn't she think of it before? There are no eyes but she can depict this band which, since it is the blind giant guiding the ship, reveals the inner eye that is present through its absence and abundance. She kisses Oedipus and scrambles up the scaffolding. Down below Clius lights the fires which splutters merrily beneath the drops of a passing shower of rain.

She works all day. First she finishes the brow, then delineates the band. The feeling returns that she is being assisted by the subterranean people and by the trust and intense devotion of her two companions. From time to time Clius obliges her to come down and get warm. Oedipus joins them but neither speaks to her, aware that she is still up there gazing at the giant face who has entrusted his laughing mouth to posterity. She returns to her task and a hazy thought comes into her head: 'The blind man singing.' The forehead is vast, smooth, superb, above the slightly protruding nose. She completes the band, it is worn and frayed at the edges like the one Oedipus wears for work. She steps back to get a better view, returns to the stone, makes a few adjustments and steps back to look at the carving as a whole once more.

She cannot believe it. Everything tells her that she can do no more, for within the limits of her abilities she has done all she can. It is not finished and will never be. Abandoned, left to himself, the master of the boat is ahead of her, well ahead of her. With the action of the wind and that of the sea, he will continue to advance into the immensity of time and the distance between them will always increase.

She is tempted to call Oedipus and Clius over, to shout: 'Look! It's finished. Come and see how magnificent, how much greater than us, our unfinished work is!' Yet she cannot and her whole body is gripped by a pain which becomes a crushing sadness.

It is done. She turns away and looks at the sea, black under a leaden sky. Encouraged by the two men she has given birth to this giant on which she now turns her back. Gazing at the waves beating up against the cliff, she is horrified to discover a desire to destroy herself as her mother had done. The alternative is that blind man confronting the storm, the action of starting again every morning and never-ending, unrelenting yearning. She is at the edge of the platform, she grabs the rope and leans out. It is born, she has done enough, they do not need her any more.

Clutching the rope as she sways, mesmerized by the sea, she is on the verge of falling when a powerful hand seizes hers, and strong arms lift her up. Is it her child, the father of the sea, bringing her with unexpected ease down from the scaffolding? Who is infusing her with his strength and courage? Who, without obvious effort, is bringing her back up the narrow path? At the headland, the effortlessness, the omnipotence dissolve, leaving Oedipus staggering with her in his arms, his strength ebbing away. In a strangled voice he calls to Clius for help. After having been carried by her child of stone, she finds pleasure in crawling alone, held up by the two men. Her child is big, he will have to live without her. All she must do now is gradually absorb the pain of having finished a task that was never meant to end.

Antigone has spent two days being nursed by Isis. Clius has

come to tell her that Chloe's husband, the old fisherman, will take them out in his boat the next day so that they can see the wave from the sea.

'What's Oedipus doing?'

Clius tells her he has stopped working on the cliff, that he seems to think the wave is finished. He is cutting rocks; he wants to build a fire-tower above the cave like the one he saw in Egypt.

The next day is cold. At sunrise the headland is still shrouded in mist. Having rounded it, the two sons start rowing to the north face. At first it is indistinct but the mist lifts abruptly and suddenly the wave is there. Their hearts miss a beat when it appears. It is as though Clius and Antigone are seeing it for the first time. Little did they realize it was so immense, so very extraordinary, so much more terrifying than they imagined it to be when viewed from the path. The wave, dark at its base, becoming lighter as it rises, springs up out of the sea. Level with the overhanging rock, it unfurls the whole of its foaming mass encircled by pillars of water that fall like arrows into a sparkle of fiery drops. Nothing can stand up to it. It is about to fall back into the vast trough but the boat gets there first and uses the power of the wave and the gap it has created to project itself forwards. White, slim, graceful, with its three oarsmen at the apex of their effort, it is guided towards the port by the blind man of the sea.

They get as close as possible to the cliff without endangering their lives so that they can get a good look at it. They admire the great, pale and dark figures that imbue the cliff with a new meaning, sending out a message of hope to all sailors and to King Theseus.

Antigone is lost in thought. Clius turns to her: 'We should add some colours, different shades of blue and grey, some brilliant white, a touch of red.'

She is seduced by this colourful vision but does not agree with him.

'But the colours would exalt the stone,' Clius argues.

'Oedipus doesn't want the stone to be exalted. He wants it to be visible.'

'He wants to give it a meaning but it has no more meaning than do the sea, the headland, the cliff. They exist. And that's all.'

The old sailor chuckles: 'Whoever did that wave understands the sea. He has made a boat and fishermen who will get back to port with their catch. And that's what counts for us. The fish.'

Time is pressing. They must return. From the top of the headland comes the steady sound of Oedipus's hammering.

That evening Oedipus and Clius eat in silence, listening to the sea beating tirelessly against the foot of the cliff. Clius builds the fire for the night.

Oedipus says: 'You are now a potter and a sculptor but colour is your true vocation. It will develop alongside you and will take up an increasing amount of space. Clius will have to move over. People like us who have been steeped in crime can only escape from it through freedom, complete freedom and the ceaseless struggle to achieve it.'

'What about Antigone,' asks Clius, 'she has committed no crime? Is there no other way for her?'

'No. Freedom is never easy.'

The following day when Antigone comes up from the village, Oedipus takes her down to the foot of the cliff. The third oarsman is incomplete. And yet there is no doubt in her mind that it is Polynices. Polynices with his princely ease, that incomparable grace inherited from Oedipus and Iocasta.

'Why? Why him?'

Oedipus offers no explanation, all he says before leaving, is: 'Finish the face, the mouth . . .'

She stands there, confronting Polynices – the idea, the vision of her brothers, formulated over the years since she was a child. And now she is having to do this face which has weighed so heavily on her destiny. For it was Polynices who, instead of turning against Eteocles and Creon, shut the last door of Thebes on his father, condemning him to perish in some burrow or other. Which he would have done, had she not drawn around him those protective murmurings of compassion which she herself unwittingly instigated.

Is Polynices's face still capable of being endowed with hope? His inexcusable conflict with Eteocles and Creon's secret hostility cast doubt upon it. But as she has come to learn since she has been on the road, there is more than one path to choose from.

She goes back up the headland and fetches her tools from the cave where she had left them, thinking the work was finished. Clius waves to her, grinning. Oedipus does not raise his head. He is squatting on the ground, cutting rectangular rocks with a large hammer which Clius then prepares for assembly. And so, he who once held the sceptre and the royal bow, he who first had the idea of the wave and then accomplished it, does not find it unnatural to do the same work as a quarryman. She thinks: it is all the same to him. Everything has become the same.

For several days she works ceaselessly on Polynices's face. She is troubled by the smile she has given him – it is weak and supercilious. It seems to denote that his joviality, if joviality it be, has nothing to do with the outcome of this deed. To vanquish or perish, kill or be killed are one and the same to this face, have the same sense or, as Clius would say, the same no-sense. She gazes for a long time at the boat as it escapes the storm, with its three glowing oarsmen and its blind pilot. This time she feels that the work, the adventure that has wrecked their bodies and united their minds, is complete. The product of their labours, their patience, their fascination with the rock-dwellers, has been yielded – yielded up to the sky, the sea, the stars, to cataclysms, insensibility and finally to oblivion. It is no longer theirs and she understands what they have to endure up there having finished – no doubt as planned – the task before her.

She runs back up the path, falls to her knees beside her father and calls Clius. She says: 'I am filled with sadness. I have understood. I too am suffering.' She puts her arms around their shoulders and weeps, her face pressed up against theirs, letting flow the tears they cannot release. Huddled closely together in the icy wind, they recreate for a moment the binding circle of their deed which has just been broken. Clius lights some brushwood at the centre of the ring and spreads their linked hands over the tiny flame. He says: 'Let us bless this moment and these tears with fire and ashes.' They return to their work. Oedipus raises and lowers his hammer on to the stone. As Antigone makes her way to the village, she only thinks: 'How fast the night is falling.'

VI

THE SUMMER SOLSTICE

The fire-tower is built. It is not very tall but, standing high above the cave as it does, it can be seen from a long way off. On the last evening a thick mist rises from the sea. With many of the fishermen not yet back home, Antigone lights the fire; as the flames leap to the top of the tower a great cheer rises from the port. When Antigone returns to the village the women are waiting and present her with a dress they have woven specially for her. Next day the trio leaves. Only Isis and Chloe have read – in the stars or in their hearts – that they will never return.

They spend the winter with Diotima. Antigone works with her or Larissa all day. Clius sets off at first light to join Narses in his workshop. Left alone, Oedipus forces himself to sit by the fire and sculpt or goes for interminable walks in the woods. Time weighs heavily and drags by so slowly that he becomes incapable of doing anything. At these moments he buries himself in his bed, at times biting frenziedly into his staff to stop himself screaming out his distress.

Antigone tells him there is a message from Ismene. He refuses to listen. She persists – Eteocles and Polynices must be prevented from rushing headlong into catastrophe. He stands, towering over her. Relieved she waits for him to speak. Nothing save a strangled sob escapes his lips. She senses his unbearable loneliness. Overcome, she murmurs: 'You're not alone. You've got us.'

He cries: 'Who else is there who would dare speak to me?'

Antigone pronounces the first name to spring to mind: 'Diotima!' She wants to run and find her, speak to her, implore her.

He restrains her: 'I don't want pity!'

'You have a right to justice.'

'To freedom, the same as everyone else.' His great frame looms over her as he smiles at her forlornly. She would like to kiss his hands but she does not feel brave enough and runs off.

Antigone realizes that Oedipus's solitude has been on Diotima's mind for some time. It is in fact within his power to remedy the situation; for a king of Thebes, albeit deposed, reserves the right to revoke any judgement or sentence passed during his reign. The day Oedipus does this, she says, will be the day he returns amongst us. She looks at Antigone tenderly: 'He needs more time, you will have to be patient.' Antigone reflects how time, which wounded Oedipus in the first place, is rapidly closing in on him. Perhaps they will unite and keep pace with one another.

Oedipus feels encompassed by Diotima's distant but nevertheless beneficial presence. He accepts that he needs time and allows new strengths and activities to germinate inside him – entreaties, supplications, pleasures, aspirations that he ends up calling prayers. Come from he knows not where and destined for no one in particular, they flash through him, devouring his anger.

One evening, when Antigone and Clius are with him in the hut, he describes a dream he has has about Iocasta. He was lost, it was a night full of celestial messages he could not decipher. He was blind and yet he was not for he could see Iocasta's thoughts. Once again he had found his former courage and happiness but illuminated by a different light. He could not understand everything, he was a long way behind her but her mind said: 'The time has come to lay down your burden.' He thought Iocasta was going to help him but as he awoke he understood that setting himself free was something he had to do alone.

'Tomorrow,' he informs Antigone, 'I will go with you in the four directions of space and proclaim that I, Oedipus, tyrant unto myself, rescind the sentence I pronounced on my own life.'

The next morning when she arrives, Oedipus is already waiting for her composed and smiling, proud and upright, supported by his staff. She is too nervous to speak. He has told Clius not to follow them. Father and daughter set off together, she with a heavy heart.

They go north up a hill where shepherds are grazing their flocks. Antigone can see them, hidden in the bushes, watching them approach. She tells Oedipus when they are within earshot. He draws himself up and after issuing a long call she hears his voice – which in Thebes decreed laws and unfolded liturgies to the city's gods – ring out and say: 'I am Oedipus the former king, today a man amongst men, a blind man amongst the blind. It was I who cursed King Laius's killer. Then I discovered that I was he. Since that time, I have carried the weight of this curse on my shoulders and lived isolated from all men. Today I lay down the burden of the edict, whereby in Thebes, I violated my rights. A man cannot remain forever segregated from his fellow men. I ask you all to acknowledge me once more as a blind supplicant, a man amongst men.'

Behind their bushes the shepherds do not stir. Antigone can see the glimmer of their eyes between the leaves. They listen without throwing stones or abuse at them. But they do not stand and approach Oedipus to invite him to join them.

Oedipus waits and then says: 'We will go west.' They arrive at a small hamlet where three women, gathered around a well, listen in silence and then return to their houses.

In the south the men are working in the fields. They are moved and troubled by what they hear but on a signal from the oldest they pick up their tools and move off without uttering a word.

Oedipus remains impassive, he is not disheartened. The dignity of his expression sustains Antigone and prevents her from becoming despondent.

They make their way to Narses's house and workshop in the east. Antigone knows Oedipus's undertaking has Diotima's blessing but she has no idea how Narses will react. As they draw closer to the house, closer than Oedipus has ever been before, he sends out his call. Narses appears followed by Larissa and Diotima. Then from further away Clius and the men from the workshop emerge. Oedipus announces the lifting of the curse and repeats his request. Clutching Oedipus's hand Antigone kneels down in front of him. As she looks up at him – standing there defenceless, offering himself to the blows of providence or the brotherhood of men, his face illuminated with the peace of sightless light – she finds him even more imposing than usual.

There is a lull. As between life and death thinks Clius. At such a critical moment how can this father and child remain so composed? He has not noticed that Antigone is still holding Oedipus's hand. Her face breaks into a smile to which Narses, tense and uneasy until then, eventually responds. Seeing this, Larissa, with a barely noticeable gesture, nudges him forwards. Standing before him, Narses bends his knee slightly and then straightening, says: 'Since, as is your right, you are now repealing this unjust sentence, be once more one of us: a man amongst men.' Taking Oedipus's hand he raises it to his forehead: 'Tomorrow, I shall call on you. If you wish, you can visit us another time and you will be received by the clan as a guest and as a friend.'

Stooping, Oedipus lays his hand on the boundary stone that marks the limit of Narses's property: 'To me, this marker is the symbol of the start of a new era.'

A few days later it is the summer solstice. Members of the clan from other parts of Greece and from across the sea come to Narses's house and join the neighbours and Diotima's sick for the annual celebration. As night falls, Antigone informs Oedipus that Narses has invited him to the feast as guest of honour. At first Oedipus appears not to understand. Twice he shakes his head and then, without further ado, follows Antigone.

As he steps into the light of the fires and torches, Narses, Diotima and all the guests rise. Clius is struck by the anguish and dignity apparent on his face. As the meal draws to a close it is obvious that the guests are expecting something momentous and remarkable to take place, but it does not. Diotima leans across to Oedipus: 'We have no bard. Could you sing for us tonight?' To Antigone's amazement he accepts and rises. Diotima leads him over to the large millstone in front of the fire and helps him climb on to it. He towers above the whole assembly. Diotima sits on the millstone, an anxious Antigone is seated beside her.

At first, all Oedipus does is rotate on the spot with those same awkward movements that periodically accompany Clius when he dances in the evening. He attempts to sing but all that issues from his lips is a jumble of sounds, a rasp with neither rhythm nor lyrics. Antigone has the impression that she is watching him drown slowly. Diotima stands and addresses Oedipus: 'Remember that you are a Clearsinger.'

He relaxes, exhales then inhales and a sound – the one they were anticipating without ever having heard it before – emanates and soars into the evening air. Oedipus's voice caresses the body, stirs it, lifts the spirit which – when it understands the significance of the song – rejoices. As it touches their hearts they realize it is the inspiration, the exploration of mysteries and treasures as yet dormant in their psyche.

Oedipus's voice had never been intended to confine itself to giving orders and solving riddles. Antigone and all those listening are now aware, to their amazement and joy, that this voice had always been predestined to sing.

When Oedipus finishes there is a sigh. The sound of glasses being refilled and the murmur of conversation return. Diotima turns to Antigone and says: 'Now we have our bard.'

A soft, silvery light emerges above the brow of the hill and suddenly, cascading over fields and woods, the full moon is mistress of the sky. She illuminates Oedipus and makes him glow with the pallor of another world. He bows then falls to his knees before her. From the millstone, he raises to the sky a startling mask – a long silver muzzle – and emits a distressing howl that reaches into infinity. Many feel their hair stand on end, for what they hear baying at the moon is the most ancient of wolves come out from the dark recesses of the unholy ages. The wolf who followed Apollo before he became the charioteer of the sun; the wolf who lived before the plague-rats and who always excites man's instinct to destroy. All those present whose roots still reach down into the ancestral soil rise, spurred on by their desire to howl with Oedipus and form into a pack around him.

At that point the clan members from Persia, seated by Narses, feel welling inside them the memory of their own ancestor. With one blow they overturn the tables. As glorious descendants of wild beasts, they trace their origins back to the sun. The howling of these wolves, this craving for primeval darkness is an insult to their lineage. The Persians are on their feet – nostrils dilating, eyes wide-open, their faces taking on the terrible aspect of the lion.

Clius is about to launch into the swirling dance of the people of the shadows. If he does others will follow, and those who became men by glorifying the sun god through the cult of the lion will find this dance by nocturnal Apollo's followers intolerable.

Any confrontation between these two primal forces will end in battle, for everyone present is either in a trance or, like Diotima and Narses, petrified by the inner struggle raging between the call of the blood and the call of the spirit.

Antigone stands: 'Father!' Oedipus stops howling his anguish to the moon. Antigone goes over to him and forces him to stand. She bids him sing: 'These are bodies and souls in torment.' Seeing that Clius is on the point of hurling himself into his vertiginous dance, she repeats his name quietly. Stunned, he recognizes her and stops instantly.

Oedipus's voice reverberates once more. Placated, they return to their places. He is singing of those three mute sisters, whose powers on the night of the solstice unite in their triple incarnation with those of the star: Artemis who hunts, Helen who causes delirium, Hecate who kills.

Behind the sisters – more ancient still and even more remote – are those he cannot name; whose extraordinary yet repellent beauty breathes life into the universe, enabling it to reveal itself. Unlike the creator of the world, these do not shine neither are they ambiguous. They are inaccessible, insensible and silent. In the same way that the sun is powerless to stop himself from rising, they crushed Iocasta the Queen and Oedipus the Parricide.

He goes quiet. A long silence ensues as all are conscious of the lethal company he has evoked. Some are afraid he will bay at the moon once more but Diotima knows he will not. She senses the spirit has left him and stands to denote this. In the form of a procession the guests leave. Oedipus remains standing on the millstone inert. Clius helps him down and leads him back to the hut where, without a word, he sinks into the elemental world of sleep.

VII

THE LABYRINTH

The following day, seated in the doorway of the hut, Oedipus strives to recall what he sang the previous evening. He cannot. His concentration is poor, his thoughts assailed by mournful supplications and snatches of prayers. He hears Diotima coming up the path. Annoyed, he stands and before he can stop himself says: 'Prayers, nothing but prayers – what's the point.'

The reply is immediate: 'They help.' But did the reply come from him or Diotima? No matter, since it is engraved in the very centre of his being and is not the purpose of Diotima's visit. 'Some of the sick who've been staying with me will be leaving soon. They'd like you to sing for them as you did last night.'

'It was not me singing, something took my place.'

'Something that had your voice, your thoughts, your life. Will you come tonight?'

Maybe this is what he has been waiting for and what he has been dreading. He replies: 'I shall come as it appears I sang.'

She thanks him and retreats silently down the path. Turning around she sees him standing at the entrance, imposing yet perplexed, like a small boy who does not understand what is expected of him.

That evening when Clius leads him into the room where the sick are gathered, he is immediately struck by the familiarity of their anguish. They too are about to set off on the road, abandoning the safety of the spring, the heart of the clan, from which they drink each day. Each of them will soon have to seek the itinerary of his thoughts and trace upon the earth and sky the alien path which corresponds to these innermost images. Antigone and Diotima are present and these people, whose faces will always remain unknown to Oedipus, are already pressing him with questions.

You ask me to tell you of my life's journey. I shall begin with the one I made as a newborn baby, with the shepherd who rescued me. That slow distance was covered to the rhythmic pace of the sheep which still remains within my body. I was adopted as the son of King Polybus and Queen Merope of Corinth – city of the sea. They loved the sea passionately and in their palace, whose doors were open to all-comers, they reminisced with nostalgia about the marvellous voyages of their childhood. Before long I also set sail from Corinth, first in humble fishing boats that never ventured far from the coast, then in ships that would set out for several days. One day Polybus told me that it was not enough to be a skilled sculptor and a good sailor. In order to succeed him I would need to become a ship's captain and know how to navigate over great distances.

When I was old enough to undertake longer voyages, I was assigned to Nestiade, the most acclaimed of Corinth's captains. He was a man in his prime, who was not only a shrewd merchant and the best sailor we had but also a much sought-after geographer and an expert on the histories, ancestries and religions of sea-faring nations. Set in this serene face, tanned by the sun, was a pair of clear and exceptionally perceptive eyes. He was above all, a zealous, humorous man who was always even-tempered.

We made a relatively short trip that took us around the islands, and during a storm I was able to observe his qualities first-hand. Though still too young to appreciate the extent of their contribution to the internal stability and prosperity of Corinth, I had grown up conscious of Polybus's and Merope's humanity. But this was the first time I had been close to a man who had the breadth of vision and depth of understanding that Nestiade possessed. I was fifteen at the time and my love for him grew out of my admiration for him. Touched by this trust and devotion Nestiade agreed, much to Merope's relief, to be my instructor.

After this first trip we set sail for Crete and Egypt. The crossing to Crete was enthralling. Nestiade was an exacting teacher but I enjoyed the tasks I was given to do. The longer I was with him, the more I learned about being a sailor and a leader of men. In the evenings he taught me about the stars, winds and sea currents. He also taught me about the Cretans and Egyptians – their religious beliefs, courtships and the long history of their kingdoms and wars.

When the King of Crete learned from Nestiade that the son of the King of Corinth had disembarked at Knossos, he granted me an audience. I asked if I might visit the Labyrinth. He refused.

'The Labyrinth,' he explained, 'is inhabited by the Minotaur, a seductive but vicious monster; capricious and unpredictable. If you are attacked by him you must be capable of fighting him in the dark regions in which he dwells. Should any harm befall you, it could result in a hapless conflict between our two kingdoms.'

This rejection of my request only served to fuel my desire further. Consequently, all the time we were engaged in the profitable sale of our cargo and the purchase of another to sell in Egypt, I could think of nothing but the Labyrinth and how to find a way round the king's ruling.

Nestiade sensed this: 'The problem is not the king's decision but the difficulty of finding the way out once you are in the Labyrinth.'

'I'll find the way out.'

'And what about the monster?'

'I'll defeat him.'

He looked at me sadly: 'You are in no position to take on this monster, Oedipus, for he is already inside you.'

At this, my affection for him changed to enmity. I felt the urge to leave him, to abandon the ship without delay and run to the Labyrinth. There was a brief but violent struggle between us and he had to restrain me forcibly.

When I woke the next day, the lure of the Labyrinth was as compelling as the lure of a body. Realizing I could never assuage it and my trust in Nestiade restored with the clarity of the morning, I spoke to him about it. He could see that, body and soul, I had been taken over by the blinding and absurd image I had of the Labyrinth and that I was beyond redemption.

He informed me that if I did not relinquish this lunatic obsession and continued to display the violence of the previous evening, I would alarm the other sailors for they would take me for a madman. And because they were superstitious they would see it as an ill omen and refuse to have me on board. If that happened I would never obtain the command of a ship and never succeed Polybus.

In an attempt to avert this, he went to find the king. His fears and devotion to me must have prompted him to resort to unprecedented arguments, for, against all expectation, the king gave me the authorization I needed. He imposed one condition: that Nestiade should accompany me. In case of mishap he wanted to be able to prove to Polybus that he had only given his permission in order to prevent me from going mad.

We set off that very evening. I told Nestiade that I accepted his presence but that he had to allow me to take the initiative and stay behind me. There was no response.

The entrance had none of the fantastic features I had expected. It was in fact a somewhat ordinary opening without even a door. The corridor in which I found myself soon dipped underground and narrowed. We were forced to stoop and then crawl. It was like a nightmare with the added sensation of suffocating. The tunnel opened up abruptly to reveal three entrances. The central one was dominated by a garish, multi-coloured sculpture representing a woman's head. She seemed to be staring at us belligerently, screaming out some sarcastic secret, thereby revealing a menacing set of teeth. I took the opening on the right which gave on to several corridors but, sensing I had made a mistake, I turned back.

Nestiade was waiting for me. On closer examination he had discovered that by pressing down on the woman's lower jaw, a passage appeared at the back of her throat. I was ready to climb in and go down the steep slope. Nestiade said: 'Once we go in, there will be no turning back. We will have to find the exit if there is one.' I had no desire to reconsider and slid down the throat. As the mouth shut I heard a burst of shrill laughter. For a long time I slithered down a slope which gradually became more vertical. The mocking laughter rang out again and I knew Nestiade had come after me. I landed in shallow water, closely followed by Nestiade. The incline we had just come down was so steep and slippery that we would never be able to return that way. We had no choice but to cross the water that lay in front of us. It looked neither wide nor deep, yet we quickly lost our footing. Although we swam for a long time and had the impression of getting nearer the other side, it was as though something was holding us back. After struggling for several hours we at last felt land beneath our feet. I was exhausted and had great difficulty pulling myself up on to the bank. When I eventually succeeded, I lay prostrate on the ground and slept while Nestiade kept watch.

When I awoke, he told me we had lost our weapons and provisions during the crossing. I was not concerned, 'Our only chance of getting out of the Labyrinth is to find the exit. So let's go.' He agreed and went on to tell me that while I was asleep the extraordinary peace that enveloped us had been broken by the sound of an animal cantering about, as well as snatches of hilarity and music.

With Nestiade a few paces behind me we set off again. The terror and anguish I had experienced in the water had gone. I moved forward quickly, spurred on by my desire to understand the Labyrinth and possess its secret. Much later, I remembered with sadness how I had never once turned round during that long walk to look upon Nestiade's wonderful face or to enquire what he might have been thinking or feeling.

In fact, the further I advanced, the more I fell under the spell of the Labyrinth. The stone walls of the corridors seemed to widen and be covered with frescoes or silk. We heard, or thought we heard, music: enchanting, soft and faintly intoxicating. We passed through rooms, colonnades, gardens with fountains encircled by green trees and flowers. We sensed the proximity of a town with its turrets, marketplaces, its bustle and sensuality. I felt a thrill of pleasure roused by the salacious reverbations emanating from this city of desire, and longed to revel indefinitely in this gratifying state. It was not so much that I was discovering but rather rediscovering, after a long absence, the place where I had lived in another life. I had reached my goal – I now had to make time stand still so that I could establish myself forever in my rediscovered house, which I should never have left.

Nestiade was behind me, a reminder that we had to cross the Labyrinth and find a way out. He was urging me forward against my will. Because he was there I moved on but the esteem I held him in was rapidly being replaced by hate. Alert and taciturn, he was forcing me to abandon the Labyrinth and the possibility of bliss being offered me through the magic of these mysterious memories.

We came to a room with tables laden with bread, fruit and various drinks. I was hungry. Calling Nestiade, I rushed at the food. We ate the bread and fruit but he advised me not to touch the drinks as they could be drugged or inebriating. I ignored him and took a deep draught of an exquisite, light liquid. As we ate, we heard manic laughter from the woman's head that had barred our entrance, reverberating several times in the distance. I sensed that I would soon be encountering the monster and made Nestiade promise he would leave me to confront him alone. I was invincible.

Deeply troubled by a meaningless yet intense yearning which

overcame me, I lay down on a bed nearby. Nestiade kept his distance to show me that, as requested, he was doing no more than tailing me. He could also have lain down but he chose not to and stood there like someone waiting to leave. This rekindled my hate. I wanted to hit him, drive him away. But the grieved expression on his face made me realize that he was there against his better judgement and because he loved me. Seeing him thus afflicted my anger abated and I lost interest in extending the rest I desired. I took one of the three corridors that led out of the furthest side of the room. Already it was my body guiding my choice of direction for, under the influence of the beverage I had drunk, my thoughts were becoming confused – and the light, so bright earlier on, was growing dim.

I was not afraid, on the contrary; for as if to challenge my adversary, I launched into a phallic paean learned in my child-hood. I had forgotten the words but had no trouble making them up. Groping my way along the walls, I reached the entrance of an enormous room. I heard the noise of something galloping, charging towards me: the monster was on top of me. I came into contact with a man's powerful body, covered it seemed by a robe, with a mane like that of a horse. A hand grabbed me. Turning his momentum to his advantage, the beast threw me to the ground. This contact with both man and beast in one being aroused such revulsion in me that it saved me, for it gave me the strength to leap up instantly. A grim fight ensued but, because of the drinks I had foolishly imbibed, I could not decide whether it was taking place in a dream, in delirium or exclusively in reality. I did not know if the monster could see in the gloom or if, like me, he was a victim of the dark; for I had the feeling that our battle, broken by dream-like interludes, was sluggish and terribly ungainly; like that of two blind men. I could feel the hairiness of the beast, hear its nostrils snorting. To escape his horns I clung to them, periodically sensing the pressure of a face against mine. I struggled against hands lunging at me gripping my throat or trying to push me over. At times it felt as though I was bound to the body of a man or woman but, more often

126

than not, I felt overpowered by the enormous bulk of an animal. In the muddled and no doubt demented state I was in, I seemed one moment to be experiencing profound horror and disgust and, the next, to be on the brink of sensuous ecstacy or already immersed in it.

In the end, the beast had me at the edge of a pit and I thought I would end up falling into it forever, as in a nightmare. My body alone compensated for the stupor my mind was in. As I shouted, lashed out, overwhelmed my adversary maybe, the most important part of what I had until then thought of as me was absent. We persisted with our battle but it was as though our limbs were embedded in sand. Our movements were being hampered by an invincible force from which we each attempted to escape. Suddenly I thought I was alone and that the enemy had disappeared, but then he was on me again, endeavouring to drag me into the void with him. In a last desperate effort I tried to free myself and momentarily felt a curious delight as the beast cried out. The din became intolerable and I escaped by dragging myself along the ground to the entrance to the cave which his attack had prevented me from entering. At last the air was purer, the darkness less intense. I could see my body once more – I was exhausted but no more than badly bruised. It was not that which prevented me from standing up though, but a strange compulsion to remain close to the ground and smell my way out. As I continued to edge forwards I visualized myself, though I know not from where, crawling along the rough ground of the cave, sniffing out scents to guide me. The body that was inching its way along, mine in fact, was after one thing only: to get out of the Labyrinth as quickly as possible. My eyes and mind were useless, only my olfactory abilities, a throw-back to an earlier epoch maybe, could help me.

Having completely forgotten about Nestiade I continued to haul myself onward for an interminable length of time. I had forgotten about everything except my lungs, my nostrils and their yearning for the open air. I longed to be lifted by a wave, projected forth and vomited out of those walls and that suffocating atmosphere that had not been completely devoid of pleasure.

I have no idea how long I pursued this hunting-dog-like method of nosing out the exit. It was perhaps several hours before the air began to circulate more freely. Daring at last to lift my head, I glimpsed a faint light in the distance. I detected the proximity of water and crawled over to it. It was doubtless the river or moat encircling the Labyrinth. I was parched – the water saved me. I plunged my head, arms and shoulders into it and drank like an animal, revelling in its earthy tang.

The fight with the monster and the effort required to drag myself to the water's edge had sapped me of the last of my strength. I would never be able to cross the river and felt quite indifferent to the fact that I was probably going to die. I must have dozed off. I opened my eyes to see a giant looming over me. I presumed it was the Monster come to destroy me but the man laboured to drag me into the water with him, where I floated momentarily, swam a few strokes and then lost consciousness.

When I came round I was lying on my back, naked. The Labyrinth's maze of suffocating corridors and caves had vanished. All I could see was the night, the stars and the great arena of the sky. And I felt for the first time that I could actually understand its language. I was once again in the great, wide world, our world, the real one – with all its splendour and poverty. I heard a feeble barely audible and extremely gloomy sigh reverberate in my heart and realized that my head was resting on the damp clothing of Nestiade's knees. As I gazed at the sky he, normally so confident and cheerful, stared at me with an air of weariness and sadness I had not seen before.

Grasping his hand, I said: 'Don't look so gloomy. You saved us.'

'Not me. It was your body, sniffing like an animal, that led us out of that deadly nightmare your mind had driven us into.' He said no more and we both fell asleep.

When at last we woke up, he gave me some of his clothes so

that I would not have to remain naked. As we walked I noticed he was limping: 'Was it the Monster?'

He gave a grim laugh: 'You went over his belly – I followed. That's when I was injured.' He turned to me and added: 'It may be your destiny to pursue your hopes and dreams through to the bitter end but it isn't mine. When we get to Egypt we shall go our separate ways.'

I did not grasp the full significance of what he had said and took the matter no further. He was in agony physically and mentally. I did what I could to help him along and we eventually reached the ship. Our prolonged absence had alarmed the sailors for, although it seemed as though we had left the previous day, we had in fact been away for several days.

I cared for Nestiade as best I could. We left Crete sooner than expected, raising anchor the next day, our cargo incomplete but perfectly stacked. His leg was causing him much pain but he could still stand. He would only speak to me when he needed me to pass on orders to the sailors. To begin with the weather was good and the wind favourable. But on the third day he gave the command that the sails be taken up, for by the look of the sky a gale was brewing.

That night the storm blew up and we took the watch together. By dawn the sea had become wild and treacherous. The two pilots were exhausted. I replaced one, Nestiade the other. We lowered what was left of the sail and the sailors took to the oars.

Nestiade ordered a rope be strapped round my waist but refused to do the same. Huge waves rolled at us. By fixing my eyes on him we synchronized our movements and rode out the highest of the waves without too much difficulty. The storm, the battle, the need to inspire courage in the men served to help him regain his former cheerfulness and each time we tackled a new wave he beamed confidently. The great foaming back of one of these waves reminded me of the touch of the Beast's hairy skin on mine. I roared with jubilant laughter and turned to Nestiade yelling: 'Look! The Monster!'

The howling wind and crashing waves prevented him from

hearing me but my shout may have distracted him. It is also possible that we were the victims of a sudden change in the wind. At the exact moment that he turned his smiling questioning face to me, for what was to be the last time, an enormous wave sent the ship veering sideways and swept across the bridge throwing the two of us overboard.

Concerned for his injured leg I struggled to reach him. My hand brushed against his body but before I could catch hold of him, the rope that held me, bruising my waist, wrenched me away. I screamed out to him in vain. By the time the sailors had pulled me aboard we were already far from the place where he had fallen in, and without a rudder or sails, there was no hope of finding him.

I wept bitterly but sparingly over the next few days, for the storm demanded that the whole crew and myself give it our full attention. With the disappearance of Nestiade I became captain and was forced, together with the sailors, to tackle the mysteries of the sea. The ship and cargo safe, we arrived in Egypt at a propitious time to make a profit on our transactions. I had left Corinth an adolescent owning nothing. I returned a captain with the command of two ships – one of which belonged to me. Proud of my achievements and acquired wisdom, I considered myself to be an expert – worse, a sage. That was the beginning of my misfortunes.

On the eve of their departure, Oedipus returns to the sick. They gather around him with their questions: 'There is a mysterious character in your life. The Sphinx. Who was she, this woman, this assassin, this man-eater? Tell us how you defeated her.'

Without answering, he begins to sing:

Fear was the killer and not the Sphinx.
Fear of puerile questions that seemed to conceal a snare.
Day begetting night. Night pregnant with light.
Life that begins on all fours, rising to two,
  succeeded by three.

How could they believe that the essential clue was birth
When having searched so hard for the reply, they had lost
   sight of the question?
They shut themselves away to find it, but fear overpowered
   them in their hideouts.
People spied the terrible tracks, spoke of annihilation.
But the listener did not kill, she waited
For the one bold enough to accept the challenge of her
   riddle.
Having crossed the sea and killed the stranger at the
   crossroads — I arrived.
As with all omens, the Sphinx might have known
   but she might not.
She was beautiful, black and white with her mysterious
   smile. How we yearned
That after the first veil, there would be another, always
   another, forever another.
There is nothing more beautiful than the enigma, that great
   loving enigma, which constantly renews itself.
There she was the mad stranger, there we were two strangers
Stopped before the hostile gates in the ramparts of Thebes.
My salt-eyes beheld this girl of the forests, clothed
   by the wild-flower
The strong lines of her body, her powerful animal curves
   discernible beneath her dress,
Igniting the passionate desire to adore, to rip and
   tear off her fur.

I was not afraid of the questions, I was the son of a king
With ships on the sea. I was the man with the answers.
The likeness of a woman, with the body of a leaping doe
And I perchance the stag, King of Stags, in the forests
   of love.
If she was inventing herself in my eyes, I was discovering
   myself in hers
Burning, we gazed at one another, bewildered by the sudden

appearance of this ardour.
True, I heard a voice: Say nothing, only your name –
  Oedipus,
Your name, like a beckoning to infancy to prophetic
  splendour
Which must never be revealed, neither through wisdom nor
  the power of love
While it is enough to remain there, where nothing,
  desiring nothing, seeing nothing, observes
His totally nebulous fiancée and her translucence in the
  depths of the waters.
Thus Oedipus was the most appropriate of terms, that name
  with its wounded feet caught between four parents
But suddenly, all I could see was the shimmering promise
  of Aphrodite's dark pet.
I longed to touch her love, I yelled out the replies and
  thought I had captured my sibyl.
Her face was close to mine, she was crying, the vanished
  one. She fainted, washed away by her tears
She who carried my enigma beneath the great ancestral
  she-wolf.
When the Thebans found me, they hailed my deed a victory.
Sapped of my strength, I wept, the Sphinx had
  disappeared.
They proclaimed me victor and loved me in that mirror
  which reflected my new face.
And that is how the god of fishes caught Oedipus
On his hook.

Oedipus's song is over. No one dares speak. All those present, thinks Antigone, like him, one day threw themselves on to that invisible hook.

Diotima's voice rings out: 'But that was not the end of your journey. After the Sphinx there was Thebes.'

'After the Sphinx, there was Iocasta,' declares Oedipus.

A clamour of questions: 'Iocasta, who was she? How could she not have known? Why didn't she recognize you?'

Oedipus collects his thoughts. Delving into his still smarting wounds, he unearths the recalcitrant images lurking beneath the words which transmute them. He continues:

Iocasta, you knew her from your dreams.
  Your eyes had pictured her for some time
And when at last you beheld this woman in all her
  physical splendour
It was with eyes blinded through contemplation of the queen.
Not the queen of a mercantile city, not Merope returning
  from the port, a blue basket of fish upon her head.
Rather the queen of a proud nation, a seven-gated citadel,
  gates thrown open each morning by the sun and closed each
  evening by the night.
A thoroughbred mare, a white unicorn with its horn of light.
As proof of this, the object of desire, visible beneath
  her veil of gold or silver,
Could quell the unruly people of Thebes with one look from
  her huge eyes.
After vanquishing the Sphinx I met Creon. To him I was
  a mere adventurer
Become a hero of the Thebans by solving riddles.
But I had without question exhibited courage and was
  the son of a king.
I would not be his rival. Neither for his beloved sister,
  nor for the city.
She kept her word. I was cleansed, attired in red,
Initiated in the rites of Thebes, led in a cortège to the
  palace
It was not she I saw but the queen, gilded and silvered
  by the moon,
As magnificently blonde as Aphrodite when she emerged
  from the sea.
A queen, so long without a king. A widow with forbidding

depths, inner spaces and stretches of unrequited love.
Her life in danger, her kingdom desperate to be cherished
and protected.
That is what the advent of my passion for her darkness,
my compassion for her light
And the numb terror of my spellbound eyes, enslaved by hers
demanded.
While Creon guided me and she thanked me for delivering
the city
I remained tongue-tied, more bewildered and discomfited than
a child, by her proximity.
Fortunately, at that moment Creon addressed me:
'It is the tradition in Thebes for people to prostrate
themselves when they first see the queen.'
I answered: 'If I am to be king, I shall abolish it.'
She smiled: 'It is abolished. You are king. The king
who delivers us from enigmas.
He who materializes from nowhere and bursts in. Love
has disconnected us from ourselves to bind us to
one another
Overfilling the cup, inundating Aphrodite's lair,
Aphrodite's double lair.'
An unbearable lapse of time ensued. In its stillness
and dread
I discerned the paradox, yet endless similarity
between the woman who was dead and the one who was alive.
She so fair with her boundless vision and the Sphinx with
her African radiance and untamed body.
The one who asked the question, the other who seemed to be
its answer.
When, for the first time after many a long day, we were
alone at last,
Knowing that shortly our exploration of one another would
lead to transports of delight,
Iocasta began to weep, I thought she would vanish as the
Sphinx had done.

She held me in her arms and murmured: 'I have found you,
  I have found you again.'
Gripped by a sense of foreboding, I should have fled.
How lovely she looked as she talked, it was the queen who
  spoke:
'In Oedipus, I have a man once more. Laius deserted me so soon.'
I did not flee. We loved. We were delirious in our love.
I was the king, she was the kingdom. A kingdom torn asunder by
  the shrieking pythonesses.
I am the child she did not defend. Why did she abandon me?
Why did they not assassinate me when the oracle predicted
  I would murder my father?
Antigone replies: 'Oedipus she was no more than a child when
  that choleric man took her.
Remember her tears, the recurring grief that would cloud
  her face.
And were you not, before the ordeal, before the plague,
  for a long time a part of this amazing happiness?'
'I lived it too,' Oedipus affirms, 'but when misfortune
  struck, she confronted it without me,
Left me alone, forsook the life we had had together
  while I lived in the hope that
My vertigo might take on some meaning and my madness
  a future.
Queen of a blind man's dreams, I feel your darkness
  guiding me towards unhoped-for light
Just as the tower of fire, that starless night
  many years ago,
Helped us as we sailed, battered by seven days of storm, to
Discover the wonderful existence of Egypt.

At Diotima's request, Oedipus makes his way to her house. He
stops and savours the calming sound of her footsteps and dress.
'Now you know my life story,' he says, 'and I know practically
nothing about you. Your voice has become familiar to me but I
can only see with my hands. Allow me to discover your face.'

She guides his long work-hardened hands: 'My hair is grey – almost white. Touch my wrinkles too, I want people to know me as I am.'

Like the fluttering of wings his hands skim her face as he gathers information, surmises. He lingers a while over her closed eyelids: 'You were loved so very deeply,' he says, 'What a loss Ares's death was to you.' His hands drop down. 'And how you loved him. What you are is confirmation of what he was and that makes me regret very much that I never knew him.'

They are both profoundly moved. He feels somewhat awkward in front of this compassionate woman who replies: 'You have just paid him and me the greatest of tributes.'

'What did you do after his death?'

'I wanted to withdraw to the mountains for a year and devote myself and my thoughts to his memory. I had barely arrived when I was summoned to return to nurse a dying woman. I refused. The man did not leave. As evening fell I saw him settle himself in front of my door the way Ares used to lie on the bridge of his ship if he was worried there might be a storm in the night. So I returned with him. After that there were others. As a result I spent three years mourning Ares. I thought about him constantly and yet never had time to think about him. Then it was I who fell ill and Narses made me come back here. I've never told anyone what I've just told you.'

'I know. But I needed to hear it.' He bows.

She follows him to the door. As she watches his tall silhouette move away, she thinks: 'Such forces battle inside that man!'

VIII

CALLIOPE AND THE
PLAGUE-VICTIMS

A few days later a nervous young highlander approaches the hut. Laying down his work, Oedipus beckons him over. Disconcerted by the dark band over Oedipus's eyes, the boy has to pluck up courage to speak: 'A traveller passing through our village told us about you: the blind man whose songs have the power to heal. Last year, a sickness entered our village, killing many of our people and leaving the survivors despondent and indifferent to their work. We invite you, your daughter and your companion to a feast so that you can sing for us – the living and the dead.'

'Do you know who I am?'

'The traveller told us you were the former king, Oedipus, and that Diotima released you from the curses that were on you.'

Oedipus smiles: 'We will come to your feast. Here, take this to your village,' and Oedipus hands him a wooden carving only recently completed.

The boy takes the sculpture, delighted but perplexed at first by what it represents: 'It's a dance! I'll be back soon to fetch you. It's a three-day walk.' Then putting the statue into his bag he runs off.

He returns to escort Oedipus, Antigone and Clius. The paths are steep and eventually bring them to a village perched on the banks of a swollen river. In the valley there are well-tended fields and gardens, on the lower slopes vineyards and on the upper slopes of the mountainside goats and sheep graze in the meadows.

Some of the houses are derelict, blackened by fire. The boy explains: 'Whole families were wiped out, others practically decimated. We managed to save the crops and livestock. But to halt the spread of the disease, we destroyed the houses.'

'This disease. Was it the plague?' asks Oedipus. The boy is too petrified to answer.

They arrive at the home of the village chief. Despite being in the prime of life his face and body are ravaged by grief. On their way, the boy informed them that the chief had lost his wife and children in the epidemic.

'Why have you sent for us?' inquires Oedipus. 'Is it so that we may join in your feast or because of the disease?' As he speaks Antigone is reminded of the firm but kind voice with which he used to receive supplicants in Thebes.

'Both, for the man who spoke to us of your songs also informed us that once you saved Thebes from the plague by sacrificing your wife, your crown and your eyes.'

A weary Antigone slumps down on to a step and a young slave-girl brings her some water. Too upset by the word 'once' to hear Oedipus's response, she weeps at the realization that to the people here, the events that revolutionized their lives have already been relegated to history.

The young slave-girl sits next to her and does her best to console her. Her name is Calliope. She shows Antigone around the house. It is cool and clean but parts of the roof and windows are still open to the sky. Having lost his wife and children, the chief burned down his home and built this one, but depression and lack of time prevented him from completing it.

The heads of the principal families gather for the evening meal. Being in a country where making a living is a constant struggle, these are men used to an arduous life. However, Oedipus is reminded, by the way they walk and talk and the subject of their conversations, of the atmosphere of mourning and oppression that struck him when he first reached the valley. The procedure of the feast is agreed. Oedipus is informed that in the course of the evening he can sing or speak depending on the inspiration of the moment. Thanking them he asks what they expect of him. There is silence until one of them speaks up: 'We have lost many of those we loved through this disease. At first we were optimistic. We nursed those who fell ill. But with each day that passed, the illness spread. We took fright and fled into the mountains leaving the sick behind. They either died or survived as best they could. When we returned we were unable to rid ourselves of our fear, our guilt. We raised an altar and erected tombstones in the hope that with the arrival of spring life would return to normal and we would regain our sense of purpose. But "it" gradually returned and now we are more dejected than we were when the sickness was at its peak.'

'What is this "it" which has returned?' queries Oedipus.

The chief speaks at last: 'When we wake up in the morning we wish it were evening. When we go to bed at night it is in the hope that we will never wake again.'

There is a general consensus. One of them adds: 'Restore our faith blind man, for we hear those who died in the charred ruins of the houses calling us to join them.'

Oedipus stands and Calliope leads him to his room. Clius and Antigone join them. 'There is something they haven't told you,' she says. 'Another three have fallen sick. They can't decide whether to abandon them or stay and look after them. That's why they sent for you.'

'Are you afraid, Antigone?' Oedipus asks.

'Very.'

'Clius?'

'I didn't think I would be, but the idea of dying like that terrifies me.'

'Right, in that case we'll leave tonight when everyone's asleep.' No one says a word. They will stay.

Oedipus wakes in the middle of the night to a sensation of intense pleasure. Calliope has crept into his bed and is snuggling up to him. Taking her face in his hands he discerns her surprising beauty: 'Did your master send you?'

'Yes.'

'Aren't you frightened?'

'No.'

'I am very grateful Calliope but go back home.' Kissing him tenderly on the shoulder she slips out. He sighs contentedly and goes back to sleep.

The following day as they begin the ritual offerings to the gods who protect the village, Antigone is struck by how few children and old people are present. It is within these two groups that death has been most active. The children look bewildered, forlorn, taciturn and when it is their turn to sing they do so in listless and halting voices that pierce the heart. Antigone goes over to them, holds hands and joins in with them. Encouraged, their troubled faces brighten.

In the evening, with all the villagers assembled in the main square, a huge fire is built up. They are waiting for Oedipus. He arrives, followed by Clius pulling a cart that Antigone and Calliope push from behind. Lying on a litter of straw inside the cart are the three afflicted men. Oedipus is holding the youngest (a boy of fifteen) by the hand, chatting to him and smiling now and then. The other two are very ill, one looks unconscious.

When the cart comes to a halt, Clius lifts the boy on to a table where Oedipus examines him and massages him gently with oil. He speaks: 'Let go of your fear and stand!' The boy sits up and steps down cautiously; petrified he glances at Oedipus who commands him: 'Go!' He takes one step then another, effortlessly. He jumps – and again. Dumbfounded, he goes to sit

with the other children of his age, who calmly make room for
him.

Meanwhile Clius and Antigone wash and minister to the other
two. When they have finished, Oedipus announces: 'There was
nothing wrong with the boy. Like the rest of you he was frightened. As to the others, we shall look after them. Allocate a house
to us and together we will defeat this disease.'

An old man speaks out: 'My name is Peleus. I refused to burn
down my ancestors' house after my wife died there. Obeying
the chief's orders I moved out and now I live in a hut near my
flock. My house has now been purified. You, your companions
and the sick can go there Oedipus. I will take you there.'

'Do you have Antigone's and Clius's support for this undertaking,' asks the chief, 'and are they aware of the risks involved?'

'Yes,' replied Antigone.

The sick are returned to the cart and the old man leads
Oedipus, Clius and Antigone to his house. By the time Oedipus
and the others come back, the young people have built up the
fire and the flames are soaring up into a moonless sky shrouded
in clouds.

The chief takes Oedipus to the front of the assembled people.
He is illuminated by the flickering rise and fall of the flames
which trace mysterious patterns all over his body and face. He
remains silent, waiting, listening perhaps. At that moment Calliope's almost child-like voice speaks out: 'Blind brother, who
hears what we cannot yet see, speak to us of disease.'

He turns to face her: 'Disease, Calliope, toils in the pastures
of life and of death. It terrifies and torments us but like a young
child, is life itself not vexing, not exacting? Disease is watchful,
it cautions us, for it understands that good cannot exist without
evil and that evil is indispensable to good, that it can assist it
even.'

From out of the crowd comes the voice of the village wise-
woman: 'Blind brother, every one of us owes a life to life itself
and the man who lived with me relinquished his without a
murmur when the day came. How can I accept he is dead when

he still abides inside me, when we each still exist in the shadow and light of the other? When a thought is alive, can it stop itself from thinking? Can the love of a lifetime just be snuffed out?'

They wait for Oedipus to reply. Suddenly he speaks with a voice that is not his, a scathing voice charged with irony and sinister rapture:

Can Oedipus answer you? Who are *you*, blind king, poet of the broken sceptre, to expound on what you have always ignored? Your life does not belong to you, it is not one of your chattels. How can he who lives for the moment untangle the barbed language of time? Life, death and disease are like beasts from the wilds or fearless gamblers who never falter as they throw the dice.

Without death what terrible battles there would be between the young, craving land and sovereignty, and those unable to die.

What would it be like if wheat could not be harvested and you refused to leave your temporary homes? This is why love is possible. Study this man through whom I speak. The Sphinx advised him: Oedipus, forgo your knowledge, await the day of your enlightenment. He would not listen. With his volatile wisdom and the slaughter of his enigma. He, misguided child, returned to Thebes, city without compassion where the queen's omnipotency awaited him.

With the confidence of the rising sun, the voice reverberates loudly:

Go, while you live, ephemeral survivors, return to your houses, banish your qualms. Life in the physical world is desire and Oedipus will still dwell in your thoughts long after I am nothing more than a defunct god.

The crowd disperses. The fire, having devoured the last of the

142

logs, subsides into the ashes. It is almost dark. Only Oedipus is left; Clius helps him sit down.

When he is strong enough to stand, Antigone says: 'What you have sung is true. And yet there is someone, somewhere who loves us.'

As Oedipus remains silent, it is Clius who replies: 'There is indeed someone who loves us; all the time there is Antigone.'

Oedipus makes a slight gesture with his hand as if to say: It's the same thing. Antigone has taken his arm and is guiding him. Clius takes the other. The three of them move off in the direction of the house where the plague-victims await them.

They have sent a messenger to Diotima asking for advice and remedies. Time passes slowly as they wait for him to return. Antigone takes charge of the cooking. Clius makes additional windows to let in extra light and limes the walls. Oedipus stays with the sick, playing them the occasional tune on his flute. As evening falls they become delirious. He envies them as they embark on their fitful journeys.

The messenger returns with remedies. The next day Antigone reads out to the assembled villagers Diotima's advice. At the foot of the tablet Diotima has added: 'To comply with the gift bestowed on Oedipus, each day he will lay hands on the sick. He will also lay hands on each member of the community. Should Oedipus die, Diotima must be informed so that the gift may be passed on to another.'

The villagers return to their homes heartened but distressed. They feel they are on the road to recovery but are disturbed that the seer has envisaged that Oedipus might die.

Oedipus admits to Clius that the laying on of hands stirs up horrendous memories; for after the death of the Sphinx all the infirm of Thebes tried to touch him, believing that his body possessed the power to heal. He puzzles over the gift Diotima has passed on to him.

One of the men is awake. They attend to him and Oedipus lays his hands on the places specified by Diotima. Appeased he drops off to sleep. It is not quite so straightforward with the second, who is in great pain and begins to scream whenever Oedipus touches him.

It is a sinister night for Oedipus; he finds it impossible to sleep. He can no longer recognize himself in the person he has become, a man constrained to lay on others the tainted hands that struck down his father and espoused his mother. Hands capable of unleashing hidden and possibly perilous forces in the afflicted. He is gripped by a longing to die. The fallen king, the king that he once was, comes to his rescue. Today it is these poor stricken people, decimated by disease, who are his subjects. He must stay with them until the epidemic passes or death comes to claim him. Diotima's instructions are harsh but it is good for him to receive orders and be able to transmit to others the resolve, above all else, that he possesses.

The following day his two patients are still alive and Antigone moves him into the shade of the great oak tree where he shall lay his hands on the village-children. Each child goes up to him in turn and places his or her hands on his knees. Oedipus takes them in his and clutches them for a long time. The first child was petrified at finding himself standing before the huge eyeless man whose hands, despite the silence, seemed to commune with his. What transpired next was best described as vibration passing through the hands of the one into the hands of the other. Returning to his place among his friends, he said: 'It doesn't hurt! It's fun!'

Over the next seven days he lays his hands on each and every inhabitant of the valley. He holds the hands of men and women of the soil – hardened, formed, deformed by their tools and by the passage of time. In these hands he is growing so fond of, he can feel the parameters of the fields, gardens and dwellings, and the meaning that any item must have for it to be of value and be used. He, a son of Corinth, native of the sea, through the imposition of his hands compels them to communicate with that inexhaustible element of his nature. In exchange for a measure of his vitality and greatness they pass him some of their stamina. He finds these long mysterious encounters that he dreaded so much gratifying. Each time one of them sits opposite him and places his hands on his knees, he enters that person's life with his whole body. By the time he withdraws his hands – without having seen, spoken to or heard the man's name – Oedipus knows all there is to know about him and the other is aware of this and knows something of Oedipus too. Each discovers in the other what cannot be voiced, even though it is what unites them. By evening, Oedipus is so exhausted he has to entrust the care of the sick to the others.

On the eve of the seventh day, Clius declares to Antigone: 'The village may well be saved for the people are busy and things are getting done. They seem to have rediscovered their former pleasures and tribulations. Our patients might pull through but I'm worried about Oedipus.'

'So am I. When I look at him face on during the laying on of hands, I see only his grandeur, his composure, his smile. But if I look at him from the side, I sense his anguish.'

On the seventh day, it is the turn of the last man in the village, the chief, to seat himself before Oedipus who discerns, beneath his own, hands that are firm, courageous and astute. The entire strength and vitality of the village resides within them. The full force of a terrible weariness presses down on him and the colour drains from his face. The chief looks up at him startled and then anxious: 'You're in pain! Are you ill?'

'Call Clius, get him to take me back to join the sick.'

Racing up to him, Clius is appalled by what he sees. Trembling, unsteady, his teeth chattering, Oedipus has broken out in a cold sweat. Propping him up, Clius leads him away. When the chief moves to assist him, Clius yells at him: 'Keep away – can't you see he has the disease!'

Oedipus collapses just as they reach the house. Clius cannot support him on his own. Just then Peleus appears: 'Let me help you, we can carry him together.'

'He has the sickness,' says Clius. Peleus shrugs his shoulders and says nothing. Together they drag rather than carry Oedipus's rigid, unwieldly body up to the house. By the time Antigone arrives Oedipus is stretched out stark naked and unconscious on his bed. Devastated, the two men make futile attempts to bring him round. Antigone forces the most potent of Diotima's concoctions down his throat. Despite his burning temperature he is shivering. She instructs Peleus to send a messenger to Diotima. She heats some water, then together with Clius wraps Oedipus's body in hot, damp sheets. He groans but his body relaxes and his breathing becomes more regular.

Oedipus comes round. Through a distant haze he can feel Clius cover what was once his body with hot sheets and blankets. Between himself and the others there is now an overpowering chill and an ever-increasing distance. His body had been sapped of its strength, its heat and life. He shouts out, crying for help. Calling out for Iocasta. Only she can cure him of this cold. He yells and a woman materializes, her gentle, dismayed face bent over his. He is shaking, his whole body racked by appalling spasms. It is not Iocasta, it is Antigone. She loves him, is suffering with him. But he retreats – from her and from life. He must breach this wall separating him from Iocasta. Only she has the power to deliver him from this intolerable pain. He shouts, calling on her to wait for him, struggling to catch up with her along the remote path she is treading. He battles to escape the arms of Clius and Peleus who are hanging on to him to prevent him from smashing into the wall. At last he is free. But now it is Antigone clutching on to him, detaining him another second, a single but agonizing moment. His two hands free at last, he strikes her in the face and knocks her to the ground. This is more than Clius can bear; seizing one of the sculptures he is about to bring it down on his head. Peleus restrains him, tripping Oedipus at the same time, who cracks his head on the ground and lies there prostrate. Clius goes to help Antigone stand. She is injured, blood is streaming down her face: 'Get him back into bed,' she orders, 'he's delirious.' They lift him back, his icy body now shuddering and burning with fever. Antigone stoops over him, the blood from her face dripping on to his. Licking it, Oedipus lets out a chilling scream. He thinks he is tasting the blood that sprang from his eyes the day Iocasta died. He spits it out and howls, a long, continuous, interminable howl, which Antigone can no longer abide. She turns and, covered in blood, runs out into the night, sobbing. Clius is about to follow her when Peleus stops him, his voice unexpectedly authoritarian: 'What about these men who are sick. I don't know how to administer the potions.'

In the grip of the plague that has hounded him all his life, Oedipus rants and raves all night, while any image offering him a lifeline recedes further into the distance. Once in a while he thinks he can see Iocasta but just as he is about to run to her the vision fades away. And then the wolf within him from the grey pack he was once part of long ago, howls.

Clius has taught Peleus how to nurse the sick and administer the remedies. At dawn, tormented for too long, he goes into the village to look for Antigone.

As he reaches the houses the sun bursts over the mountaintops and slides down into the valley. After a dreadful night of Oedipus screaming as the disease hounded him, Clius is struck by the tranquillity and reassuring familiarity of the sounds that indicate that village life has returned to normal.

He is sure that he will find Antigone at the chief's house with Calliope. The two are seated together by the fire where food is cooking. Recognizing his tread she leaps up and covers herself with a veil, but not before he has seen the injuries to her tear-stained face. With a strange tremor in her voice she asks: 'Is he dead?'

'No but he is very ill.'

'Why have you left him?'

'Because you're the one who matters. Come back with me. He was just delirious!'

'Then let him be delirious without me. As he was with my mother in Thebes.'

There is an unfamiliar ferocity in her voice. She escapes into the garden. Calliope stops him from following her: 'Leave her to cry. She doesn't want you to see her, she's worried she's going to be disfigured. Has Oedipus gone mad?'

'No. He's just ill. He'll die if Antigone doesn't return.'

'She'll feel better when Diotima arrives tonight. Until then she can do nothing.'

She opens the door slightly and points to Antigone, her head on her knees, hunched sobbing in the middle of the vegetable patch. Clius feels his universe crumble around him. First Oedipus. Now Antigone has lost her sense of identity. Calliope shuts the door quickly: 'Leave her. Go back to the sick and wait for Diotima.'

Diotima arrives, having crossed the valley and seen people back at work. She has been into freshly limed and cleaned houses and seen for herself that peace and hope have come back to the village, and that even if Oedipus's sickness does mark a new outbreak of the disease it will eventually be defeated. The chief leads her into his house where Antigone and Calliope are waiting for her. She painstakingly examines Antigone's face. She will not be disfigured – time and the application of the correct remedies will heal the wounds. But she will require careful nursing. Diotima shows Calliope which ointments to use and how to apply them and then shows her how to massage and which pressure points to concentrate on. Observing Calliope, she is amazed at her skill. When she has finished she announces: 'My child, you were born to heal. You are very gifted.'

Antigone is taken aback to hear Diotima call Calliope 'my child'. Diotima has never addressed her in that way. She realizes that something momentous has just transpired. She now feels better and even if she cries again, this time it is because Diotima's presence allows her for a moment to return to being the child she was and is, but will not always be.

Diotima and Calliope set off to minister to Oedipus. 'Stay here. You have been the calming centre of this village and shall be so again.'

'Is he going to die?'

She does not know and leaves, accompanied by Calliope who says to Antigone: 'Look after the men.'

Finding herself alone, Antigone sits by the fire and weeps. It does her good but she has the feeling that she has overlooked something. Calliope spoke to her of the men – the chief and those working in the fields. They will be returning soon, hungry no doubt. She finishes the meal and sets the table. Clius appears, completely drained: 'Oedipus was raging all night. I couldn't take any more. I left Peleus in charge – that little man is twice as tough and fearless as me.' She insists he sit down and eat. The chief and the others appear. She serves the food. They are too exhausted to speak but look happy enough with what she has dished up. Filled with admiration, Clius watches her, oblivious of the injuries that distort her face. When the meal is over she urges him to sleep before he returns to the house where the plague-victims are.

Oedipus is at sea in the nucleus of a storm. The wind howls over him, the waves crash deafeningly against the bow of the ship, at times engulfing it. But worse are the cries, the cries of those who, terrified, are pushed or washed overboard. And yet these screams sustain him, for they are proof that he is there, still fighting. Already numbed by the icy cold of the waves assailing him, he is convinced he will drown – though the fact that he is still screaming means he is alive.

By morning the ship has disappeared along with the sailors, leaving behind his prostrate body, calling out ever more feebly in the middle of the stormy sea. He is conscious of a presence that he can neither see nor touch but which exacerbates the pains in his body. The torture becomes excruciating making him wish he were once more that Oedipus unconscious and scream-ing, in the sinking ship. He hears Diotima's voice coming to him from a very great distance – but how can she be here in this tempest off the coast of Egypt saying: 'Lay your hands on him!' A pair of hands touch his forehead filling him with a warmth that provokes such intense pain that he loses consciousness. Cal-liope then places her hands on his and Oedipus's body contracts.

She is terrified by the blueish pallor of death that spreads across his face. Diotima's steady voice is comforting: 'Don't be afraid. Nothing worse can happen to him that he hasn't already experienced.'

A deadly cold from the sick man's hands permeates her own. She responds to it by willing some of her own warmth and peace into Oedipus's body. She rests her hands on his icy knees and then, not knowing what else to do, prays, entreating this great recumbent body, its muscles, blood and feeble breath to come to her assistance. Driven by an overpowering compulsion, she slides her hands slowly down the muscular legs to the feet that still bear the scars of his early days on earth, testimony to Iocasta's treachery. At that point Oedipus howls and hurls himself about on the bed, a man in agony but still alive. Calliope hears him whimper like an infant and releasing his abused feet goes up to his head and, cradling it against her, rocks it gently. She has lost track of time, all sense of where she is and who she is. When she comes back to herself she sees that Oedipus has fallen asleep.

Not knowing what else to do she goes to find Diotima, for with her experience she will be able to advise her. Diotima and Peleus are busy tidying the house, left in total disarray by Antigone and Clius's sudden departure. As Calliope enters the room Diotima is saying to Peleus: 'Continue to nurse the sick. You learn fast, your life is about to change direction.' Serene and gratified, the old man is compliant. She turns to Calliope: 'Your life will also change. You have the gift of healing.'

Unaware she possesses this gift, Calliope is astounded but pleased. She beams. 'Oedipus is asleep. What should I do now?'

'That's for you to decide. Stay near him. Compose yourself and do whatever your heart and body dictate. He is in need of your strength. You must determine how to give him that without sacrificing your own.' Diotima returns to her chores.

Calliope goes and sits next to the bed where Oedipus is asleep. He is cold and the blankets covering him afford him little warmth; he moans quietly. She holds his hands but they remain icy. So taking off all her clothes, she lies down next to him — naked.

Tired from having walked half the night, Diotima is resting. When she wakes, Peleus says: 'Oedipus is asleep with Calliope next to him.' They go into the bedroom where they find the two sleeping figures huddled closely together. It is now Calliope's turn to be shivering and icy cold. They make up another bed and manage to move her into it. They give her a brisk rub down and cover her with blankets. Peleus brings her a bowl of hot soup. She complains of terrible pains without being able to tell them where they are. Then, quite suddenly she falls back to sleep.

Towards evening she begins to have painful convulsions. Clius and Peleus are convinced she has the disease but Diotima assures them she does not. She instructs Clius to warm some sheets and blankets in front of the embers. The two men sit quietly by the fire, in the certainty that something is about to happen.

Just before dawn Calliope lets out a piercing scream. Diotima who has been dozing goes to her, then quickly fetches the warmed sheets. When Calliope begins to groan Diotima calls in the two men to help. A white sheet covering her head and torso, the young woman has left her bed for Oedipus's, where, having turned him on to his front, she is sitting astride his shoulders. Yelling and moaning she seems to be straining to expel him from under her. Standing next to them Diotima orders: 'Help them!' Petrified they dare not move. A louder, more piercing cry from Calliope makes them see the urgency of the situation. While Diotima attempts to drag back Calliope, the men pull on Oedipus's arms to extricate him from under her but they cannot shift his unwieldly, leaden body. Just when Clius thinks he must be dead he feels Oedipus's body stir and inch forward.

Calliope continues to yelp and gasp but not in that same helpless, desperate manner. 'He's moving!' she yells, thrusting his body forwards until gradually it emerges from under hers. His progress is slow and the men wonder if Calliope will survive it.

151

She does; her face concealed beneath the large white sheet, her dark body shuddering under this awesome labour.

Oedipus is alive, panting in time with the young woman. His body slowly slides out from beneath her and when he has emerged Calliope's rhythmical cries cease. It is like the breaking off of some frenzied music or the silencing of a thundering waterfall. Am I dreaming? Clius wonders, but he has no time to think, for Calliope quite drained has slumped back, semi-conscious, into his arms. Her body is bleeding and drenched in sweat. Diotima ministers to her needs silently and swathes her in warm sheets. Calliope comes to and, smiling, asks: 'Put him near me so that I can rock him, it will make him better.' They move Oedipus's bed next to hers and Calliope cradles him and kisses him as if he were a child. 'Look,' she says, 'his hair has changed colour!'

Clius notices that Oedipus's hair has gone from tawny to grey. A silvery grey that lights up his face. A face that betrays his suffering but which is no longer haunted by that air of distraction which appeared in the aftermath of the tragic events in Thebes. Distressed, he turns to Diotima to ask for an explanation but she anticipates his question with a light shrug. He realizes she has no need to know, that she accepts that night's mysterious events, whereas he is unnecessarily perturbed by what has just transpired between Oedipus and Calliope, which must forever remain undisclosed.

Over the following days and weeks Oedipus slowly returns to consciousness. The extremes of his suffering have weakened him so much that it is with dread, almost terror, that he returns to the land of the living. It is Calliope's unassuming love and her devotion that bring him back. She nurses and cradles him, coaxes and chats to him expecting nothing in return. With her nearby he is able to spend the first few weeks of his convalescence as free and as dependant as a leaf on a tree. Something has taken place between them; something tragic and still spurned by memory, yet something unspeakably light and sublime.

Occasionally she goes away and Clius or Peleus takes her place by the bed, for he is still bedridden. All the time she is absent his face remains fixed on the door through which she left as he awaits her return. When she does it is with news from the village. The epidemic has been checked. The people await his recuperation with impatience. One day she makes a mistake and refers to 'his resurrection'. They both laugh at this. He feels comforted by the knowledge that the villagers love him. Their lives were in danger. He did all he could and fell ill. Antigone and Clius took the same risks as him. They are all right. He was unlucky, that is all.

Diotima has gone home. Before leaving she asked the chief to release Calliope so that she could help her nurse the sick; for Diotima can foresee a time when Calliope might take over from her. The chief agreed and after a brief ceremony, Calliope is free. She informs Oedipus that once he is strong enough to make the journey she will leave with him and join Diotima.

Speaking is still too much of an effort for Oedipus so he remains silent. He does not seem to need to understand what she is saying, he just cherishes the sound of her voice. He appreciates Clius and Peleus's conversations too and likes to see Antigone walk in and that tender moment when, having checked his heartbeat, she says: 'You are getting stronger. Soon you'll be able to get up.'

Yes, it is good to see and hear them, but the times he treasures most are those spent alone with Calliope. Those when she cuddles him, suddenly kisses him for no reason and begins to sing the songs of the little village girls or snatches of those in an African tongue, those which her mother must have sung to her. He listens as she goes in and out of the room, responding to his every request, relishes the way, when she thinks he is asleep, she jumps and dances on tiptoes or plays and giggles to herself. One day it occurs to him how wonderful it must be for a small boy to have a young mother, still almost a child like Calliope. Merope was kind and jolly but too old, and Iocasta abandoned me so that one day she could have me all to herself. His response is not one of condemnation, in fact he realizes that Iocasta, his

153

anguish and the memory of Iocasta's bitter splendour – have now receded. To him, Calliope is like the sun. The others have distanced themselves. Even his relationship with Antigone has changed, it is as though he were weaker and younger than her now.

Clius has set up a wheel in one of the rooms of the house and has taken up working again. Antigone, as well as keeping house for the chief, has borrowed a loom from a weaver. The village does not have to support them and Oedipus need not trouble himself over how long it will take him to recover.

Autumn and winter pass in this way. One evening, an emissary arrives from Diotima, and another, an Athenian, who conveys a message from King Theseus:

Oedipus, on my return from the north, I saw the Wave you carved for the sea, the sailors and me. We stopped the ships to take a long look and to learn from it how to survive a storm. May this image enlighten me and Athens.

Events in Thebes give me cause for concern, dangers lurk, threatening you. Should you want to come to Athens we will protect you.

Oedipus is touched by Theseus's message but in his present blissful state, developments in Thebes are so remote he cannot spare them a thought.

It is spring. Oedipus is stronger, able to walk around the house and with Calliope's help around the garden. Whenever he hears her though, he still breaks into that childish grin – much to Clius's irritation. Could the disease have affected Oedipus's mind?

The cherry blossom is out in the garden, alive with the hum of bees. It is late afternoon and a gentle euphoria hangs in the air. When Clius, weary after his day's work, hears Antigone returning from the village, he leaves his wheel and invites her to dance with him in the meadow. His back against the wall, Peleus sits and accompanies them with a song. As soon as Calliope hears

154

them she rushes to join them. Oedipus, flute in hand, sits on the step and begins to play. His music quickens, becoming increasingly insistent. Carried away by the rhythm, they surrender themselves completely to the dance. Oedipus stops: 'Antigone, teach Calliope the dance of the young Theban girls, the one they used to do, naked at the spring festival. You never danced it, for you were never the right age, but your mother taught you well.' He takes up his flute and the merry, voluptuous notes of the dance rise up. Antigone is astonished that he should remember this tune to which she, her mother and Ismene danced so often. She takes off her dress and Calliope, as she devours her with her eyes, does the same. Watching Antigone, she has no difficulty in imitating the steps – like flowers on the brink of bursting into bloom. The two girls, one white and the other black, take their places in this rite which has survived through the centuries and which Iocasta, burning the hearts and senses of the Thebans, developed to an unparalleled level of perfection.

Calliope follows each of Antigone's moves. They are both flowers not women, swaying on their stalks, synchronized with the movement of the sun. How beautiful Antigone is, she thinks, white and golden, how mysterious, wise and blithe.

How dark she is, thinks Antigone, deliciously dark with that small pink interior which one imagines is there. How well she has grasped the rhythm and essence of the dance.

Their actions, scent and youth intermingle in joyful harmony, they look as though they could go on for ever but Oedipus's music slows and gradually fades away. Calliope skips over to him, embraces and kisses him on the cheeks, shoulders, hands; the way she has done so often since he became her child. She has forgotten she is naked, does not see Antigone rooted to the spot, stunned, nor the expression on the men's faces. Suddenly she feels Oedipus's shrewd, blind hands move hungrily over her body. They clench, withdraw and in a changed voice, he orders her: 'Go and put on some clothes!'

He is back in his room. She and Antigone get dressed. She feels no shame – after all, he is cured, no longer her child to be

155

cherished, nursed, fondled. He is a man again, maybe an unhappy man like so many others but that is not her problem. He is not a man she loved, or still loves; he is a child.

They watch Clius dancing until nightfall, delighting in the perfection and daring of his movements. They prepare a meal. On this occasion though, Calliope does not take Oedipus his food, Antigone invites him to join them.

This idyllic period has not come to an end but it is fading. They suspected it might; they realize it will. There is still affection – a soothing spontaneity in the way Calliope looks after him. Oedipus senses that she is still fond of him and so allows himself to be loved and waited on by her. But it will only be for a short while. He is regaining his strength and with it the constraints and barriers of reality.

Summer is approaching. Oedipus sends a message to Diotima informing her that as soon as they receive her answer, they will set off with Calliope. He is healed. The young woman will be able to work with her as soon as they arrive. If other villages need him to go and sing for them, he is ready to do so.

IX

THE GATES OF THEBES

For months the trio wander from village to village. When the temperature drops and twilight falls, Oedipus sings. His song over, Antigone and Clius take him to wherever he is staying. Clius attends to his needs and helps him to bed before escorting Antigone through the quiet village. As they walk together through the night, the responsibilities that have absorbed so much of their time and thoughts now behind them, they are conscious of their love for one another; an impossible love. They hear it, live it in silence, but cannot pronounce it.

For over a year they are constantly on the road. Eventually it brings them to the outskirts of Thebes. The following day Oedipus asks Clius to lead him to the Seventh Gate. It is not his intention to enter the city but only to sing before its ramparts. Pointing out the potential risks of such a venture, Clius refuses. Determined, Oedipus asks Antigone. In vain she begs him to abandon the project. But knowing that once he makes up his mind nothing will persuade him to do otherwise, even if it means doing it alone, she finally agrees and the next day they set out.

Begrudgingly, Clius trails behind, but he is so furious that he cannot stop himself from berating Oedipus vociferously. Were it not for Antigone's presence he would force Oedipus to give up this nonsense and surrender to the overwhelming compulsion he has to strike him. Fully aware of this, Antigone advances undaunted.

As they near the Seventh Gate and the imposing high defensive walls he helped to fortify, Oedipus instructs them to leave him as he wishes to proceed alone. Once he is facing the gate, he drops to his knees and in a low voice begins to sing of the greatness of the city. He describes the remarkable construction of its ramparts and towers and the erection of the seven gates – symbols of his power and now the envy of visitors. Two soldiers stand guard at the entrance and one armed sentry is up on the ramparts. Too young to remember him, all they see is a tall, blind beggar singing for alms who does not realize he is too far away to be heard.

Oedipus's voice grows louder as he sings of Thebes's more recent history, of the banished blind king reduced to begging by his sons and brother-in-law, Creon. The city, conspirator to this heinous crime, is in danger of being punished – for a war threatens which, if it is not too late, must be averted whatever the cost.

Growing alarmed, the soldiers summon the commanding officer who, once he has witnessed the events at the gate, sends word to the palace. A group of men emerges from the city shouting: That's him! That's him! Oedipus persists with his song through their taunts. They pelt him with earth and pebbles. Clius seizes his javelin and is about to hurl it when Antigone utters: 'Leave him!' in such a way that he desists. The men demand that Oedipus go away. He falls silent but does not move – at which point they begin to gather stones.

While Oedipus sang, Antigone was surveying the city whose high walls resemble the prow of a ship. A sense of pride and satisfaction surged through her, for this is her city, the one where she was born, where she grew up, where the world slowly

158

unfolded before her. Life has become difficult since she left, often gloomy and yet so much clearer; for the appalling battle between the strong – those armed and equipped for life against those who are poor, defenceless and destitute – has persistently revealed itself to her since she has been on the road.

Thebes, white-walled city, paid for by the sweat and misery of the peasants, is a terrible reminder of this struggle. And yet it is her city, the one that touches her heart. Her soul is bound to it and she knows that one day it will be up to her to challenge and placate its tyrannical spirit and to perform an as-yet unnamed deed that is hidden within her.

Seeing these poor wretches preparing to stone Oedipus the bard, the supplicant, arouses the conviction within her that she is the integrity of Thebes. With a confident step she goes to his assistance and makes her way towards them. Clius is by her side. He had wanted to bring his javelin but a gesture from Antigone made him see she did not want him to. With a laugh reminiscent of his old self he says: 'This is our last journey, Antigone. We escaped the plague but we'll never escape these stones.'

She says nothing but he hears her muttering under her breath: 'Thebes will never allow that.'

At that moment it becomes clear to him that she is Thebes – Thebes city of the heart, more real than the one of stone.

Seeing her come closer – fearless and defenceless – many flee not wanting to be a party to such a shameless act. Three giants remain, intent on stoning them. The first grabs a large rock, raises it and takes aim. Just as Clius throws himself forwards to protect Antigone, Oedipus, who has stood up, lets out a piercing cry. The stone shatters in mid-air and the pieces fall at the feet of the one who threw it. Panicked, the three louts turn tail and take refuge in the town. Orders ring out and the gate is shut. Eteocles appears on the ramparts, armed, his face concealed beneath the high, black plume of his helmet. Behind him: Creon. Antigone approaches the gate alone. Her eyes fixed on Eteocles, she waits. They stare at one another without saying a word. She will not be the first to speak. Neither will he. Creon has disappeared. Eteocles turns and leaves. The gate remains shut. There is no one on the wall. Once more, Oedipus is banished from Thebes.

Clius's anger has subsided. He and Antigone return to where Oedipus is standing. He picks up a fragment of the shattered stone and makes Oedipus touch it. 'How did you perform this marvel?'

'That is no marvel. One of the Pharaoh's guards taught me when I was in Egypt.'

His anger returning, Clius shouts: 'But what if it hadn't exploded?'

'I must obey the road. It is an unknown journey that today brought me here.'

'As it brought me,' adds Antigone.

They take the track that circumvents the ramparts. Despite the feeling of being spied on, they see no one. They go along paths that are barely visible; it is a lengthy, tiring route since travellers normally cross the city by going from one gate to another. The heat is unbearable. They pass two closed gates, the soldiers on duty are invisible. The Gate of Alcestis which opens on to the path leading to Narses's house is shut; but clustered around it is a handful of houses that make up a small outlying community and at the base of the wall is a fountain gurgling into a basin. The three are thirsty, sweaty and dusty. Two young women emerge from one of the houses with a jug and some bread for Antigone. Clius gives Oedipus some water then helps him freshen himself at the fountain before leading him back to the track to make his own way, for he does not want to leave Antigone alone. She takes a long drink, hands him the jug and, while he is quenching his thirst, goes over to the fountain to wash her hands and face. She springs back suddenly, her cry of disgust provoking loud guffaws.

It is the three men from the Seventh Gate now slightly drunk. The giant who had aimed the stone has taken his revenge by tipping excrement into the basin. In front of Antigone, Clius is quietly requesting the dagger. She takes it from her dress and says: 'Be careful, it's three against one.' From his sinister laugh she realizes he is going to kill. A strong feeling of elation and terror rushes through her. Polynices's dagger in his hand, he makes his way slowly towards the three men. They watch him draw closer, mesmerized by his smirk as he tests the sharpness of the blade. He is almost upon them; two turn tail and run but the giant has raised his cudgel and is bringing it down. With a sideways skip Clius avoids it and, taking advantage of his opponent's loss of balance, he grabs him by the hair and slits his throat. He discards the body, carefully side-stepping the stream of blood spurting out and spreading across the sand. Appalled, the other two have disappeared. Clius carefully cleans out the basin. Antigone recoils in horror at the suggestion that she go back to the fountain but she feels she must. She plunges in her face. Never has water seemed so cool nor so delightful. Meanwhile, Clius thrusts the dagger several times into the earth and, when Antigone has finished, he cleans the blade in the fountain and without a word returns it to the precious sheath which hangs between her breasts.

The silence is shattered by the voice of Eteocles who has witnessed the scene from the ramparts overlooking the fountain. Leaning over he calls out to Clius: 'I would make you captain of my guard.' Before Antigone can stop him Clius, with a reflex action, seizes his spear and hurls it at Eteocles. With a speed equal to Clius's, Eteocles deflects it with his shield, catches it with one splendid movement and flings it effortlessly into the distance, almost as far as Clius could have done. Antigone hears him mutter: 'Pity!' before vanishing.

Without so much as a glance at the massive corpse lying face down in a pool of blood on the ground, the flies already buzzing around it, Clius drags Antigone away. Subdued, she follows. Oedipus is now a long way ahead.

When they reach the edge of a stream they stop and Clius leaves them to hunt in the nearby forest. Antigone gives Oedipus an account of recent events: 'Clius could have just hit the man, but no, he slit his throat as though he were an animal. As for me, I felt exalted by the killing, exhilarated by the blood.'

'Clius treasures you above all else. That Theban humiliated you. To a man like Clius – chief of a clan that resists all authority – blood was the only vindication for such a deed. Eteocles understood that, which is why he didn't interfere.'

'Will Clius always be a man of blood?'

'He is a painter. Red pigments could replace blood. But first he will have to work his way through the whole range of colours. The terrestrial, the infernal and the celestial.'

Soundlessly Clius has returned, over his shoulder a pheasant he has just killed. The bird's magnificent colours complement his long black locks and dazzling smile which tonight is full of tenderness. He goes up to her: 'As you see Antigone, I can capture terrestrial colours, but the celestial ones lie within you.'

'Does that mean you will have to relinquish me in order to find them?' Her words surprise her.

There is a long silence, broken by Clius: 'My decision is not yet made. I do know that I cannot go on down this road for much longer.'

Overwhelmed by a sense of anguish, her voice tremulous, she asks: 'But why? Why?'

Brusquely he says: 'It is too long. Too slow. I shall end up hating Oedipus.'

Antigone is confused: 'That can't be true. You love him.'

'I love him and I often hate him.'

Irritated that she does not believe him he yells out: 'Impatience, Antigone! This endless road! This blind man's sense of time that leads nowhere! Don't you know what impatience is?'

Alas, she understands only too well. And she knows that for some time now Oedipus has also understood what it was. And because she understands, understands so well the life these men of blood lead, she weeps. Clius prepares a meal; she dries her eyes and joins him. The two men eat. As an ebony night descends around them she forces herself to do the same.

Back at Narses's house Antigone settles down to working with Diotima once more and Clius returns to his place in the workshop. Oedipus sends a message to the village communities that have requested his presence saying that at present he needs to rest and will visit them later.

Sculpting in his hut, he thinks about Clius and his young fiancée. The years have passed and the marriage proposal from Clius's former enemy still holds, though the appointed time is fast approaching. If he does not take the young woman as his wife a final reconciliation and the union of the two clans will not be possible. He confronts Clius who explains: 'Antigone is the one I love. But when we were at the Seventh Gate the other day, I heard her mutter: "Thebes will never allow that." She is the heart and soul of Thebes. It is too important a destiny. Antigone is either too great or too crazy for me.'

Diotima asks Antigone whether she would like to marry Clius and settle in his country.

'And who'd look after Oedipus?'

'I'd find someone.'

'No. I have to stay on the road with him.'

'For whose benefit Antigone – yours or his?'

Without hesitating she replies: 'His and mine.'

Diotima is satisfied with the reply, as are Oedipus and Clius when she passes it on to them.

Clius spends two days deep in thought and then announces to Antigone that he is leaving to return to his homeland to marry.

'You will marry your little fiancée?'

'Now that she's older, yes.'

'When will you leave?'

'Tomorrow?'

She makes no attempt to hide her tears as she repeats: 'Tomorrow.'

The previous evening Narses had suggested that he and Clius should go into partnership manufacturing and selling painted vases. Narses gave Clius the money from the sale of his vases, thereby enabling him to rebuild his house and reconstitute his flock.

The following day, the three find it impossible to conceal their misery. Having taken his leave of Diotima and Narses, Clius, accompanied by Antigone and Oedipus, makes his way to the bend in the road where they have agreed to part. Saying goodbye to Antigone and noticing how thin and pale Oedipus has become since his illness, cause Clius to waver. The old bitterness flashes momentarily across his face only to be wiped away by the great love he bears them. This is so obvious from his expression that Antigone cannot repress a last smile of admiration and pleasure. He swings round, grabs his bag and runs off. Without a backwards glance, his body sprinting to the rhythm of a dance, he vanishes into the distance.

X

CONSTANCE

S omething is evolving. With constant practice, Antigone's use of the Phoenician script is improving. She has reached the stage where she can record the thoughts and songs she would otherwise have forgotten. When Oedipus heard her reading fragments of these songs, he wanted to learn to write. This was not easy for he needed strong materials and shapes which his fingers could recognize. Thanks to Antigone's simplified characters, he now writes by carving into stone, slate or clay slabs which he then leaves out to dry in the sun.

He spends a long time considering this new ability which, though not the same, does allow him to capture the songs with which he addresses villagers and those around him, whom he can hear but cannot see. If the power and passion of his song can hold their attention then they enter into communication with him. Sometimes, it is at that moment that the god takes over and following clamorous, grisly paths speaks through him.

While this other voice is richer, more expansive and edifying than his, it is also more forlorn; like the one Iocasta used, when with words and an enigmatic smile, she beckoned him across the years to join her. It stirs the memory's forgotten treasures, stimulating the functions and inspirations of the mind; but man, given the nature of his powers and the brevity of time granted him, cannot surrender himself completely to them. It may be that the restrictions that writing imposes on him are an essential factor enabling him to find his place in the house of time and to isolate what is humanly possible or impossible from what is beyond.

A ship is about to set sail for Asia, bound for the city where Calliope is teaching the clan-healers the art of Diotima's therapies and the use of new medicines. Oedipus has completed a carving of her profile: tender and sharp like that of a bird. On the reverse side he has engraved some verses which amaze Diotima: 'Antigone, Larissa and I have been writing for many years. Everything we have written could just as well have been spoken. What Oedipus has inscribed could not have been voiced. Maybe writing will become more humanized than speech.'

Rumours abound, substantiated by a recent oracle which claims that following Oedipus's death the city which holds his ashes will be blessed and become the most powerful in Greece.

With the oracle pledging superiority to the holder of the ashes, the sympathy, honour and respect that Oedipus attract are now, in Narses's opinion, critical factors in the forthcoming conflict. Eteocles and Polynices will both need Oedipus's presence to bolster their cause and may try to take him by force. As Narses has no means of protecting Oedipus and Antigone, he offers to arrange a safe refuge for them in Asia.

Oedipus declines, for his place is in Greece. But since he does not wish to jeopardize the safety of the clan he decides to travel to Athens. He turns down the offer of a sea passage, for he belongs on the road. They will walk and beg their way to Athens and arrive as supplicants. They will endeavour to avoid Eteocles's and Polynices's troops by wandering from one small rural community to another. In the event of their encountering soldiers on their way, Narses advises them to make a westerly detour

166

to the High Mountains where a small tribe resides, independent of all Greece's kings and religious cults. An ally, Constance has been regent since their last queen died. He has established trade links with Athens and is in a position to protect them.

On the day of their departure, Oedipus hands Diotima a stone bearing a carving of her house. Engraved in the door-frame are the words: 'Where the blind King heard his crown sing.'

'This isn't your golden crown that you're giving me,' Diotima tells him, 'the one that could be usurped – but your writing crown.'

'It's the one I heard in your house.'

Knowing they will never see one another again, they embrace.

Keeping to goat tracks, Oedipus and Antigone make their way from one hamlet to another, from farm to derelict cottage. They have no idea how the peasants of these isolated regions will receive them. Many are destitute and primitive, and with the threat of war, suspicious of strangers. The shepherds they encounter are true to their pact with Selenus but can offer them no more than a place by their fire, milk, cheese and the occasional piece of bread. Antigone is trying to hide the fact from Oedipus that she is weary and ailing but she cannot, for a chill caught crossing a gorge has left her with a cough.

Aware of her growing discomfort, Oedipus decides to take Narses's advice and makes for the High Mountains. The area is a wilderness, desolate and difficult to access. One morning, after a cold night out in the open, as they follow a narrow hilltop path, Oedipus stops abruptly and signals to Antigone to go and hide in the woods. There are troops in the vicinity for he has heard the jangle of weapons. They crawl back towards the slope. Antigone is exhausted and parched. They have nothing to drink. Oedipus hears the sound of footsteps approaching and identifies the noise the pike makes as it hits the shield when held in the marching position. He is in no doubt that it is a Theban. Fortunately Antigone doesn't cough and the soldier retraces his steps.

They cannot go in that direction. They hear the babble of a

stream coming from the bottom of the ravine. They have no choice but to take that way down, picking their way carefully so as not to dislodge any rocks. The descent is arduous. Antigone stumbles on a stone, dislodging it, and she falls, conscious of a sharp pain in her ankle. She cannot stand unaided. His arm around her waist, Oedipus helps her down to the stream. They immerse their faces and drink eagerly. They remain there for some time quenching their thirst, refreshing themselves in the cool water and sharing their last piece of bread, postponing for a while the inescapable moment when they will have to attempt what Antigone thinks is impossible – the ascent of the far side of the ravine in order to reach the High Mountains.

Oedipus stands: 'I'll carry you.' She gazes at him, convinced he will never have the strength for he is as weary and famished as she is. With apparent facility he hoists her on to his back, crosses the stream and begins to clamber up the first incline. She does not think he'll succeed, he tumbles several times and is eventually unable to get up.

'I'll stay here,' she tells him, 'you go and fetch help!' But the foolish man still thinks he can do it. Panting into the soil she hears him murmur with that familiar determination in his voice: 'We will make it!' After a long pause she senses mounting in Oedipus's body a great rage – born of despair – and knows that this embodiment of rage she with her eyes will guide to the ridge, despite the stones loosened by his feet and the branches and brambles tearing at him. This rage seems to make his body, that cherished body supporting her, even stronger and larger. He has become immense and she weightless. It is the body of a giant that charges the gradient, his shoulders towering above the treetops as he grabs their trunks to propel himself upwards. As the climb eases, he begins to run, leaping effortlessly over any obstacles. And she, his beloved eyes, becomes a child once more, her peals of delighted laughter urging him ever onwards, faster and faster.

They suddenly come crashing through the trees of the ravine. And there before them on the path is a soldier, a ridiculously small pike in his hand. Horrified, he swoons at the sight of them. Oedipus is about to trample him but with her small hand, Antigone directs him around the obstacle. As he passes the soldier, Oedipus seizes his pike and shield and hurls them into the distance. Elated, she laughs loudly, and he, glad to hear her, sings at the top of his voice of goodness knows what marvels as he lunges through the trees heading for the huge rounded peaks discernible against the skyline: the foothills of the High Mountains.

With a terrifying, frenzied crash, they emerge near some pastures, a short way from a group of shepherds' huts and a smoking chimney. A cloud bursts overhead and rain beats down drenching them. The huge body which the two of them form pursues its course for another hundred paces or so before disintegrating and collapsing. Antigone finds herself lying sprawled on the ground, conscious of a pain in her injured leg. The giant and the little winged girl have vanished leaving Oedipus on his knees, his face to the ground, panting as he catches his breath: 'Summon the shepherds!'

Antigone remembers how when she was young and Thebes unbearably hot, Iocasta would send her two daughters to join the flocks on their way to their summer grazing. Their bags on a donkey, they would set off with a couple of servants. As they approached the huts, the servants would send out a warble that the children would try to imitate. A loud trill would come in reply and everything would spring to life. Four shepherds would emerge with mules bedecked in ribbons, the music of the jingling bells of their harnesses contributing to the general merriment. When they were near, the shepherds would bow to the young princesses, lift them on to the mules and hail the servants with loud guffaws. Antigone takes a deep breath and retrieves from the depths of her childhood the rhythm and inflections of the call. It soars like that of her old servants.

An incredibly rich voice brings the reply: 'You are welcome as our guests, we have been expecting you.'

She sends out another call: 'I am injured, my father unable to carry me any further.'

The voice returns: 'We are on our way!'

A moment later, to the tinkling of bells, two mules emerge from the huts. Sitting up, she watches them draw near, preceded by two men.

Oedipus rises to greet them: 'I am Oedipus the blind man. My daughter Antigone is hurt.'

Antigone sees standing before her a tall man, unusually tall like Oedipus, and next to him a young man of similar height, gazing at her compassionately. Unlike the Theban mules, these are not decorated with ribbons but the numerous bells on their saddles and harnesses tinkle melodiously.

'The mules will carry you,' the man informs them, 'and my son, who is familiar with the art of healing, will tend your daughter.'

The young man moves over to her, kneels, picks her up and seats her on the mule. She feels light in his arms, and despite her shame at the state of her dirty, wet clothes, she is reminded of Clius, of how strong he was and how she longed to be carried by him.

Oedipus turns to the older of the two men: 'You must be Constance, Regent of the High Mountains.'

'I am indeed Constance, and this is my son Constantine. How did you know my name?'

'My daughter and I are friends of Narses and Diotima who have on many occasions taken us into their home.'

'Why did you leave them?'

'Soldiers from Thebes and those of my son Polynices are searching for me. To have stayed would have exposed them to grave dangers. They told me that if ever we were in trouble, you would offer us shelter and assistance.'

'My alliance with Ares goes back to the time he saved many of our people from drowning. Any friend of his son will always be a friend of ours. No soldier would dare follow you here.' He leads Oedipus to his mule and helps him mount.

'How, with your daughter injured, did you manage to climb the slopes which surround us?' Oedipus stays silent. Constance's sharp eye scrutinizes his face: 'The woods seem to have been cut in half by a herd of enormous, stampeding animals. Taking the furore to be that of a storm breaking, I came out to have a look and thought I saw a giant materialize from out of the valley. But there are no such things as giants. Suddenly there was a cloudburst and everything went hazy. Then we heard your daughter's call and found you both lying in the grass. Tell me, what do you make of what I thought I saw and heard?'

'This might seem strange to you, but we just found ourselves here. How it happened, I don't know.' Constance is disappointed but then life is mysterious and he has no reason to believe that Oedipus is hiding anything from him.

They have moved into a stone and log hut divided in two by a partition, thus giving Antigone a room of her own. At Constance's request, as soon as she can walk again, she spends her days working with the shepherdesses and evenings helping out with the children.

When Oedipus feels stronger he begins to familiarize himself with his environment. Constantine brings him stones that he either carves or covers with characters.

They have been there for some time when Constance invites him to a feast so that he can meet the leaders of the shepherds. He is greeted by six women and six men, for in the High Mountains all responsibilities are shared equally between the sexes. There is an enormous fire, musicians and simple but well-prepared dishes.

When the meal is over they ask Oedipus to sing. 'Tell us of your life,' adds Constance, 'so that we may know you better,' and he leads him to the front of the fire where the leaping flames frame his dignified presence.

In recounting the story of his life Oedipus feels he has never sung better. His voice soars, resonates, plumbs the depths of the tragic and the cryptic and captures images of light which touch the threshold of serenity.

He stops. There is a whisper of approbation then a murmur of repressed mirth. He is stunned. Never before have his songs prompted such a reaction. And yet this laughter – at first nervous, an emotional response maybe – persists. As it grows louder, he is drawn by his body to abandon himself to it. Yes, Oedipus the criminal is howling with laughter at himself, overpowered by a curious, jubilant inebriation that sends him reeling. Constantine and one of the shepherdesses rush over to support him and bring him back to the table. He laughs so hard that the anxious shepherds and Constance fall silent. Oedipus is aware of someone refreshing his face with a cloth, of Constantine holding one hand, a shepherdess the other. Her head resting on his shoulder, she strokes him the way Calliope used to when she wanted to calm him. She speaks: 'Your song was exquisite, the most wonderful, along with that of the birds, I have ever heard. The hilarity of we women was the result of our delight at hearing a true story, the kind we like, that of an unhappy child.'

'You are the greatest bard in Greece,' announces Constance, 'since you've been with us we have grown to respect you. Now that we've heard you sing we can also love you. We have a saying: Man thinks and the Goddess laughs. That was the laughter you heard earlier when you disclosed how you were forever searching and planning, only to become further ensnared in the traps laid by the oracles. Unaided, you transformed your destiny into the tragedy of Thebes, an affair of state and the tragic tale of a king and queen. And all the while, as Melane pointed out, it was in fact the story of an unhappy child. You are indeed blind but that hasn't prevented you from being a man capable of creating great beauty with his hands. Moreover you are a bard and have Antigone as your companion. Could it be, Oedipus, that you are not willing to relinquish your crimes and misfortunes?'

The following day Oedipus declares: 'It would seem that we each have something to learn from the other. How would you feel about lending me a horse or a mule so that I can accompany you on your trips and get to know your country better.'

Constance is delighted. He had wanted to suggest this to Oedipus but feared the idea might be unwelcome.

They go out almost every day, on horseback if the terrain is not too precipitous and by mule if it is. Constance likes to inspect everything himself: the state of the flocks, pastures and crops, checking the shepherds' vigilance should there be a threat from wolves, predators or brigands; but more particularly to survey the breeding stocks of the dogs and horses on which their trade and the independence of their mountain community depend.

Constance turns up one morning and announces: 'I have warned Antigone that we shall be absent for a few days.'

Sleet falls and turns to snow. It is a day no different from any other. In the evening they come to a hut, sheltered from the wind by the rocky peaks. A layer of snow covers the roof. Constance ties up the mules in a small stable partitioned off from the only room in the hut by a beam and a manger.

When they have eaten Oedipus turns to Constance: 'I have given you an account of my life, perhaps it's time you told me yours.' They settle down in front of the fire. Night has fallen and it is by the light of the flames that Constance begins his story.

XI

THE HISTORY OF THE
HIGH MOUNTAINS

For many years I was unaware of my origins and of those of my people. I was already an adult when my brother Adrastus informed me that we were directly descended from the tribe that had once occupied the whole of Greece. Indeed, Oedipus, we were here before you, before your pythonesses and sibyls came along with the disgraceful imposition of their language and oracles.

Your early ancestors, the Achaeans, invaded us. Their weapons were of bronze, ours of stone – consequently we suffered a heavy defeat despite the bravery of our warriors. As was the custom in our armies, women fought alongside the men. This was alien to the Achaeans, so not satisfied with victory, they raped and killed the women whom they referred to as the Amazons. Inherent in metal is the consuming desire to satisfy its lusts and dreams through the incursion and control of men's minds.

Fire, the cornerstone of family life, established a clear divide between man and the animal kingdom but to the Achaeans it also became a means of maintaining their supremacy. They burned down our houses and settlements and set fire to our boats as they had no use for them. The survivors fled the coastal plains and took refuge in the forests and mountains.

Our queens were either slain or burned to death during successive invasions. When all seemed lost, a new queen came forward who succeeded in gathering on to the High Mountains the pitiful remnants of our race. This queen, known as the Widow, saw that our only hope of survival lay in our ability to safeguard our independence with metal weaponry, thereby preserving not only our heritage but the right to our language. We were in great danger for they besieged us with images of their Achaean gods and accounts of their many conquests, thus striking at the very heart of our individuality, beliefs and way of life. The assault on our language was just as bad: forsaking their own dialect they adopted ours and began to massacre it. There was an almost noble quality to the conqueror's infatuation with his victim's last and most elusive treasure. Those ruthless, barbarous men, whose women either submitted to them or mocked them cruelly behind their backs, began to study, under the tutelage of their slaves, the language that had moulded us and encouraged our continued evolution. Intrigued, they hoped it would add a certain refinement and style to their lives which they had never encountered before.

Unfortunately the Achaeans have always venerated war as the father of all things. Their legacy to our mother-tongue is this notion of superiority and its almighty logic. What still threatens and contaminates us to this day is not just their weaponry but also this alarming passion.

The Widow managed to rescue some of the slaves fleeing the Achaean mines and forges they had been sent to work in. They soon passed on to us the art of excavation and forging, giving us the skills of defence and trade that led to our acquiring the valleys adjoining our hills. We were optimistic that the Widow's reliable policies would soon lead to our regaining access to the sea.

Then other invaders came to Greece. In Asia they had learned to forge iron against which our bronze weapons were useless. We hurtled towards catastrophe. Our valley and hill settlements, so painstakingly reclaimed, were overrun; the inhabitants massacred or taken into slavery.

We fled to safety up in the High Mountains but it was clear from the great number of our people taking refuge that we would eventually starve to death. Aware of this, the Widow put the proposal to the Assembly that we sacrifice our carefully amassed treasure and return to a policy of acquisition, thereby securing land and a sea-port from the king whose domain abutted ours.

The king found the proposition attractive, for like their gods, these new Achaeans had an insatiable appetite for gold, silver and other riches. A meeting was arranged and both parties agreed to attend unarmed. After hours of negotiation, the king came up with further demands. When the Widow rejected them he drew out a weapon concealed in his clothing, threw himself upon her and, disregarding her great age, killed her, while his companions slaughtered her advisors. They no doubt hoped that, deprived of a leader, we would be at their mercy. When they attacked the High Mountains the following day, those of us hiding in the sacred forest launched a desperate counter-attack that cost many lives but which cut the opposing army in two. Unprepared, they suffered a bloody defeat that left them without a king. We found an amulet on his body that had failed to protect him. It depicted a crude Prometheus with a firebrand in his hand.

A sense of elation and loss followed the death of the Widow and the victory that had cost us the lives of so many of our people. Who would lead us now? How could we withstand further onslaughts from an enemy better placed than us to regroup and return to battle? The Widow's favourite servant, Antiope, chose that moment to inform us that unbeknownst to us the Queen had named a successor. When she revealed her identity our shock and disappointment were profound, for this woman was a fugitive from one of our ancient valleys and was living with other miserable wretches in an outlying village. When the invasion took place, her husband was killed as they stood together defending the village. Wounded and repeatedly raped, she had been left for dead by the Achaeans in the ruins of her home. Leaving the mountains that night, a party of our men discovered her and saved her. The rest of the village had perished. She seemed to have lost her mind and spirit as a result of the tragedy and could only remember the sight of her dead husband, run through by an Achaean spear, plummeting from the village wall, spewing out vast quantities of blood which streamed uninterrupted from his horrified face.

Nothing about this woman, who no longer even knew her own name, could have singled her out as the indisputable heiress of the assassinated queen. Incapable of anything beyond working in the fields, she was almost always silent and withdrawn and occasionally apt to rave. Many felt the Widow's choice should be rejected. Extremely concerned, the members of the Assembly were busily airing their conflicting views, when a sometime prophetess – from whom age had long since erased the ability to foresee the future – suddenly recovered her powers. The voice of her youth momentarily regained, she stepped forward shakily, and entreated the Assembly to accept the choice, however incomprehensible, made by she who had guided them safely through a succession of catastrophes. She prophesied that this new queen's revelations and deranged intuitions would save us from annihilation. The past had been so completely erased from her memory that she would have no trouble leading us down the unknown paths of the future. As she spoke, her body, for years twisted by pain, straightened and, her words and life concluded, she fell back into her daughter's arms.

The seer's statement and subsequent death made such an impact on those present that a wave of hope swept through them. It was decided that the queen should be enthroned that same evening. Priestesses and members of the Council went to fetch her. Having clothed her in royal raiments and prophetic insignias they returned, the priestesses carrying her on their shoulders. She was seated on the bronze three-legged seat from which the Widow used to listen to Mother Earth, explaining what she heard. Alarmed and sceptical, their hearts quavered at the sight of their new queen – her head swaying, her extraordinary eyes quite blank, her body racked with sudden convulsions and beautiful ovoid face marred by dreadful nervous tics, she was a poor deranged creature, inspiring pity rather than confidence.

There were those who, quite unabashed, expressed the opinion that we would gain nothing from this lost soul and her senseless deeds. Having held back up until then, Antiope came forward with the vociferous reminder that this woman had indeed lost her mind but that this was what we needed so that the spirits of the Great Goddess, the Widow and our forebears and descendants could speak and act through her.

She seemed however to lack any desire to speak or act. Her head wobbled and her face occasionally broke into a guileless, inane smile. To the disillusionment of all, she finally fell asleep. There were noisy demands that the priestesses wake her and give her prophetic infusions but they refused, as if her sleep were in itself something sacred.

She slept for so long that the waiting crowd lay down. When she woke in the middle of the night everyone was asleep. The moon, almost full, shed its light on to the large, square stone on which she lay, and on to the hollow of the hill that was the site of our assemblies. She rose, prostrated herself before the star of the Great Mother, and cried out as she stared at the great slumbering ellipsis around her: 'We are an egg. Our shell has become brittle.' Antiope and the priestesses rushed up to calm her and administer ritualistic drinks.

She stood on the stone for some time. Her yellow dress was the only colour in the sea of white garments worn for the coronation by those who, wherever they sat or knelt, now turned their anxious faces towards her. Again she shouted: 'The

178

Achaeans! They will return!' Her face contorted in terror: 'Look! Prometheus is come to burn our forests!'

They had all heard tell of the talisman of Prometheus the fire raiser, found on the king's corpse. Stirred by her cries the people visualized the Achaeans climbing the High Mountains, bearing torches to incinerate the forests that had sheltered them and brought victory. They understood that death would strike the following summer, death by fire, for they were neither adequately equipped nor sufficiently numerous to fight against the Achaeans in open terrain.

The people were overcome by a terrible sense of anguish. The queen fell silent, her face once more devoid of expression. The priestesses said nothing for fear of hindering a prophesy. Eventually Antiope spoke: 'What can we do against the fire?' The queen's face glowing, she shouted: 'Against the fire, the fire! Let it burn the arsonists!'

'But what about the people?'

'The white egg must shelter in its yolk.' Head raised, nostrils flared, she murmured: 'The yolk? Where's the yolk?' She turned her triumphant, excited face towards the ravine which separates the hill where our assemblies are held from the Sacred Mountain, the site of our places of worship. 'There!' and she began to run in the direction of the ravine. There was pandemonium as everyone rushed down the slope after her. Already tainted by the Achaeans, many thought the yolk symbolized gold and there were whoops of delight at the prospect of unearthing treasure. The queen led the way. When she reached the bottom of the ravine she stopped in front of a huge boulder. She stared at it, touching and sniffing it. When a breathless Antiope appeared, she said: 'Send for tools. This stone must be loosened. Dig. Dig. We must get to the yolk so that the whole egg can be protected.'

As soon as the tools were bought she set to work along with everyone else, contributing substantially to the task for she was a strong peasant woman, not averse to strenuous work. Two days later, with ropes and the added assistance of hundreds of men and women, the stone was rolled back revealing the entrance to

179

an underground cavern. She had not been mistaken; there for all to see was a vast cave whose walls and ground were yellow. Beyond it were several more caverns, large enough to shelter us all and store our weapons, animals and all our supplies.

This amazing turn of events restored our hope and confidence in the directives of she whom we now called the Young Queen. Her requests however, remained difficult to decipher, so the priestesses called upon Antiope to be the queen's attendant and interpreter.

Antiope had wished to be no more than her servant but she eventually agreed. Despite the bizarre, obscure manner in which they were delivered, her directives were simple. They were to use the treasure, untouched since the Widow's death, to purchase as many provisions and weapons as possible and keep them in the safety of the caves. We had the winter and spring to prepare for the Achaean offensive. As part of our defences we set traps in the forests and built fires ready to be lit. As soon as the attack was under way we would retreat to the underground caverns.

We divided into two groups the dogs that were so much a part of our livelihood: sheep dogs and fighting dogs. These we trained to remain completely silent and to pounce unexpectedly on anyone daring to cross our frontiers.

Each and every one of us launched enthusiastically into the task allocated by the Queen. No one doubted for a moment that the Achaean incursion would take place as she had predicted. The difficulty lay in persuading our people to do as the queen advised and to move into this subterranean world. Accustomed to daylight and the open air, they had a fear of caves, of their size, their darkness, the stifling air, and the awesome shadows cast by the eerie white stalactites. Along the narrow tunnels that led into them, we had discovered huge animal skeletons and traces of fires extinguished centuries ago, which spoke of unknown creatures and men who had lived lives we knew nothing about but whose spirits still inhabited this underground world.

The Young Queen was the only one not afraid to go in. With

Antiope she penetrated deep into these caverns, taking a stock
of torches she had made and leaving them in tunnels that were
difficult to negotiate. Exploring in this apparently aimless
manner, she stumbled across the beach of an underground lake,
the shape and farthest shore of which could not be distinguished
in the dark. Presumably fed by a river, its waters were very pure
and could supply us and our livestock with water. The discovery
of the lake and the opportunity it offered of survival over a long
period of time underground, finally persuaded many of our
women and young girls to follow the queen to its shores. Under
the supervision of Antiope and the priestesses, they began to
transfer provisions and all that was needed to subsist to the caves
nearest the lake. The first few were to serve as a line of defence,
a shield, should the Achaeans learn of the existence of these
yellow caves and try to enter them. In the end the men followed
the women's example and gradually we grew accustomed to the
dark and to our subterranean citadel's incredible past.

According to tradition, when war is imminent, the queen, at
the winter solstice, must chose a king to command the army and
take a share, under her leadership, of the responsibilities of power.
To be king in this situation is a dreadful honour. He is king
solely for the duration of the war; at the solstice that follows the
ending of hostilities he must be sacrificed to ensure the welfare
of our people.

The men were gathered so that the Young Queen could make
her choice. Each hoped that the prophetic spirit would inspire her
to select an old man who would not be sacrificing too great a
part of his life for us. With that vacant smile she seemed unaware
of the significance of the assembly. Antiope steered her through
the ranks and it was impossible to say whether the shake of her
head and quiver of her lip were a sign of rejection or a symptom
of her nervous disorder. She scrutinized the best of our warriors,
priests, labourers, shepherds and highly skilled craftsmen. On
reaching the rows of young men, she stopped and beamed at an
adolescent who had only recently attained manhood. A slave to
the Achaeans in his childhood, Adrastus and his two friends had

managed to escape. As a result of the courage he had displayed, he was sent to join the frontier guards and soon became proficient at training the dogs of war. Without a word, she put her arms around him and kissed him. When it dawned on them that the queen had made her choice, there was a gasp of disbelief from the people, for this royal nomination was condemning one of our youngest and best-looking men to an early death. But when he had been dressed in royal insignias and, in accordance with the rites, lifted on to a shield carried by three male and three female warriors, there was such a rapturous outburst from the Young Queen that the crowd fell to cheering the king.

Standing straight and still, a somewhat serious expression on his face, he swayed gently with the motion of the shield. His indifference to the enthusiasm he was provoking only served to make him appear more splendid. Dancing backwards the queen passed before him through the crowd, an expression of intense, almost pained devotion on her face. Antiope told me later that it was as though Adrastus and the queen had known each other before and as if they would never know one another again so well as at that moment. Dancing backwards all the way, she led the shield bearers to the entrance of the caves. Adrastus leapt to the ground and stooping down low, went into the opening, followed by the queen and Antiope.

Having settled into the cavern closest to the underground lake, the queen undertook to serve Adrastus his meals and minister to him. This was no easy task for there was so much for him to do before the Achaean offensive that he was up at sunrise, making his way through the hills, overseeing the preparation of the defences and, most importantly, checking the progress of the runners responsible for using the Widow's riches to purchase supplies and weapons.

No boy of his age could be expected to have an understanding of all that was involved and to take informed decisions. The queen rarely left the caves for only there, where whatever existed beyond common knowledge would unfold, could she herself acquire understanding. Silent and inert for the best part of the day, she would come alive just before the king was due to return in order to prepare his meal and bed. When he was back, with a great show of respect she would remove his clothes, wash and dress him in his royal vestments and then lay out the dishes on the table. It was at this point that he took over and served her.

As they ate the king would give a brief account of what he had achieved or relate what the members of the Council had said. She seemed not to hear and never said a word. Some evenings she would sing him simple ditties remembered from her childhood. He greatly enjoyed these and often fell asleep; however, this did not deter the queen from continuing to sing in her pleasant but rather monotonous voice. They would then go off for the night, each to a different cave.

Although they spoke very little to one another, Antiope, who shared a cave with the Young Queen, saw her seek out Adrastus each night and sit down beside him. She would take his hand in hers and Antiope was convinced that the queen communicated to him, through his body rather than his mind, the ideas that issued from that unfathomable source.

Following directives from the queen, the king had boats built to enable them to explore the underground lake. One evening, having seen to the king and given him his meal, the Young Queen removed all her clothes but kept the long knife that hung around her neck. Babbling incoherently, she was extremely agitated, beautiful and wild in her nakedness. She was obviously nervous, wrestling with a mighty force that was pushing her towards the lake. She stepped reluctantly into it. When the king realized she was about to throw herself into the dark waters and abandon the bright circle cast by the torch, he rushed over to stop her. At first she seemed willing to comply and then, with a shriek, attempted to return to the murky depths. She struck him several times with her knife forcing him to release her. By the time he was back on shore covered in blood, she had already disappeared, swimming into the gloom.

The king and Antiope stayed up most of the night hoping that the queen would reappear or that they would receive a sign that she had reached the other side. They waited in vain. The next day Antiope revealed to the king that the Young Queen had been training for some time, gradually increasing the distances she swam along the shore. He sent orders that the first of the vessels on the beach be prepared. With a stock of provisions, weapons and tools, a crew of ten was to set off across the lake to assist the queen and himself for, once his strength was back, he intended to go and search for her. His injuries were in fact only superficial and healed quickly.

He smeared his body with oil and taking only his dagger and a necklace of flints, he plunged into the water. At first he swam easily, hollering now and then; Antiope and the guards had been instructed to call back. His great fear, as with all of us, was that monsters might be lurking in the depths of the lake. He did not notice, when he was some distance from the shore, that a light current began to carry him away. He paused occasionally to shout but the replies ceased. Fatigue was setting in, he was losing strength and at times nearly fell asleep. He became conscious of the current dragging him to the left. Unable to fight it, he continued to swim towards the queen. In his state of exhaustion, she was all he could focus on. The invisible bond between them reassured him that she was still alive.

The current grew stronger, the water more turbulent. He became aware of a muffled rumbling he could not identify. The waves and backwash were such that he could no longer swim in the same direction. All he could do was concentrate on keeping afloat. In his panic he felt, for the first time, the threat of death overshadowing him. As the noise grew louder he suddenly recognized it to be the crash of a waterfall. The current was so strong that he could do no more than surrender himself to it, in the hope that if the lake narrowed before the rapids, he would be able to catch hold of protruding rocks. And then he saw, beneath a foaming white head of hair, an enormous face rising out of the waters. Its eyes, blanched by moist clouds, were bottomless, promising infinity. A gigantic opening seemed to engulf the world and the sight of it kindled an insane yearning for oblivion. Adrastus gathered the last remnants of his strength ready to throw himself headlong into this inviting mouth. He was overpowered, dominated by its supreme splendour and the vitality of the falls.

The lake narrowed before tumbling into a chasm. Dragged by the undertow, lashed by the precipitous waves, Adrastus, half-drowned and transfixed by the spuming pallor of the abyss, heard a shout from the opposite bank. Standing on the glistening rocks between the gloomy lake and the hypnotic lure of the abyss and below a light that resembled that of the long-forgotten sun, he thought he could see a tiny female figure. At that moment he felt as though his body was connected to hers and that, despite his longing, she was preventing him from giving in to the current. Helped by the opposing movements of the water, the bond was pulling him into shore. Clutching a protruding rock, the woman drew him towards her. He collapsed as soon as he reached the bank and disgorged the great volume of water he had swallowed. Exhaustion prevented him from attempting to climb the slippery rocky bank. After a moment he felt the bond tighten, this time flooding him with warmth and energy. At last he had the strength to scramble to dry ground. Above him, the queen with that same wild demeanour she had had when she struck him with her knife, was infusing him with vigour and gazing at him encouragingly. When he was close to her, he cut the bond with the knife hanging round his neck, fell to his knees and vomited again. He felt her hands supporting his forehead and heard her soothing him with sounds that were more like the cooing of a bird than words. He fell asleep in a state of indescribable bliss.

When Adrastus woke after a long sleep, the Young Queen was next to him and a fire burned brightly before them. She had found an exit and introduced herself to a shepherd who had given her food and the wherewithal to make a fire. As they sat and ate together, he felt that his body had never felt so charged. It seemed to be the same for the queen although she had drifted back into her characteristic smiling state of relaxed dreaminess. Her head, too unwieldy for her body, wobbled as before. As the shepherd had supplied them with torches, Adrastus decided to make his way back along the shore to the spot where the first boat to come along would land. As he set off he was surprised to see the queen in front of him. They collected wood that had been washed up by the swell and stacked it up at certain points to make beacons delineating the shoreline and indicating their whereabouts to the occupants of the boat.

They were both naked and Adrastus found himself wondering what the shepherd had thought when he saw the queen emerge in the full light of day with no more than a dagger around her neck. She might have read his thoughts for she suddenly spoke: 'I made myself a dress of branches and a crown of leaves.'

Each carried a torch and he was profoundly disturbed as, in the shadows, every one of her movements, revealed a shoulder, breast or knee the sight of which awakened his desire. It was as though he was unearthing something buried within himself, something he had once known but lost, which that childlike expression, that tender, moronic grin of hers, reminded him of. When they stopped to rest he lay next to her and for once she did not move away. He had never known a woman. She took him in her arms. The flickering flames of the torch planted in the ground next to them sent patterns of light and shade dancing over his muscular body. Slowly and with singular sensitivity, she taught him to love her.

She seemed quite content the next day to tag along behind him, but it was in such a way, he realized, that without a word or a sign, she was leading him. 'We have to find our fortress,' she said. Mystified, he asked for an explanation but she did not seem to understand what he wanted.

The following day they lit the first of the beacons. As she watched the flames rise she was enthralled, her face glowed with enthusiasm: 'We shall soon have our island home on the sea.' Enjoying the brightness and warmth of the fire, Adrastus was none the less baffled: 'Why do you call it a sea? This is a fresh-water lake.'

Embarrassed, like a child discovered doing something adults

cannot understand, she smiled: 'This is our sea. It will thwart the Achaeans. It's called the Inner Sea.'

Time passed slowly. Their anxiety grew as there was no sign of the boat. And then towards evening she suddenly said: 'There they are! They're making the same mistake as you! They're heading for the rapids!' Seizing her torch she ran along the shore, Adrastus behind her. At the second beacon, she yelled: 'Pile it high! Make it enormous. They're in terrible danger. I'm going to see if I can find them. Keep shouting.' With that, she ran and plunged into the water. He soon lost sight of her.

He stacked up the wood until the beacon was huge. Each time he yelled out, her confident calls came back in reply. He lit the fire and continued to shout at regular intervals, more in distress than anything else. Her replies came from further away and seemed to say: 'Don't worry. I'm all right,' then nothing more despite his hours spent calling.

As the early morning mists began to lift, he heard the distant blast of a shepherd's horn and his calls were answered at last. Propelled by its oarsmen the heavy vessel came into view with the queen standing on the prow.

The crew had been unaware that the current was dragging them towards the waterfall. When they heard the queen they feared it was one of the water goddesses. Too petrified at the thought that the blinding tail of a siren might be trailing from her naked body, they would never have had the courage to haul her on board had Antiope not intervened.

Adrastus's first impulse when he saw the boat was to throw himself into the water and join the queen. But Antiope had dressed her. She was no longer the same woman he had lived with in close proximity for the last three days – as spontaneous in her nakedness as a wild animal in its fur. She had returned to being the Young Queen with her inane expression and euphoric, dazed smile. He lingered in the shadows until the craft landed and Antiope brought him a tunic to wear.

187

XII

THE YOUNG QUEEN

U p until now, Oedipus, I have only spoken of our people and of Adrastus. For years I had no memory of my childhood and find it quite difficult to talk of myself. I could only remember two things: a hand taking mine and leading me far away from a house where we had known only misery; and an ill-fated day, a couple of years later, when the hand and voice that had been my security disappeared.

I lived the life of an orphan slave. Covered in vermin, I kept sheep, was given the worst jobs imaginable, ate what I could lay my hands on and when I had to, thieved to survive. I was constantly spurned and beaten, right up to the day that I was too strong for anyone to challenge. My owner released me so that he could sell me to a man recruiting for an Achaean king. So I became a soldier and quickly rose to the rank of cavalier in the royal guard, thanks to my knowledge and understanding of horses. Never had I been so well looked after and well-treated. The king was demanding; my friends thought him strict but after all I had been through I found the work effortless and discipline slack. I was free. I had a beautiful dapple-grey mare whom I adored, a tall helmet with a red horse-tail and women could not take their eyes off me. I assumed I was the son of an Achaean who had ended up a slave as the result of some tragedy.

The recollection of that hand, too small to be that of either of my missing parents, was all that ever saddened me. For it had saved my life when I was abandoned at such a young age. It was a painful memory and one that served to remind me of how I had spent my childhood – filthy, frightened and constantly abused. But my situation had changed and even though there was not a great deal going on in my head at the time, at least I was not afraid of anyone. One day when I was grooming my horse after returning from a training exercise which everyone except me had found arduous, I was approached by a cheerful young man. I returned his smile. He was so handsome and virile that it was impossible not to feel the same delight and wholeness echoed in my own body. 'Would you like me to help you?' I laughed. I had always cared for my horse on my own and needed no one. 'It wouldn't be the first time we've tended animals together,' he added, 'those days it was sheep.' I was dumbfounded. He went on: 'You have a scar on your thigh.' This was indeed true though it was a mystery to me how I had come by it. 'It was a wolf. You were very young. He would have broken the bone if I hadn't beaten him off with my stick. I think I put out his eye.'

Everything came back to me. 'Were you hurt?'

'Yes. We both lost a lot of blood. Do you remember?'

Oh, I did! I grabbed his right hand and there was the long scar. This was the hand from my past grown larger, become like mine, a hand of iron. Running my finger down the scar I was seized by an impulse. With tears in our eyes, I raised his hand to my lips as I had done so many times before. Seeing me kiss Adrastus's hand made the guard grooming the horse next to mine snigger. Adrastus spun round: 'This man is my brother. Who has the temerity to laugh?' His tone was such that the guard, not an easy-going man, untied his mount and left without a word.

I questioned him: 'Why did you disappear? Why did you abandon me?'

'I didn't abandon you. I was a slave like you. The master sold me to some passing buyers who left immediately, leaving me no time to find you in the sheep-pen.'

'And now?'

'I was rescued by the people of the High Mountains. I'm head of their army.'

'And who are these people?'

'They're our people, Constance. Come back to us.'

'Is my name Constance?' I had only ever known the name given me by my Achaean masters.

'It is your name. You're not Achaean. If you like we can leave this very night.' And that is what we did. I took my horse and my weapons, removed the Achaean red plume from my helmet and we made our way into the High Mountains where he presented me to the Young Queen and put me in charge of a troop of cavalry.

Certain that the forests will be our battleground, the Achaeans decide to burn us to death. Warriors, arsonists bearing firebrands, group for the onslaught on the High Mountains. Retreating before the Achaean advance, small bands of our guards draw them into the sacred forest and then run for cover. They make their way back to the caves down subterranean tunnels while our adversaries burn down the trees which collapse in a fearful blaze.

The Achaeans know we have eluded them. They discover our underground entrances and swarm in. Adrastus releases the rocks that have been assembled, while I set alight the waiting fires. Those who are not buried alive, perish in the flames intended for us. Survivors are forced into a hasty and disorderly retreat by our noiseless hounds referred to by our enemies as the dogs of night.

The summer solstice falls shortly after this memorable victory and Adrastus summons the full assembly. It is his intention on the occasion of this great solar event to hand back his powers to the queen and, in accordance with our tradition, set the day of his execution.

A sharp sword at his side to indicate his choice of death, he kneels before the people, neck bared. The queen is on the mystics' three-legged seat with Antiope and the priestesses encircling her. Her head nodding in perpetual and ambivalent denial, she looks perplexed.

I stand and roar: 'You don't know the Achaeans as well as I do. They will always see a thing through to the bitter end. We may have beaten them this time, but they'll be back. They're stronger than we are. They'll materialize the moment they hear the king's dead.'

The queen, with that vacant expression of hers, does not move. I begin to find her quivering smile intolerable. Just as I am about to open my mouth again to protest, Adrastus stands and looks first at me and then at the people, calmly compelling us to be still, to pull ourselves together. He kneels once more. During the long, soothing silence that ensues, the Young Queen suddenly begins to sob: 'The time is not yet ripe, Adrastus. The day will come when we shall both give our lives in defence of the island.' No one says a word. The queen has withdrawn into her private world, seemingly out of her depth once more. We realize that war cannot be far off, that we shall indeed be in great peril if our last bastion, the island discovered by the Young Queen at the centre of the Inner Sea, is also under threat.

The queen rises and makes Adrastus stand. She returns his royal insignias, places his sword in his hand and we honour them tearfully as though they were already dead.

War breaks out. The Achaeans firmly believe we have a vast fortune secreted below ground. They torture prisoners to disclose the entrances to our caves. Over a number of years they attack us unrelentingly, plunder our harvests, decimate our flocks and destroy what is left of our forests. To avoid annihilation we become like them. During our night incursions we reclaim our livestock and anything else they have seized. But the war impoverishes us as much as them. We live under the threat of famine and are forced to think only of fighting. Addressing the Council, Adrastus says: 'Soon, we shall be no better than the Achaeans.'

For once the queen breaks her silence: 'We are too numerous and without allies. Let the strongest leave and seek a nascent town and there found a city populated by men of iron. Those who love the sea must seek a coastal town. In this way we shall have secret allies in two cities, whose complementary mentalities will support us and assist those of us forced to leave.'

We follow the queen's advice. The most warlike set off for the Peloponnese where they help found Lacedaemonia. And those who yearn for the sea leave for Attica where they contribute to the growth of Athens. We support them until they are established, then they help us. That is how we have avoided extinction.

The Achaeans' persistence eventually pays off and they force their way into our caverns. Their victory marks the beginning of a long succession of bloody battles. We fight in the dark, sucking them into the bowels of the earth, down tunnels where they fall into waiting pits or burn to death when we ignite the ground beneath their feet. We retreat inch by slow inch to secure as much time as possible for those engaged in the fortification of the island and the construction of warships. But the Achaeans are better equipped and outnumber us. In the space of two years they have driven us back to the shores of the Inner Sea. But by then all we possess has been transferred to the island and all our people are ensconced there. For a time we have the advantage. Our crafts give us mobility and allow us to find and strike at their weak points. They persevere; they fetch wood and build a fleet. Two of our ships, fitted with a powerful ram, succeed in sinking several of theirs. They set up forges and soon all their vessels are fitted with rams. The number of their warriors and ships increases and we know the final assault is imminent.

One evening, Adrastus and I are discussing tactics when the queen becomes agitated, ripping off her clothes and babbling incoherently. We see her, in a trance, in the feral resplendence of her nudity. She calms down. Antiope puts fresh clothes on her and wipes the foam from her mouth. Her face is noble and serene. It is a queen who speaks: 'The war is coming to an end. When they attack, Adrastus, you and I will both be sacrificed. Constance will reign until the one who must come arrives. Let our spies inform the enemy that the royal vessel is planning to abscond with a cargo of treasure. They will give chase. We shall lure them to the rapids – greedy for gold they will notice nothing. You shall be sacrificed when you turn your ship into a dazzling inferno. They will then pursue me and I shall drag them down into the abyss with me. Every one of them! That will be the second day after this.'

She falls silent, her eyes glaze over, her strong, handsome features relax. Her mouth quivers with that ambivalent smile.

Was it a dream? Is this the same woman? Her message was sufficiently clear and rational for Adrastus to leave instantly. He orders that our warships regroup at the point where the Achaeans will cross. Their instructions are first to attack the Achaean fleet and then to protect the vessels of the queen and king as they flee. My orders are to take my troops to the other side of the Inner Sea and rescue the shipwrecked. He convenes a meeting of the Assembly and announces that the war will end the next day with the total destruction of the invader and the deaths of many of our people. His speech is charged with such resolve that no one disputes it. We are filled with tremendous hope and a great sense of sorrow.

To the sound of raucous singing and war cries the Achaeans set sail next day, confident of victory. There is no sound from our side of the water. As their fleet nears the island, ours – concealed until then – takes them by surprise. We concentrate on their flank but only the royal boats, fitted with rams, succeed in sinking any of theirs. Some attempt to break the Achaeans' oars and board their ships. Initially in our favour, the course of the battle suddenly changes. We have sunk or burned some of the enemy vessels but most have broken free to attack and ram ours broadside-on. Adrastus gives the order: 'Retreat! Protect the queen!'

The remainder of our fleet pulls back in a southerly direction and moves in behind the royal vessels. The Achaeans put off landing to pursue them, confident that the queen's boat – larger, better equipped and visibly more heavily laden – carries the treasure they covet. They pull hard on their oars to catch up with and board the slower vessel. The call goes out from what is left of our fleet: Save the queen! Our ships regroup to create a barrage to prevent the Achaeans from passing. To do this they will first have to ram our boats and sink them. Meanwhile, the queen's ship is slipping away with dignified slowness. To sacrifice our fleet in this way is further confirmation to the Achaeans that the treasure is on board. Once through the barrage they resume the chase oblivious, in the darkness of the Inner Sea, to the current dragging them away. As they gather momentum Adrastus swings his vessel round with remarkable skill and launches an attack on the first of the pursuing ships. He rams one and his men seize several of the others. Once there is a seething mass of ships, Adrastus throws a burning torch into the inflammable materials on his boat. These ignite and the flames spread rapidly to the enemy ships. The whole becomes a giant conflagration in which Adrastus, his men and many Achaeans perish.

The Achaeans cannot tear their eyes away from the brightness of the flames. Blinded, they still do not see the current, stronger now. Those who have escaped the blaze throw themselves into the pursuit of the queen but the number of her oarswomen has doubled. Ringed by her attendants, she stands on the poop. The women drop their veils to reveal their naked bodies adorned with gold jewels. Her radiant face glowing beneath a golden mask, the queen sings the glory of Adrastus' death; her eyes and mouth – huge and fearsome diamonds – a fatal lure to the Achaeans. Her face enlarges, becomes the treasure, then greater than the treasure: the certainty of consummate bliss. The enemy oarsmen row frantically, propelling their ship towards the queen's. Our women pull harder on their oars. The royal vessel, helped by the current, skims over the water. The thunder of the waterfall can now be heard. But the spellbound Achaeans – tormented by the queen's face, her naked body, her ever-growing eyes – hear and see nothing. Her eyes hold theirs, her fragrance infiltrates their nostrils, her song their ears. They shout and howl out their lust, their hopes, their duplicity. By the time they see the giant white face and its yawning black maw rise up before them, by the time they see it devouring the queen, her love song and her beautiful crew, it is too late. They drop their oars and, appalled, prostrate themselves in their boats before being hurled over the brink.

The whole Achaean fleet was destroyed that day. We found the torn and bloody remains of their leaders and warriors in the valley, on the banks of the river where it emerges and levels out. It was there that we also found the bodies of the queen and her companions. Since Adrastus and his men had been consumed by fire in defence of her vessel, we erected a stone in their memory on the shores of the Inner Sea.

The queen's triumphant death and that of Adrastus heralded a new era of peace. It was also a time of mourning and great sorrow. Their heroism was an example to us, pointing the way to the future. But we could not adjust to their not being with us. Personally, I could not come to terms with the fact that the companionship of Adrastus, his physical presence and his intellect, had gone; that once again and for always I was to be deprived of his comforting hand. The queen's inane smile and quiet bewilderment – as though she had strayed from another world into ours – were also missed. Deep down we all expected, as we wandered up mountain trails and island tracks, to feel her protecting us once more.

The depth of my grief and distress were such that I felt unable to assume the regency entrusted me by the queen. An oppressive sense of my inadequacies tempted me to call a meeting of the Assembly so that I could resign. It was then that Antiope came to my rescue. Throughout the long years of the war, whenever we were threatened by defeat or great peril, the queen had sometimes fought at the head of the army. Adrastus and the Council had ruled that she stay on the island where she embodied the spirit and aspirations of the people. Antiope stayed with her, deciphering the muddle of words and lengthy silences that punctuated the queen's thoughts before passing them on to us. It was she who heard everything, retaining much of what the queen had said – fragments of dreams and visions, revelations as she fought by Adrastus's side, the outcome of her solitary hours swimming in the waters of our underground sea.

Realizing it was my wish to renounce the regency, Antiope, whose time left on this earth was now limited, moved into my house. By way of comforting me she would recount observations the queen had made when they were alone together. A whole universe of thought was opened up to me, one that was as rudimentary and wholesome as bread. The affection that Adrastus and our people had shown me since I had returned had helped me mature. But what matters at times of war is efficiency. Unknowingly, I regarded efficiency as Achaean. Only when Antiope repeated what the queen had said did I see this: 'Constance is valiant but he speaks Achaean and is introducing our people to Achaean ideas.'

Her words appalled me: 'So the Queen didn't like me!'

She was amused: 'On the contrary she was very fond of you. She loved you as much as she loved Adrastus.' I found this hard to believe, but she had so much evidence of this affection that eventually I accepted what she said. I asked her to explain how I spoke Achaean. She made me recognize how a belligerent spirit governed my opinions: 'You never listen to or converse with others. You argue in order to convince, be informed, command.'

'But Antiope, it is imperative to be informed if one is to command people.'

'There is nothing wrong with knowledge but the queen never claimed it to be imperative. Obligation is not a characteristic of our language. This "imperative", this obligation you impose on yourself, is Achaean. Whenever the queen was in need of knowledge, it came to her. Her most memorable words and her greatest undertakings simply came to her.'

'Before any undertaking Antiope, it is imperative to train and to prepare.'

'The queen was always ready for any eventuality. She never shrank from anything. There was always the memory of a future governed by the Goddess.'

'She never spoke of the Goddess. Did she believe in her?'

'Your question, Constance, places those who believe in opposition to those who do not. Had she heard you, the queen would have said you were speaking Achaean. It was the Great Goddess who believed in her, as she now believes in you despite your doubts. It was not a question of whether the queen believed in the Goddess or not – she lived through her whether present or absent.'

Antiope informed me one day: 'It was the queen's desire that you marry. Her greatest wish was that you have sons and daughters so that your blood and Adrastus's be perpetuated in our people. Open your eyes and your heart; the right one for you is among us.'

I did as Antiope wished and wandered through our country my heart and eyes alert. I encountered love. It gave us children and it was while I listened to Callia as she talked to them that I at last understood the essence of our language and the role it had played.

An incident at the frontier which cost the lives of several of our people rekindled my hatred of the Achaeans, this time stronger than before. I asked Antiope: 'Did the queen loathe the Achaeans as much as I do?'

She and Callia laughed. She explained: 'As far as the queen was concerned, she was defending our right to exist. She referred to the Achaeans as cruel but courageous. She certainly didn't loathe them. They were infatuated with power and wealth but nevertheless appreciated beauty and although they spoke it badly they cherished our language. In fact she used to say that setting aside our differences and conflicts we were one and the same people.'

I was stunned. I found it hard to accept that someone who had suffered so much at the hands of the Achaeans and who had lured so many to their deaths could think we were of the same race.

Antiope's death soon after this deprived us of our last great source of wisdom. The priestesses collected her sayings and those of the queen, adding them to those of the great teachers of the past. There has been no one since to equal them. Our independence has been safeguarded, new riches discovered on the banks of the underground sea, but we are without the inspiration and guidance of a woman. We are fewer in number and no longer have bards, heroes or heroines to encourage us. These will only return the day we have a queen again.

'Where is your story leading us?' asked Oedipus.

'The first time I saw Antigone seated on Constantine's mule with her injured ankle and her torn clothes dripping wet, the thought crossed my mind that she might be the one who must come.

'I have seen Antigone almost every day over these past few months. I have observed the way she ministers to you, writes, sculpts, helps the shepherdesses with the sheep. I listen to her whenever she is telling the children stories, or joining in their songs. More and more I am convinced she is the one.

'I sometimes fear that the arrival of the one who must come will herald the day we are overrun and engulfed by a huge wave of Achaeans. It is not a possibility I shy away from but as regent I have to do everything in my power to prevent that from happening. The danger is there. Poverty, and often famine, are around us.'

'Why don't you distribute the residue of your resources from the subterranean sea among the poorest of your neighbours?'

'Because I have no faith in man, or perhaps because I have no faith in myself, I cannot take such a risk. They would know I did not trust them and that would stop them from trusting me. But an exceptional queen, a heroine, could fire us to undertake deeds that would cleanse our hearts and those of the Achaeans, thereby releasing us from our mutual fears.

'Antigone is one such heroine. She has begged for you, given up everything and risked her life to be with you. Patiently, she has cleansed the terrifying mask that parricide and incest left on your face. We as a people, and our women in particular, find the appalling image of Achaean patriarchy odious, but with Antigone's help we have all learnt to understand and admire you. For the first time since the murder of the Widow, our children have been taught our language, the myths and the history of our forebears. If anyone can perpetuate our heritage Antigone can. One day I asked her from which fountain she had drawn this barely remembered treasure. "From listening to Oedipus sing," was her reply.

'If Antigone were our queen and you – our greatest bard – were also to stay, the future of our people and that of Greece would be an enlightened one. Is it still your intention to journey to Athens?'

'I have been summoned to go there.'

'By Theseus?'

Oedipus shrugs to signify he does not know and adds: 'By an invisible bond. Like the one connecting your brother to the Young Queen as he crossed the Inner Sea.'

'May I approach Antigone?'

'Indeed you must.'

When they leave the next day, the vestiges of their recent experiences linger within them for a while. And then a blank. Just the long road, the snow becoming heavier and turning to rain, reality unfolding before them and the inability to distinguish certainty from uncertainty.

Allowing a few days to elapse, Constance asks to speak to Antigone in the presence of his wife Callia and Antigone's closest friend, Constantine's older sister, Arga. He speaks without ceremony or preparation, getting straight to the point: 'We need a queen. We have been without one for twenty years. Since you've been with us many feel you're the one we've been waiting for. Accept and the Assembly will crown you our queen. It would be the greatest of blessings for us and the Achaeans since you might be able to prevent another war from taking place.'

Never having foreseen such a role for herself, Antigone is obviously taken aback: 'I am deeply honoured. But what of my father?'

'We need him to inspire us. Oedipus is safe here; were he to stay, he would once again have a sense of belonging.'

'But he would no longer be on the road. You are his friend, Constance, do you think he is ready to give that up?'

Constance is startled and dismayed by the question. From the look in their eyes, he can see that Callia and Arga anticipated Antigone's reaction and that they regret it as much as he does. He says: 'I was thinking only of us and of you, Antigone. You have made me see that Oedipus cannot abandon his journey.'

XIII

THE DOGS OF NIGHT

One morning Constance spots twelve heavily armed Theban soldiers at the end of the path that leads up to the huts. He sends word to Oedipus and Antigone then despatches Constantine to speak to them. They have orders from King Eteocles to bring Oedipus and Antigone back to Thebes.

'And if they refuse?'

'Then we shall use force.'

Constantine reports back to his father. Constance is amused: 'With only twelve men! What arrogance. Send the dogs to sort them out and post a few archers.' Turning to Oedipus, he inquires: 'Is it all right if I tell them you accept?'

'Of course.'

Constantine informs the soldiers that Oedipus and his daughter will obey the king's command. He returns to the boundary stone, sits down on it and starts to whistle. Antigone guides Oedipus to the head of the track. The soldiers see no one else, it is as though the High Mountains were deserted. Not even the rustle of the wind. And yet . . . there, on either side of the track leading to the huts, the tall grass is stirring. 'Look!' exclaims one of the soldiers.

The officer turns and catches sight of black shapes silently moving closer: 'Dogs! The dogs of night!' He gives the order 'Raise pikes!' Twelve long Theban pikes are pointed at the harmless-looking hounds, standing twenty rows deep, blocking the path and preventing Oedipus and Antigone from taking another step. They endeavour to push their way through but the dogs, huddled tightly together, force them to move back.

Constantine is moving away. The officer calls out: 'Call off your dogs!' With a shrug of his shoulders he signals his powerlessness and disappears. Several hundred dogs now separate Oedipus and Antigone from the troops. The silence of the dogs, their way of moving as one body without supervision is most impressive. Ordering his men to get ready to charge, the office hollers: 'We're coming to get you!' Pikes lowered, they are barely in position when other dogs, until that moment concealed, pounce on them from behind. Several of the soldiers are bitten and one – assaulted by three dogs – falls and drops his pike. An order rings out. They step back a few paces and form a square around the wounded man.

Antigone admires the precision of the manoeuvre which forms the Theban wall of iron. With each attack the men move as one, each protects the other with pike and shield against the dogs. Quite a few dogs are killed, while others keep out of reach and stand their ground. Those encircling Oedipus and Antigone have pushed them right back up the slope.

A step at a time the troops retreat to where the path begins and the dogs go back into the high grass and guard them. Now that the path is clear the officer can see the wounded soldier's weapon and sends a man to fetch it. He has barely taken two paces when the dogs reappear and bar the way. They stay there, a silent threat. Once he is back with the others, they vanish.

The two they came for have gone. Were it not for their painful bites, three canine corpses on the path and the pike glinting in the sun, the Thebans could be excused for thinking they had been dreaming. Dejected, they about-turn, the deadly silence of the dogs echoing in their ears. To take Oedipus and Antigone will be impossible all the time they are here, says the officer. The king will need an army. I will send him a message then he can decide what to do.

Antigone is approached by Arga, two female and two male archers: 'We saw how the Thebans handled their weapons when the dogs attacked them. Constantine has told us you are familiar with this manoeuvre and could teach us the Theban wall of iron.'

One of the women gives Antigone the captured pike. It is long and heavy and no longer communicates with her hands and heart the way it used to. 'Do you believe the pike to be superior to the dogs? After all they very efficiently prevented the troops from advancing.'

'There were only twelve of them,' the young woman replied. 'Had there been two hundred, the dogs couldn't have achieved much.'

Arga speaks up: 'We had hoped you might become our queen and help us achieve a lasting peace with the Achaeans. You declined. When the Achaeans next attack we must be able to cripple them long enough to allow our Athenian and Lacedae-monian allies to come to our assistance. Our infantry must be as good as that of Thebes. Only you can help us.'

Antigone has not handled a weapon for ages – not even Clius's javelin. But she has not forgotten the nature of that uncompromising passion for iron. Why have they come to pester her when she is content to sit in the shade of the hut with Oedipus, busy chronicling the ancient songs of the High Moun-tains? Is that not more important than the Theban wall of iron? 'No,' says Arga – Arga who has experienced the enchantment of the deep valleys.

Antigone turns to Oedipus. He says nothing. She knows that his silence signifies that in her heart she has accepted. She sighs sadly: 'I'll do as you ask. But first I'll have to practise. Come back in twenty days and I'll teach you all I know. But Arga, do you really believe that handling the pike brings happiness?'

'No, not happiness, Antigone. Survival.'

Every morning Antigone runs through the complete sequence of exercises for the pike followed by the more complex drill involving pike and shield. Beating out the tempo with various long-forgotten tunes, Oedipus directs her, helps her get the timing right. At first she feels clumsy, uneasy and, most of all, ridiculous. But the movements gradually come back to her; she remembers how to shift her weight, where to stand in relation to the others, the space she must occupy fully but never exceed. Beating his staff on the ground or banging two stones together, Oedipus inflames the cruel circulation of her blood and makes the world dance to her footwork.

When the twenty days have passed she summons the archers. Six men and six women. To Antigone's relief Arga is not amongst them. Arga whose lot it is to have children, breed horses and retain her optimism.

Despite their being adept warriors and accomplished athletes, they find the first morning's exercises gruelling. Manoeuvring a pike requires you to use different muscles and to adapt caution, courage, intensity and strength to conform to different cadences. You must never allow yourself to forget that you are one of several muscles, a constantly controlled part of a larger body of iron whose power at any given moment can become indestructible if all its components function together in harmony. You must be exclusively yourself as well as another, moving to execute the dance of iron, beyond fear and unbridled pleasure. It is the antithesis of what they have always done; a fact of which Antigone is always conscious as she witnesses the pain of the twelve bodies as they capitulate, then gradually adjust, in order to master this intricate skill which will eventually become their passion.

But is this compatible with happiness; with the happiness of Constantine, Arga and the valley where the deer roam? Probably not. But to her surprise it is in harmony with her inner labyrinth and that of Oedipus, who was at first so absorbed in her training sessions and those of the warriors. Perplexingly he stopped and she was obliged to take over, pacing their moves with stones or shouts as he had done. She asked him one day why he no longer came: 'You didn't need me any more. Besides I still like all that. Too much. Far too much.'

As she progresses through the drills, she rediscovers her former fascination with and passion for iron. She pictures herself – the only girl – training with Polynices, Eteocles and other Theban boys. Much to Eteocles's displeasure, Polynices far outstripped everyone else. She can still hear the ring of pikes crossing, the clash as they hit the shields and Eteocles's exasperated cry as his brother disarms or corners him.

Polynices! How she loved practising with him. It used to infuriate her that he always held back when they were fighting together. Then one day, with a clever tactical move she forced him to unleash the full force of his strength and she – cunning and elusive – was able to withstand the ensuing onslaught by hurling it back at him. They fought for a long time until he stopped abruptly. 'It's hard to believe but my pupil has become my equal.' With a laugh as engaging as Oedipus's, it was he who now went to fetch the pitcher of water and cup from which they both drank as always. As she lunges at her partner, whose progress is more marked each morning, she acknowledges that that day was a triumphant one. Mad Antigone's absurd triumph. All her strength suddenly unleashed, she sends her opponent flying, fears she might have injured her, and seeing she has not, embraces her – sweaty and iron-clad, seething and ready to do battle once more.

The thought darts through her mind: this one will soon be ready, ready to kill, ready to die, stepping in time to the beat of that mad Theban music.

Training the twelve has been a long process but each of them is now ready to instruct others who will ultimately form a detachment capable of influencing the course of battle. It is almost time for the shepherds and breeders of the High Mountains to pay the heavy toll that allows them to take their animals across Achaean provinces where they shall meet merchants from all over Greece and Asia in the market of the Blue Valley. Constantine and the shepherds moving out their flocks is the only opportunity Oedipus and Antigone will have to outwit any Theban soldiers posted to look out for them. However, it is with heavy hearts that they will leave the High Mountains which have provided them with a safe haven for over a year. And yet they both long to be back on the road.

Oedipus has carved a giant monolith out of black diorite surmounted by a waking face. Before they leave, Oedipus has it erected at the spot where Constance retrieved them the day they arrived. As though clothed in light, the highly polished statue gleams for an instant as the rising sun falls across it. At dawn Oedipus takes Constance to see it. First Constance is dazzled by the brilliance and then overcome by the re-emergence of the dark stone. 'It blazes the way the Young Queen did in her moments of inspiration, and is then consumed as Adrastus was. How did you manage to bring them together in a single stone?'

'By using my hands to hear their story.'

Constance takes Oedipus's hands in his and kisses them as he used to kiss Adrastus's. The one with the long scar.

Constantine is herding the flock to the Blue Valley. Antigone, dressed as a shepherd, is one of the young men assisting him and Oedipus, too easily recognizable, is hiding in the cart.

Some time before they left, Antigone sent Clius a message. She feels sure he received it and that as far as possible he would help them overcome the perils of the road.

A Theban patrol has been posted at the top of the pass. As Constantine's sheep are all around the cart, the soldiers allow them through without checking it.

They stop for the night at the next pass. In the morning Constantine will take the track that leads to the plain while Oedipus and Antigone continue through the mountains. They are filled with great sadness by the prospect of parting. To ease their sorrow Oedipus offers to sing. The depression lifts. 'What would you like me to sing about?'

Constantine thinks of the tall stone that now marks Antigone's point of arrival and departure; 'Sing us the Young Queen's farewell, Oedipus.' Were Oedipus's thoughts also on the High Mountains' turbulent past and Adrastus's greatness?

He sings:

Elected king by the chaos of my mind and an explosion of physical
joy,
Together we are borne away but you, spark of the great
fire, you must leave,
Proud spirit, fighting spirit; while I, in these final
moments, sing
As I tempt these rapacious men, who see themselves as our
enemies, to the place of their annihilation.
I offer my entire golden body to their eyes
I sparkle, I blaze to lure their lust to death.
I, the forlorn, cryptic queen without a name or memory,
incarcerated by an ancient murder
Periodically raising the prophetic torch to tear aside the
veil of divination,
While you, each morning, with the energy of the sun
delivered us from fear.
Farewell presence and transparence, screens of semblance.
The Achaeans believe in death, can be defeated by it, but
we the offspring of the Celestial Earth
Can never be separated or removed from life.
Farewell, dearest body of my love, void in which we lived,
void into which we plunged,
Farewell translucence, leading light of our transient
lives, farewell to the heart and soul's exchanges
beneath the trees.
Hail to the few days we have lived, to the time
required to invent love.
Crying I leave you, ephemeral being, evanescent bliss.
A smile on my face, I follow you over the threshold.
In our new life, may a winged memory

Remind us of the transitory.

His song over, Oedipus leaves them and goes off into the nearby forest to sleep. They gaze at the moon as she rises over the mountains, their thoughts on Adrastus, the Young Queen and the Great Goddess who by night inspires Oedipus but by day blinds him. With sudden elation, Constantine and the shepherds collect wood and build a bonfire as huge as the one that blazed on the headland. Antigone does not shy away from their mounting euphoria nor from joining in the shepherds' dance. She thinks of Clius and of the uncertainty of the next stage of their journey, and smiles at Constantine.

XIV

THE ROAD TO COLONUS

That night Antigone wakes several times to the shrieks of night predators, terrified that she and Oedipus might have to endure, as they go through the mountains, the same miseries as they did before their stay in the High Mountains. She recalls their parting and Constantine's grief. As they were about to go their different ways she said: 'What the High Mountains needs is a woman who can teach you Diotima's remedies. When your business in the Blue Valley is finished, go and find Diotima and ask her to send you Calliope.'

Oedipus's face breaks into a smile: 'That's right, Calliope's the one you need.'

The sheep are moving away. Oedipus keeps the farewells brief and they leave. The tracks are steep and rugged. Antigone can sense that her father, as he toils and stumbles over stones, shares the same misgivings and is no doubt wondering where they will find food and shelter in these remote areas.

But that evening a peasant appears and offers them his barn. His wife brings them a blanket and some bread. The next day is extremely tiring since the paths they take are treacherous and virtually non-existent. They arrive at a crossroads and to their horror encounter two Theban soldiers, who until that moment had been screened by trees. It is too late to run or hide. But the soldiers ignore them and move away; when Antigone hesitates, one of them turns round and signals to her to move on quickly.

Over the next few days they discover there are numerous soldiers scouring the countryside or posted to look out for them; and yet no one has any qualms about helping them or offering shelter. Each time they think they might be lost, a woodman, goat-girl or shepherd with his flock appears and sends them down the right road. 'Do you think someone, Clius perhaps, is assisting us?'

As though he had had the same thought, Oedipus replies, 'Possibly.'

After long days and countless detours, it is with relief that they arrive in Attica. The rugged terrain of Thebes and the wild hills and mountains through which they have wandered for so long are now behind them. Here everything, particularly the sky, is open, more elementary. Oedipus never tires of asking Antigone to describe the colours of the earth and the gradations of light as they walk through the day. She does not have Clius's gift for translating into words what she sees and feels. She will suddenly remember a turn of phrase he used and, delighted, repeat it, relishing the sensation that he is back on the road with them, albeit momentarily. It is almost night. At an intersection, a young woman is waiting for them and invites them to her house. Her name is Aeolia. Antigone would like to know how she knew they would be passing this way. Two days before a man had appeared announcing the arrival of a blind man and his daughter. He had said they would need to rest. She and her husband Aeolus are ready to receive them. Antigone describes Clius and asks: 'Was he the man?' Aeolia tells her it was not; she is not someone who would lie. Antigone is pleased to have crossed the mountains and to find a friend in Aeolia but at the same time she is intensely disappointed.

They rest for a few days before setting off with Aeolus who will guide them to the sea. On the outskirts of a forest they hear a sound like the rustle of silk in the sky. Looking up they see two swans pass overhead. Oedipus pauses, concentrating as they fly into the distance. 'They sound like Aeolia and Antigone – somewhere between music and silence – something one never tires of listening to.' Delighted, Aeolus, who loves his wife deeply, beams but Antigone cannot decide whether she is pleased or confused to discover that Oedipus enjoys listening to her voice so much.

On a cliff-top they stop and while Aeolus builds a shelter, Antigone and Oedipus sit together. She finds the view disturbing for the reefs that rise from the sea have that wild, windswept look reminiscent of the descendants of her race. The waves have already engulfed Laius and Iocasta. She wonders whether Oedipus and his children, washed out to sea with such violence, will also be submerged in time? Her thoughts are interrupted by Aeolus. Would they like him to take them all the way to Athens? Oedipus thanks him but refuses. Next day he asks Antigone to guide him to the centre of an open space. Once there, he declares: 'We have lost our freedom. I feel as though someone is protecting us and I find it oppressive!'

'What if it's Clius?' she stammers.

'I don't need help. Not from him, not from anyone. This road is for you and me. We've been lost since we left Thebes and lost we must remain.' He pauses. 'We must become even more lost, you and I.'

Like a pledge, an oath, she quietly echoes his words.

He senses she understands: 'Move right away from me. Don't turn round. When I stumble, and I will, leave me. When I'm ready to set off again, keep your distance. From now on, you and I will both be blind.'

She obeys. She moves away and gazes out to sea and watches a ship with a red sail pass by. She hears him spinning round, stamping loudly on the ground. She hears him panting. He drops his staff. She reiterates the words: We must become even more

lost, you and I; these words are no longer representative of the
bond which unites them, but of the suffering which threw them
out on to the road. She kneels and covers her ears with her
hands, she does not want to hear him fall. She hears him getting
to his feet, rotating now the other way. The sea is out of sight,
all she can see is the pointed tip of the sail which has turned
black not red. She has lost count of the number of times she has
heard him pick himself up off the ground, howling to draw
strength from his wrath. She too would like to scream but she
cannot. She prostrates herself on the ground, biting ferociously
into the earth. He falls again. 'What power,' she thinks, 'what
power there is in that great body!' Everything has gone quiet.
He has fallen for the last time and is lying motionless. The
scorching sun beats down on them but she has relinquished the
right to help him. Despite her anguish she has the sensation of
dozing off every now and then, like him perhaps.

When she hears him stir she cannot help but look. He has
come to and is on his hands and knees groping for his staff
without which he cannot stand. Oh misery, he is going in the
wrong direction. How she longs to run to him, pick up his staff,
put it in his hand and pour him a drink. But that is not what he
wants! He has that now. He strains to crawl beneath the fiery
sun, he has almost reached his staff. He has it. He tries to stand.
As she watches him, it dawns on her that she has a mouthful of
soil and pebbles. She spits it out. She spits on Thebes, on Creon
and Eteocles, on beloved ineffectual Polynices, and finally on
Clius and Antigone who thought they could help Oedipus. He
had known all along that it was with her and only with her that
he had to be lost on this alien road.

Oedipus has at last managed to stand. Clutching his staff he is
walking, staggering in an unfamiliar direction. Blood pours down
his face from a wound in his head. Looking out to sea, Antigone
sees that the ship has gone and that the sun is beginning to sink
beneath the horizon. He has taken his time, such a long time to
lose himself. He who always knew which path to take, goes off

towards the east. Athens is in the west. No matter, they will take their time, all the time they need to go anywhere, anyhow.

Oedipus is disoriented, lacerated by brambles and bracken. He pushes down a fence and wanders into a garden where a woman is stooping over the earth, weeding her vegetable patch. He stumbles. Will he fall? The woman has seen him and runs over to catch him, as Antigone longs to do, steering him to a hollow tree-trunk into which water from a small spring flows. She summons a big red-haired fellow working in the neighbouring vineyard. They make Oedipus sit and drink. Antigone, standing upright, has stayed at the entrance to the garden, keeping the distance proscribed by Oedipus. The man catches sight of her and the woman turns round. Surprised, she speaks to Oedipus. In a husky voice he calls out: 'Come, Antigone. You must be very thirsty.' Her eagerness and vitality return, she rushes nimbly over to him. They take it in turns and gulp down the water the woman has poured out for them. He called her over; now she can cry and drink and, with the help of this woman named Gaia, take him to the house and look after him. They undress and wash him. Gaia reassures her: 'It's not as bad as it seems. Some oil, your healer's ointment, a few days rest and he'll be on his feet again. He's very sturdy your blind man.'

'He's my father. Oedipus.'

'Oedipus the Bard. And you are Antigone who brought him to us, guiding him from behind.'

'I didn't guide him. He brought himself.' Gaia smiles and says nothing.

Oedipus spends a day in bed. The following morning he settles down, leaning against a wall and takes a sculpture out of his bag. The weight of it worries Antigone. When she questions him about it he explains it is the mask of Athene. The striking simplicity of its features is more evocative of the woman who lost her memory and became Queen of the High Mountains than it is of a goddess.

While he is occupied, she and Gaia go down to the river to wash their clothes and bathe. The water is clear and Antigone is astonished by her reflection – she is tall, her face tanned below her unkempt hair, her faded, worn clothes billowing around her skinny body. She is slightly reassured when she notices Gaia's admiring glance as, naked, she steps into the water. When she has finished, they darn and clean Oedipus's clothes. She is upset to see that washing has not removed the bloodstains of his count-less falls.

Oedipus has worked all day on his mask. He goes back to it after their evening meal. Antigone wakes in the middle of the night, anxious, for she can hear that he is still working. She gets up to look. The garden, the well and the distant sea into which a forceful headland appears to slide, are bathed in the softly shrouded light of the moon. Oedipus is on his feet, the mask of Athene he has placed over his face, making him appear to be taller than he is. There is something quite menacing about it. The eyes which were closed, soothed by sleep, are now two dark holes.

He hears her: 'Athene is like me, unable to see except inside herself. Through these empty orbits I glimpsed our road to Athens. Will you paint this mask, Antigone? White with red circles around the eyes and touches of black and blue wherever you think they're needed.' She finds the strangeness of the moon-light, the fact that he looks so tall and remote behind that mask, so disturbing it makes her want to paint it right away. He removes the mask and smiles: 'There's no point in hurrying Antigone. The road will be hard and tortuous. We'll walk around Athens many times before we reach it. I'm still not clear what is drawing us there.' He looks tired. 'You should sleep.'

'This night of light which I cannot see is evocative of too many memories. Walk to the sea with me and tell me if the colours I imagine to be there are indeed the ones you see. Do you remember that game we used to play?' Of course she remembers. She remembers the game and recalls the times they spent together in the garden in Thebes when it was too hot to sleep. She will never forget the amazing words he would find to describe celestial events or the loveliness of Iocasta and his young daughters. Those words whose mystery he has recaptured and transcended since he became a bard.

As they make their way to the cliff-top, the sky pales and the moon, its failing light disconcertingly reminiscent of Thebes, gradually fades. When she tells him the sun is about to emerge from the water he sings softly to her of what her brilliance has meant to him. At that moment – which she will never forget – she feels composed and self-assured, beginning at last to understand herself. No more than the world before her, no more than the dawn that sends a shiver through her body; but no less.

They spend a few days at Gaia's house. When her colours are mixed Antigone paints the mask white, then circles the eyes with a traditional, ancient red earth she has found in a niche in the cliff. She paints the Gorgon on the helmet blue to symbolize the dreadful yet intrinsic relationship Oedipus sees existing between folly and wisdom. To begin with, the mask terrifies but finally it laughs, it is the gaiety of a woman from the High Mountains who knows more about life than any man will ever know.

In the meantime Oedipus has carved on to blocks of wood two poems he has been working on for some time. In the courtyard he sets fire to them. Antigone makes desperate attempts to save them but Oedipus stops her. They had been written for the fire.

Oedipus is better and they set off again, following a strange route of detours and often retracing their steps. Antigone no longer frets about their slow progress or the clumsiness of Oedipus's tread. His attacks of vertigo and frequent tumbles have ceased to trouble her and she has stopped wondering whether it is the interminable road or an illness that burdens him, causing him to stumble and tremble as he does. She does not object to his perpetual stops, probes and changes of direction as though he has collided with an invisible obstacle. He seems to have entered an immense labyrinth where he alone encounters hardships and takes risks. Through trial and error and perseverance, he gropes to find a way through; she knows he will succeed. He can be in the middle of the wilderness or a deserted beach – for he follows no recognizable road – and he will suddenly begin to move forward cautiously, stooping to explore with his staff a rock-face that is perhaps not a figment of his imagination, as if he were in the underground caves and passages that lead to the Inner Sea. Even if it were possible, she does not try to understand this strange undertaking of theirs. Her task is to follow, keeping her distance as agreed, neither forewarning, nor assisting; just to be there, ever more present in their joint escape.

They pass other travellers, people busy working. They are not considered to be mad, as she feared they might, when people see their bizarre way of progressing. People watch them without fear or mockery, often bringing them water, bread or fruit. To Antigone's surprise they seem to know who they are, treating them with respect, affection even. Women accost her with advice about where to spend the night. Even in the most isolated of places she knows that as darkness falls someone will turn up with an offer of shelter. His day on the road accomplished, Oedipus accepts. When he abandons the labyrinth of his mind and his preoccupations, Antigone can be with him again. As they eat he is happy to chat to his hosts and sing, should they ask him, of one of Heracles's labours. Of all the heroes – why Heracles? Because Heracles had to overcome his terrors before he was able to tackle and accomplish his tasks. He does not say 'like me', although this is in fact what he thinks and does each day. When he has eaten and sung, Oedipus rises and sits with his back against an outside wall where Antigone brings him his tools, pieces of wood and stones. He then embarks on a new sculpture or carves out a few verses while Antigone finishes those he has abandoned. It is a moment they cherish. Antigone loves the smooth surfaces, curves and rhythms he creates, whereas he never ceases to be amazed at the way she always manages to discover unexpected hope in the harsh shapes he has hewn.

They journey from east to west following tracks chosen at random and then from west to east. Through the seasons they go from seashore to seashore in ever-decreasing circles around

Athens without knowing why they must take such a long, circuit-
ous route. They become sturdier and stronger in this ignorance.
One day Antigone says: 'It is the invisible track we are following
that is guiding us.'

'No, it is my feet, my wounded feet. I didn't know it before
but now I do. What I don't know, is where they will lead us.'
Antigone finds the idea of Oedipus's feet leading them where
they will, and who knows where, incredibly funny and she bursts
out laughing. This merriment is contagious and with a light
heart Oedipus joins in.

They are in a fisherman's hut. Oedipus does not leave in the
morning but tells Antigone: 'Rest. We shan't be leaving until
tonight. From now on we shall travel by night.'

Though their hosts are poor they have eaten well. As soon as
it is dark, Oedipus stands, thanks them with that peculiarly
expressive smile of his, and leaves. The wife gives Antigone some
provisions and through her tears says, 'You have only been with
us for a day and yet you feel like a friend. Come back and stay
with us!' Antigone would like to stay and console her but as
Oedipus is already far ahead she runs to catch up with him. He
has found a path, one used by day no doubt but not by night.
The sky is clear and Antigone has no trouble in keeping up with
Oedipus. But it is a long walk and as weariness sets in the distance
between them grows. She calls out for him to wait and sees him
stop. When she is no more than twenty paces from him, she also
stops out of respect for his wishes. He does not move on, nor
does he turn round and join her, so she lies down in the grass
beside the path.

Walking with her eyes so firmly fixed on Oedipus's dark frame
she had thought she was isolated and lost. Now she feels in the
grip of something tangible, a glow which completely invades
her. The deepest most hidden of her desires, those which her
daily existence denies her but the constant call of which is the
tenacious act of living, must be heard. This is audible here and
now. This is why she was born, just for this. Tonight she is sure
of it. She is conscious of a shadow in front of her. Dazzled, she

turns her gaze slowly towards it and recognizes Oedipus. She is happy and elated to see him. He is doused in the pale reflection of the astral wonders taking place in the sky, but it is sufficient to give him the aura of a beautiful star.

He stretches out next to her and asks her what she can see. 'No more than I have seen so many times before except that this time it is I who am seen.' He clasps one of her hands. She talks to him of the stars, of their immediacy, of the sea she cannot see thundering in the distance. 'Oedipus, everything has a meaning!'

'One specific one, no more.'

'One is not enough. Your words are inadequate.'

'They're all I have. After all, I'm not going so very far.'

'Yes but we're travelling the same road.'

'One day you'll be on your own.'

At that she sighs but refuses to be distracted from her present state of bliss. The power travelling through her radiates outwards and penetrates Oedipus, forever shattering the contradictions and burdens manacled to him. Not a sound passes between them, no more circumscribed words, no possibility of eluding that other language enveloping them, which is present on an uncertain threshold, despite an awe-inspiring certainty.

They stay stretched out on the grass until sunrise. Oedipus stands, they must move into the shade and sleep before setting off on their night walk to Athens. With a sigh, Antigone complies. A shepherd rounding up his sheep sees them walking side by side. Are they still encircled by scattered rays, remnants of what took place the previous night? He thinks it is the great blind god, creator of this world, and an aspiring young goddess that he can see. Awed, he smiles, and as Antigone smiles back, he approaches them. He is about to take his animals into the mountains. Would they like to use his hut? It's clean. He lights a fire, gives them some of his rations and leaves, troubled by the scene he has just witnessed which he will never forget.

In the hut Antigone drops off to sleep, a smile on her face which Oedipus thinks he can feel in the palms of his hands. What she identifies as love has permeated him in much the same way that the muse does when he sings. With the dexterity of a craftsman and within the confines of madness he is fulfilling his pact with her. Work subjects you to its laws, pares you down, fortifies you, but you remain unchanged. But love, as Antigone experienced it that night, as she has done for some time without realizing – that certainty that someone awaits you eagerly, raises you to a different level of consciousness, indeed to a level greater than life itself. When love rushed within me, overturning and shattering everything in its wake, I beheld that weighty magma, those worthless labyrinths that constitute what I and others name: Oedipus. In an instant, all that was left of me was an empty shell inside which only the music of the stars stirred. Nothing is more real than Antigone's love. Without it I would not have survived. But if that is everything and all there is to give a meaning to my life, then it is not enough. Antigone's love is only one of many routes to choose from but it does not invalidate the slow trudge, the ant-like activities and the passions which have been mine.

Someone is watching him. Without moving, for this moment is precious, he asks: 'Are you awake Antigone?'

She replies cheerfully: 'I'll soon doze off again. You should sleep if we are to set off tonight.'

He turns towards her: 'What I am endeavouring to understand, Antigone, is that neither necessity nor love are all. I'm not interested in an all that is everything.'

'But it isn't like that. We have each had our place on this road, you and I.'

Oedipus is gratified. She gets up, gives him some bread and milk and stokes up the fire for the evening meal. He lies down on the sweet-smelling bed of bracken.

He dreams he is in an underground passage having difficulty finding his way. It becomes increasingly narrow. An unexpected turning startles him. He stops. Maybe he is no longer blind for a glow announces that someone from far away is coming to meet him, compelling him to draw near.

He is in a cheerful mood when he wakes. But who was this person with the light who had come so far to meet him? Not

Theseus. Someone closer. A father-figure or son pledged by the dream without disclosing either his voice or face.

The meal is ready. The sun is setting. Their hearts are heavy for they will soon have to leave. He recounts his dream: 'I was crawling underground and everything around me kept narrowing down, making me dizzy. There was a man coming towards me who seemed to be summoning me with his light. I felt quite optimistic when I woke up. Do you suppose this light is meant to help us?'

'That's why he was coming to find you. Was it someone you knew?'

'I didn't see him or hear his voice.'

'What was his name?' He is taken aback by her question, and yet in the dream he did know the man's name. He forgot it on waking.

They eat in silence, apprehension growing inside them. They are on the point of going when Oedipus says: 'We must take nothing. We shall be supplicants for Athens to welcome or reject.'

'What about your sculptures? Your tools?'

'Every five hundred paces, leave one of the sculptures at the side of the road. Put down my tools with the last one. It's over. I shan't be carving any more.'

He might just as well be saying to her: shortly we shall no longer be together. The abandoning of his tools will be the signal that their arduous yet soothing working relationship is coming to an end. She can see that he is also dismayed by this thought.

It is then that he remembers that the man in his dream was called Sophocles. He knows no one of that name. He questions Antigone. The name means nothing to her either. Then he says: 'If you're ready we can go.'

She subdues her distress: 'You go first, I'll follow on behind.'

The night is pitch black, the sky overcast and the wind strong. Between two cloud masses she sees the stars engaged in their timeless course. Stumbling along the rough track makes her all the more aware of her own frailty. Ahead of her all she can see is Oedipus's tall stooping frame battling against the wind.

Every five hundred paces she takes a small stone or wooden sculpture from the bag. The last one is the painted mask of Athene. She kisses each one of the tools as she lays them in a circle around the mask. From around her neck, she takes the only object of any value she possesses – Polynices's dagger – and plunges it into the ground as hard as she can.

Oedipus has not waited and is already some way ahead. She breaks into a run, reflecting angrily: 'Well, I shall never sculpt again either. Not on my own. I only did it for them – him and Clius. It never was my vocation.'

She has almost caught up with him, astonished that she should feel so embittered. She wonders what her vocation is – only to find her name? That name – Antigone – forever tugging and nudging her forwards. That name – bound to Oedipus's: Oedipus the King, the Outcast, the Bard. Oedipus her Tyrant and her charge who compelled her to live her life with a passion she would never have thought believable. Oedipus, who perhaps learned more from her than from Iocasta or Diotima. All that will shortly be no more. Oedipus will be dead. Dead for the rest of the time that she, whom he named Antigone, has left on earth.

She is assailed by the most excruciating anguish and dread at this sudden vision of her life, a life without him. She has an urge to scream but cannot and discovers she has within her incredible reserves that will help her cope with future ordeals. A dark shape looms close by. She could feel afraid but does not. She allows it to hold and support her for she is on the point of collapsing. It is Oedipus, lurching, struggling to push himself forward. 'If you weren't here I'd run away,' he whispers.

She takes his hand, it is clammy despite the cold. She insists he sit and rubs him with the now faded corner of what used to be Diotima's blue coat. When they set off again his stride is synchronized once more but he keeps hold of her hand.

They walk on for several hours until she has to stop and lie down at the side of the road. Without saying a word he sinks down next to her. They are hungry and parched but there is no water and as requested she has brought nothing. Through a break in the clouds she watches the stars' distant performance. Squeezing Oedipus's hand she says: 'The stars remind me of our mother.'

After a moment's silence he says, a touch of regret in his voice, 'You and I, Antigone, were not meant to understand a true queen of this earth – one who wants only the earth, deigning to love only herself. Eteocles and Polynices are just like her. Unfortunately all that is left them of her golden image is her fury. They are under the illusion that it is a kingdom they are fighting over whereas in fact they are vying to possess the shadow of their mother in order to deprive the other of it forever.'

Oedipus rises: 'Let's go. I want to get to the Erinyes's Forest before dawn while there's no one around to stop me from going in. You'll have to wait in the square. I'll bring you water drawn from its spring.'

They move off exhausted, having to drag themselves along, each holding the other up as they make their way down a path which thankfully leads to the town.

As the stars fade slowly, Antigone discerns through the thinning mist the impoverished houses that flank the rutted roads. She had expected to see high ramparts and enormous gates similar to those of Thebes. All she finds is a small square enclosed by a few dwellings, blanched by the moon's feeble light. She wonders whether their strength will hold out long enough for them to reach the square and for Oedipus to enter the hazardous forest whose threshold of bronze she can just make out.

XV

NARSES REPORTS BACK
TO DIOTIMA

That evening Theseus summons Clius and me to the palace, aware, as we are, that Oedipus and Antigone's protracted journey through Attica is nearing its end. They are not far from the city and could arrive any day at Colonus where we have been waiting for them for so long. The king has just heard that a group of Theban soldiers has arrived at the frontier led by Creon who insists he has come in his capacity as ambassador. Theseus has sent word allowing him to cross. The king is anxious that Creon might try to take advantage of the situation to capture Oedipus and offers to put soldiers at Clius's disposal in the event of an attempted kidnapping. Clius accepts and moves the soldiers into a house in Colonus not far from ours.

Clius, his assistant Hippias, and I spent months ensuring Oedipus and Antigone would be looked after whichever route they chose. At first our various envoys kept us informed of their movements but as time went on these became too erratic and unpredictable. Oedipus has again taken to walking through everything, ignoring roads and obstacles. When we eventually pick up his trail we suspect he is determined to circle Athens rather than go straight there.

All we have done is in vain, for their journey will be much longer than we anticipated and their route does not take them to any of the places where preparations have been made. Fortunately word of their wanderings has spread through the country, touching the hearts of the people, and everyone wants to take in the tall blind man and his daughter.

One moment we have lost them, the next we pick up their trail. One of our agents informs us that a young shepherd has come across them. They look like travelling gods, impecunious yet glowing, especially the young goddess when she smiles. They stayed in his hut which is on a remote track that leads to Colonus. Our messenger thinks they should be here tonight or tomorrow.

We mount a watch. Hippias takes the first and I the second to ensure Clius has a rest should he and his men be obliged to go to Oedipus's assistance. I take over in the middle of the night. Our house gives on to the square and from the doorway I can see everything. I am nervous and find the overcast sky disturbing. It is the deepest hour of the night and a curious mist gives the small square a singularly eerie appearance. The moonlight illuminating it is sliced in half by the shadow of the statue of Colonus. Opposite the house is the sacred forest still echoing with a nightingale's song. Suddenly, I sense the proximity of Oedipus and Antigone. I move to the centre of the square from where I can watch the two paths that converge into it. I do not have long to wait. After a moment I can just distinguish through the mist two figures at the top of the slope. Leaning on one another for support they drag themselves painfully along.

With the moon behind them their disproportionate shadows precede them. These spectre-like shapes lurch towards me. Foolishly petrified I run and hide round the side of the house.

As he fumbles his way forward, Oedipus's dignified gait and Antigone's superb poise are gone. Yesterday the young shepherd had seen them radiant. Today, as the night draws to a close, they are ashen, dusty and exhausted, fainthearted even. They stop before reaching the square. Quickly, I wake Clius and Hippias. Transfixed, we watch the huge, dark, quivering reflections as they draw near to Colonus's shadow. There is a momentary hesitation as if they were frightened of breaking some imaginary interdict. Then we see the longer of the two shadows take the other over the line and move jerkily forward across the dimly lit square.

How ill they look. Clius whispers, 'Oedipus hasn't changed. He took nothing with him when he embarked on this waterless road. They're thirsty and hungry.'

The new arrivals make their way to the stone bench facing us. With tender but clumsy devotion Oedipus makes Antigone lie down. Then he makes his way to the Erinyes's Forest and boldly enters their perilous domain.

'What folly,' exclaims Hippias, 'the moment the people hear about this they will cry sacrilege and the king will have to evict them from the city.'

Oedipus emerges bringing water for his daughter from the sacred spring. The mist has suddenly thickened, obscuring our view. Clius is not yet ready to show himself and so asks me to take some food to Antigone.

Early morning noises can be heard coming from the ramparts – shouts and calls as the building sites come to life. There will soon be passers-by to see Oedipus in the forbidden forest.

I go to Antigone with food from Clius. She is in a deep sleep, stretched along the stone bench with nothing on which to rest her head. Oedipus has covered her with his stained coat which is full of holes. She is pale and thin. She has removed her sandals and her feet are caked in mud and dust.

Either the aroma of the soup Clius has made or my gaze wakes her. She is both surprised and disappointed to see me, I am obviously not the one she was expecting. Then her face lights up with that translucent smile of hers that conquers all hearts:

'Look at you, already here to help us! I am starving and thirsty, quite parched despite the water Oedipus brought me.'

She takes some bread to her father who will accept nothing more and refuses to leave the forest. She sits down next to me and eats hungrily. The colour slowly returns to her cheeks.

The rumour has spread that a stranger has entered the Erinyes's Forest. Terrified faces emerge from the houses that circle the square, others leave their building sites – soon there are some hundred people or so standing around the enclave. They fear that Oedipus's act of profanity will have dire consequences for Colonus and Athens. While some implore him to come out, others threaten him with noisy shouts. As he says nothing they send for the priests who alone are authorized to enter that hallowed ground.

The hubbub increases with the arrival of masons and sculptors who have abandoned their work. These fearless active men, with their vehement taunts, threaten to stone Oedipus if he does not leave immediately. Suddenly, a song rings out – not from one voice but many. They peer through the mist but all they see is Oedipus seated beside the spring.

Like the invincible virgins, the song uses only the purest language of music to communicate with man. It tells of Athens, her fertile soil, her gods and her vessels with their shimmering oars. Of the foals who emerged from the surrounding sea for whom Colonus, encouraged by Athene, invented the bridle, and his heirs, the saddle and chariots. We only half understand the song, recognizable as in our idiom and yet not. The words, their intonation and pronunciation have changed. Is it an ancient form of our language or the one of generations to come? I look around and see that those present – charmed and soothed by its beauty – are no more enlightened than me.

The wind rises, the mysterious morning mist shifts and swirls but does not clear. Two priests of the sacred forest appear and the crowd parts to let them through. As they approach the bronze threshold Oedipus looms out of the haze. So tall, with his long white hair and black eye-band, that despite his crown of mist, he has the aura of a god deprived. He drops to one knee before the priests, makes a gesture of supplication then stands, his air of supremacy restored. As bewildered as the rest of us the priests look as though they should be the ones soliciting forgiveness.

Oedipus speaks: 'It was imperative I enter this sacred spot where the Children of the Shadows teach contemplation. There has been no sacrilege. Go and ask King Theseus to come and speak with me. While we wait – since the place itself has honoured your city's splendour, the clemency of its soil and its illustrious future – I, Oedipus the Bard, will sing for Athens, and for you, my final song.' His voice rises, trembling, broken with tiredness and misfortune. Then the power and timbre we heard that first night of the solstice, and those many memorable evenings with Larissa and Antigone, gradually return.

Unlike the mysterious voices we had just heard, his does not celebrate the greatness of Athens and the gifts bestowed upon her by the heavens; he sings of a different, more hidden city which will issue from the other, as a result of enlightened minds and the songs of her bards. Athens, he declares, will dominate on land and reign over the seas, but other cities will eventually eclipse her. Immortality will be accorded her, thanks to that slender, flickering, steadfast light with which he and Antigone will illuminate her future. What place would Athens have in the hearts of men were it not for the tragic, supplicant characters Oedipus and Antigone will become in her history? Cities and people are spawned under the sign of dark, inescapable passions; it is a fact that, once a prey to these, the spirit is too weak to resist them. But the spirit is long-suffering, refusing to be intimidated by the pressures and perils of the road. It is courageous, not because it triumphs, but because it sets out time and again without knowing where it will end up.

While Oedipus is singing, Antigone is facing the road by which she came. Her face suddenly breaks into a smile: 'Ismene!'

Through the floating mist I see at the top of the track a young woman mounted on a pretty horse from Etna, a straw hat from Thessaly shading her beautiful blonde hair. An old servant is escorting her and despite having dressed simply for the journey, everything about her is regal.

After so many years parted from them, Ismene weeps as she embraces her father and sister. She is thrilled to see them, touched by their delight but distressed to find them in a state of such unimaginable poverty and misery. Hippias informs me that Theseus is so anxious that Creon will seize the opportunity to kidnap Oedipus and his daughters that he has sent word to Clius and his men to put their emergency plan into operation.

Oedipus has left the sacred enclosure. The priests tell him that custom demands that he make a sacrifice to the Eumenides. His response is that he is unable to leave this spot, so instead, Ismene sets off to perform the rites.

The crowd is restive. Theseus arrives with two attendants. As always, I am struck by the humility of his demeanour, that aura of independence and stateliness that emanates from him. He set out in life as an adventurer. Now that he has succeeded in uniting a handful of straggling villages and turned Athens into one of the leading cities of Greece, he needs no more than the power of his words to govern. He goes up to Oedipus and Antigone and, acknowledging them for what they are, treats them as equals. He is moved by the piteous condition in which he finds them and assures them of the protection of Athens.

Oedipus thanks him and then states that the sole purpose of his visit to Colonus is to gain second sight through words and deeds. Theseus, and this is what makes him great, senses the truth of the statement and that this man and young woman are the forebears of the future city. He excuses himself with a quick bow for he must return to the city to preside over the people's annual sacrifice to Poseidon. He leaves, swallowed up by the persistent mist hanging over Colonus, which the sun cannot pierce.

Just as I am about to go up to Oedipus to talk to him, I notice Antigone's face contort. She positions herself protectively in front of her father as she announces: 'Creon!' Turning round I see a man approach down the second road that leads into Colonus.

He is manifestly a man of some importance as he is ringed by an impressive company of soldiers. Theseus was right to be concerned, Creon has had the audacity to penetrate Athenian territory, bringing troops to the gates of Athens itself. His soldiers, helmets down over their faces exposing only their eyes, hold their weapons at the ready.

Handsome, imposing, sophisticated, this is indeed the man Antigone described to us so often. Meanwhile, forcing back the crowd, his troops deploy themselves in a semi-circle around him as he marches straight up to Oedipus, to inform him that his city and family want him to return to Theban soil. The city will ensure that he and his daughters want for nothing and that he and Antigone never again find themselves in the deplorable, impoverished state they are in at present.

Without stirring or making a sound, Oedipus listens patiently to every word. Creon finds this unsettling and falls silent but still Oedipus does not answer. The silence through the thickening fog becomes oppressive. Creon orders three soldiers to remove Oedipus but they cannot dislodge him from the rock on which he is seated and of which he now appears to have become part. When they abandon their efforts, Oedipus announces that after years of misery he has at last arrived where he must remain and that nothing can oust him against his will. Theseus has made him a citizen of Athens. This city and not Thebes has made him welcome and therefore it is Athens that his ashes and renown will enrich. These words are delivered with such compulsion and dignity that the enthralled crowd pushes through the bewildered soldiers to encircle and shield Oedipus and Antigone.

Creon knows he cannot take Oedipus by force: 'I have already captured Ismene. Now I shall take Antigone and you, in need of their protection, will have to join your daughters.' The soldiers have regained control and, pikes raised, repel the crowd. Incensed, the people pick up stones. Antigone has no wish to be the cause of conflict between two ill-matched adversaries and intervenes, agreeing to go with Creon's soldiers of her own free will. Oedipus stays on his rock, silent and inert. His terrifying silence weighs heavily on the Thebans as they group round Antigone, ready to make a hasty departure. I am standing next to her, she takes my arm. Ignoring me, they escort us both away. Unperturbed and alone, Creon remains where he is, facing Oedipus as he waits to speak to Theseus. Awed, the throng keeps its distance.

As we walk along, Antigone asks me about Clius, his young wife Io and their children. I tell her that not only has he rebuilt their house and flock but that he has become a distinguished artist known throughout Greece. When her request for help arrived he wanted to set off immediately and join them in the High Mountains. Io persuaded him it would be better if he and I went to Athens to seek Theseus's support. My news evidently pleases her and she seems confident that Clius will come to her assistance.

At the crossroads we join the troops who have taken Ismene captive. She is very frightened and Antigone does her best to calm her fears. Catching sight of me, the officer in charge orders me to leave. Antigone protests, threatening that if I am not allowed to stay, the two sisters will refuse to move and will have to be carried. When the angry officer strikes me, she turns on him without a second thought. He can see she is a woman of her word and as time is pressing, he allows me to stay.

As we approach the pass where Clius has set up his ambush, I holler loudly. A huge boulder lands in front of us and behind us a tree crashes down. We are trapped. The officer sends men to shift the rock. Two are instantly struck by javelins that appear from nowhere. The soldiers form a square and withdraw to the fallen tree, the officer thinking they will be able to go around it. Any retreat in that direction soon proves to be impossible.

Antigone intercedes and addresses the officer: 'Are all your men to be killed on account of a ridiculous command? Tell them to lay down their arms. These will be returned the moment we are released. Keep yours for the sake of the honour of Thebes.'

As the officer is unsure she disarms the first of the soldiers herself. The others lay down their weapons in a pile on the path.

Clius and his men appear above the pass. He did not expect to
see the officer still armed and raises his javelin. When Antigone
calls up: 'It was I who agreed,' he lowers it and sprints down the
incline to join her. They gaze at one another, beaming. 'You're
always there when I need you, Clius,' she says, adding: 'We must
see to the wounded.'

He chuckles: 'How could I forget my Antigone. I have the
necessary ointments for their wounds.' Antigone goes over to
the injured and I help her treat them, as I am familiar with the
remedies.

Ismene is obviously moved by the great affection she has read
in Antigone's eyes and in those of the man who has just rescued
them. She had not imagined that such love was possible. And
yet Antigone, as she stands facing this demi-god who glows
beneath his armour, has nothing that is reminiscent of Iocasta's
beauty. What she possesses is something quite different – more
independent, more harrowing no doubt, since she has touched
the heart of this man who is beyond her reach.

It distresses Ismene to see her sister reflected in Clius's eyes,
in a world to which she has no access. Yet she is not jealous.
She asks him to describe how they managed over those long
years of vagabondage. 'Antigone begged; I hunted, fished and
thieved if I had to but without her knowing. Later, once Oedipus
had begun to sing, people gave us what we needed without our
having to ask.'

Antigone comes over to Clius and asks him to free the Thebans. They retrieve their weapons, thank her and depart. We turn
back and head for Colonus. Antigone takes her sister's arm and
together they walk with Clius. Antigone questions him: 'Is Io as
graceful as her name? When I try to imagine her, I picture a
leaping doe.'

'That's just what she's like.'

'Tell me about her.'

'When I left for Athens, I wanted to bring her and the children
with me but she refused. She said: "I think Antigone must love
the one she used to call your little fiancée as much as I love her,

231

for I owe everything I have to her. But we will love each other all the more if I don't come between you." '

Antigone is moved: 'That was a good thought and it makes me happy. Happy Clius, because of Io and because we are together on the road again.'

When we reach the square at Colonus, Creon and Theseus are face to face and Oedipus is waiting patiently for their discussion to end. A triumphant smile flickers across Theseus's face when he catches sight of Antigone and Ismene. Creon chooses to ignore it. A solitary figure, he remains indifferent to the fact that he is standing in the midst of Athenian soldiers and an angry mob. He has violated Athenian territory with his armed invasion, assaulted her *protégés* and now lost his hostages. Despite Theseus's condemnation of his actions and his threat of reprisals, Creon knows that negotiations are all the weapons they have left. Each understands what the other is up to but knows that neither can win.

Clius turns to me and says: 'Just look at the three kings! Two of them have done well but they're no better than a couple of merchants haggling over a price or a wager. Oedipus is the only one of the three whose crown is safe, for he keeps it inside him.'

The girls sidle up to their father. He takes their hands in his and they, like a pair of doves, rest their heads on his shoulder.

The discussion over, Theseus decides he will escort Creon to the place where Theban troops are assembled. He beckons to Antigone and informs her that her brother Polynices came to him begging for an audience with Oedipus. As Theseus and Creon leave and the crowd begins to disperse, Polynices looms out of the mist in front of Oedipus and his daughters.

He is huge, magnificent and, although unarmed, every inch a great prince and fearless warrior. He is upset to see Oedipus and Antigone in rags. Locked up inside his inner bastion he has obviously never imagined until now what they might have endured since he sanctioned them to be banished from Thebes. Sobbing, he lunges at Oedipus's knees, clasps them and kisses them. He begs his father's forgiveness for his crime and begs him to come to his aid.

With great authority Oedipus stops him. His gestures and his whole demeanour seem to say: Yes, I know, I understand. Sensing this Polynices calms down. With great tenderness, Oedipus runs his hands over his son's face, his sturdy neck and glorious head of hair. 'My son, you are a king.' He makes him rise and then draws himself up to his full height in front of him. Polynices is taller. Oedipus feels his shoulders, waist and long hands; savouring his stateliness, strength and splendour. He repeats: 'You are a king,' then adds, 'No. More than that. You are the King, just as your mother was the Queen. And that is what Eteocles has found so insufferable. It is therefore up to you to understand for the two of you and to do everything within your power to bring about peace. A true king like you has no need of a throne in order to reign.'

Polynices's face brightens for a moment and then clouds over. He does not understand. What Oedipus is saying to him is too complex a concept for him to grasp. He cannot dismiss his army, abandon his allies. He must defend his right and push Eteocles to renounce his preposterous claim.

'Peace, my boy, peace. Stop seeing war as your only means of defending your right and it will return to you.'

With righteousness on his side and his father's support, Polynices had hoped to reinforce his position. Should Oedipus refuse, he will continue with his campaign whatever the cost.

Antigone tries to mediate. Surely after the misfortunes that have befallen their family, Polynices should abandon this ill-starred venture. He rejects her entreaties. Oedipus flies into a rage and rants against the folly of his two dreadful sons. Let them go to war since they refuse to understand. But if they do, then the only Theban land they will get to call theirs will be their tombs. He implores Polynices one last time to stop. Can he not see that if this war goes ahead his tragedy will also become Antigone's? No, Polynices cannot. Moreover he insists that his sister, whom he has always loved dearly, has nothing to do with the struggle for the crown.

'And when you are dead,' shouts Oedipus, 'who will be king?' Confronted by Polynices's silence he continues: 'Creon! He's king already, Eteocles is nothing but a front! But when he is the only ruler, do you think Antigone will be able to stand by, quietly witnessing his tyranny, and do nothing?'

Polynices is speechless with despair. He knows, maybe he has always known, that he has chosen a path that leads to death. Sadly, his heart and mind are too limited to allow him to embrace the future and understand who Antigone is. He turns around. His sisters cling on to him to restrain him but he frees himself and flees. Through their tears, they implore him to come back. But it is to no avail. Becoming one with the mist, he is gone.

Antigone and Ismene return to Oedipus with their account of how Clius rescued them. He asks them to fetch Clius and leave the two of them alone.

I witnessed the events that took place subsequently and was one of those who accompanied Oedipus to the spot where he left us. However, Clius was with him the whole time and went further than I did.

Diotima, despite his wish to remain silent, it would be better if he told you how Oedipus's journey ended. An ending which in fact marked a beginning for us and for Athens.

XVI

THE ROAD TO THE SUN

Clius's account

After the skirmish with the Theban soldiers, we all go back to Colonus where Oedipus is waiting for us in his special way. He shows as much affection and consideration to the one daughter as to the other, with no display of favouritism for she who was with him every day while the other stayed in the palace at Thebes. Antigone is overjoyed at being with her sister again and delighted by the equality between them.

Oedipus still has the look of a divine beggar and he is, quite frankly, filthy. His clothes are stained and tattered. He has not washed for at least two days and his dusty face is streaked with sweat. His long, unkempt hair and neglected beard emphasize his bewildered air. He never looked that bad all the time I looked after him. The life of the wanderer and the demands of the road proved to be too much for Antigone. He has lost a great deal of weight since I left them and his hair has turned prematurely white. It upsets me to see him like this but what grieves me even more is seeing his hands idle. He does not have his bag of tools with him which can only mean he has come to die. That distresses me profoundly. How could I have deserted him, leaving him and Antigone alone on the road? Convulsed by sobs, I fall to the ground and kiss his feet, his poor, wounded, muddy feet that I should never have stopped washing and tending.

He bends down and grabs me by the waist. Alarmed, I realize he wants to lift me. How can he, in his present weakened condition and poor state of health? But he does, and apparently with remarkable ease, for despite his broken appearance he is still as strong as ever. He hoists me over him, arching back his body as I had seen him do with Antigone on the headland, when he offered her up to the sun. Behind me I can hear the merry, relieved laughter of the girls, their pride in Oedipus replacing their qualms.

He sets me down to stand before him. He is grinning, an amused expression spreading across his sightless face. His act has erased my sorrow and guilt and all I can find to say to him is: 'Thank you!' But between you and me, thank you is all I need to say for then, in that abrupt manner of his, he says: 'You have done well, Clius. You had to leave. Your house had to be rebuilt, your flock reconstituted and your clan, with Io's help, restored. And now you're an artist, that's good.'

I detect a farewell in these words that cause me great anguish: 'What will become of Antigone if you leave us?'

'When that day comes she'll know what to do. The ordeals you endured and the high regard you have for each other have changed and matured you both.'

As we speak the sinister morning mist lifts. The sky appears, pure and calm; the breeze dispersing the mist barely stirs the trees. As so often happened when we rested by the side of the road, we fall silent, immersed in the blissful tranquillity of the moment, so welcome after the morning's gloom and agitation.

There isn't a cloud in the blue sky and yet we can hear a distant rumble of thunder. Lightning cuts through the atmosphere. 'This is the sign,' says Oedipus and asks me to send a message to Theseus. Hippias runs to tell him.

I bring Antigone and Narses closer and ask Oedipus why he

journeyed for so long around Athens rather than coming directly.
He kneels and asks Narses to take his finger and trace in the
sand the course of his comings and goings. He stands up saying,
'I wasn't aware of it at the time but it would seem I have outlined
in this country's earth, a near perfect shape. What it signifies or
might portend I don't know. As with the last dream I had, it's
always the unknown that greets me.'

Antigone speaks out: 'Since we have been here, we have been
paraded for all to see. Everyone has had the chance to examine,
ignore, or identify with us. We have been assaulted, defended
and finally accepted. The reason will become clear in due course.
We should leave Athens to discover what it is.'

The thunder rolls a second time, it does not seem to bother
Oedipus. This is still the same person who, out on the headland,
mastered that huge wave of madness and made it crash back into
the sea.

A messenger from Theseus arrives to announce that he is on
his way. It would seem that we have very little time left, so I
turn to Oedipus: 'Not only have I decorated the temples of
Athens and the king's palaces, but there is a wall in the middle
of the countryside where I have painted a fresco that evokes our
years on the road. It is a beaten track typical of the ones we so
often travelled; like the one my father and mother, holding me
by the hand, loved to walk along when I was as child – and
which they called the road to the sun. The branches of the trees
touch overhead; bushes, brambles and bracken grow alongside
and a single clump of poppies is all it takes to give it light.'

'When I was young,' says Oedipus, 'I thought that nothing in
the world could outclass the beauty of the sea or that of poppies.
Tell me more about this track Clius, for it speaks to my heart.'

'It is strewn with those half-concealed stones you were always
tripping over. And beyond, through the branches, you can see
the dazzling colour of the flowers referred to in our valleys as
suns. And that's it. It's a path no different from so many to be
found in Greece. A path that is unhurried, snaking indefinitely,
without advance warning of where it is going. I didn't paint it

for Theseus but for you and Antigone. And for all those small communities made up of people and slaves exiled far from their homelands who come in their droves time and again to view it.'

While we are speaking Narses has taken Antigone into our house, where Ismene dresses her in a white robe she has brought from Thebes. Oh Diotima, I am so pleased when I see her emerge looking as radiant as she did once before, in the blue coat you once made for her.

A long rumble of thunder reverberates in the unchanging blue sky just as Theseus comes into view. Awed and somewhat apprehensive, he goes up to Oedipus. In their youth, both men had entered the Labyrinth. Oedipus battled his way through, fought the Minotaur but did not kill him. Theseus, on the other hand, killed the Minotaur and through deception and seduction went back the way he came. He became the founder and king of a great city – Oedipus a beggar and a blind bard.

Another peal of thunder rings out and the earth quakes. Oedipus stands: 'The hour has come.' Theseus offers to be his guide and take him to the place to which he has been summoned. Oedipus smiles: 'As I have told you, I now have second sight.'

He discards his staff and with an air of authority sets off, taking the lead. Theseus is at his side and struggles like the rest of us to keep up with him. At the edge of a precipice he comes to a sudden stop. There in front of him, in the hollow trunk of a massive tree, are some amphoras. He asks his daughters to go and draw water from a spring we can hear.

Meanwhile, I attend to him the way I used to. I cut and tidy his hair, and, with respect, remove his rags. When his daughters return with the water, I wash him while they proceed with the rites. No one says a word. I sense it gives him pleasure to have me see to his needs once more. Though much thinner, his body is still that of an athlete – perfectly proportioned, the muscles strong. Antigone helps me slip over his head the new robe Io has woven for him. We are profoundly moved. 'This robe is from the wool of your sheep,' he says, 'like the one in which you dressed your dead father.'

He signals to Narses and the others that they should stay put and moves off, his face and whole being reflecting a state of ecstasy I have never seen in anyone. Theseus walks behind him and I follow with Antigone and Ismene. He strides towards the setting sun. I am amazed then shocked when I realize he is making his way to the wall which depicts the path of my childhood and of our long trek.

He arrives at the fresco and contemplates it for a while before announcing: 'This is indeed the road.'

He summons his daughters, kisses and blesses them with that same impartiality he has established between them. 'You have suffered much because of me and yet no one could have loved you more.'

He turns to me: 'You left and came back when the time was right. You have been a true friend to Antigone and to me; you will always be so to all those who come to see your work, Clius.'

A powerful voice rises from the earth; Oedipus is eager to leave so that he can answer. Theseus holds him back for he wants him to hear what he has to say to Antigone: 'Oedipus will be an Athenian citizen until the end of time. You two will be my children. What do you want to do when your father has gone, Antigone?'

In that forthright manner of hers, she replies by reciting two verses in that strange tongue we heard in the sacred forest of Colonus. They tell Theseus that she must return to Thebes so that, if possible, she can prevent Murder from marching on her brothers.

Are these verses by Oedipus I had not heard before? But the time for questions has passed; Oedipus is leaving us. He stands at the foot of the fresco. He steps on to the path and, without stumbling, walks beneath the trees. He picks some blackberries and stoops over a clump of poppies. He moves off without turning round once and we see him disappear into the distance, not knowing whether he is plunging into the colours I have mixed for him, or into our hearts where, to our surprise, grief combines with joy. He arrives at a point where the light of the sky merges with the golden glow of the suns, where distant lines converge and reach into infinity. Our eyes are too weak to see . . . he soon becomes no more than a minuscule dot which slowly fades away.

The thunder roars; we are cold and frightened. Like abandoned children, we take one another by the hand. Antigone is in the middle, leading us on, urging us back to Colonus. The sky is now quite black and the lightning crackles around us.

Ismene and I are petrified. Antigone's calm, determined step is all that prevents us from running away. Something compels me to look back. The wall has been struck by lightning and what is left of the fresco is now ablaze. I tell Antigone. She neither pauses nor turns round. She says: 'The path may have disappeared, but Oedipus is still, and always will be, on the road.'